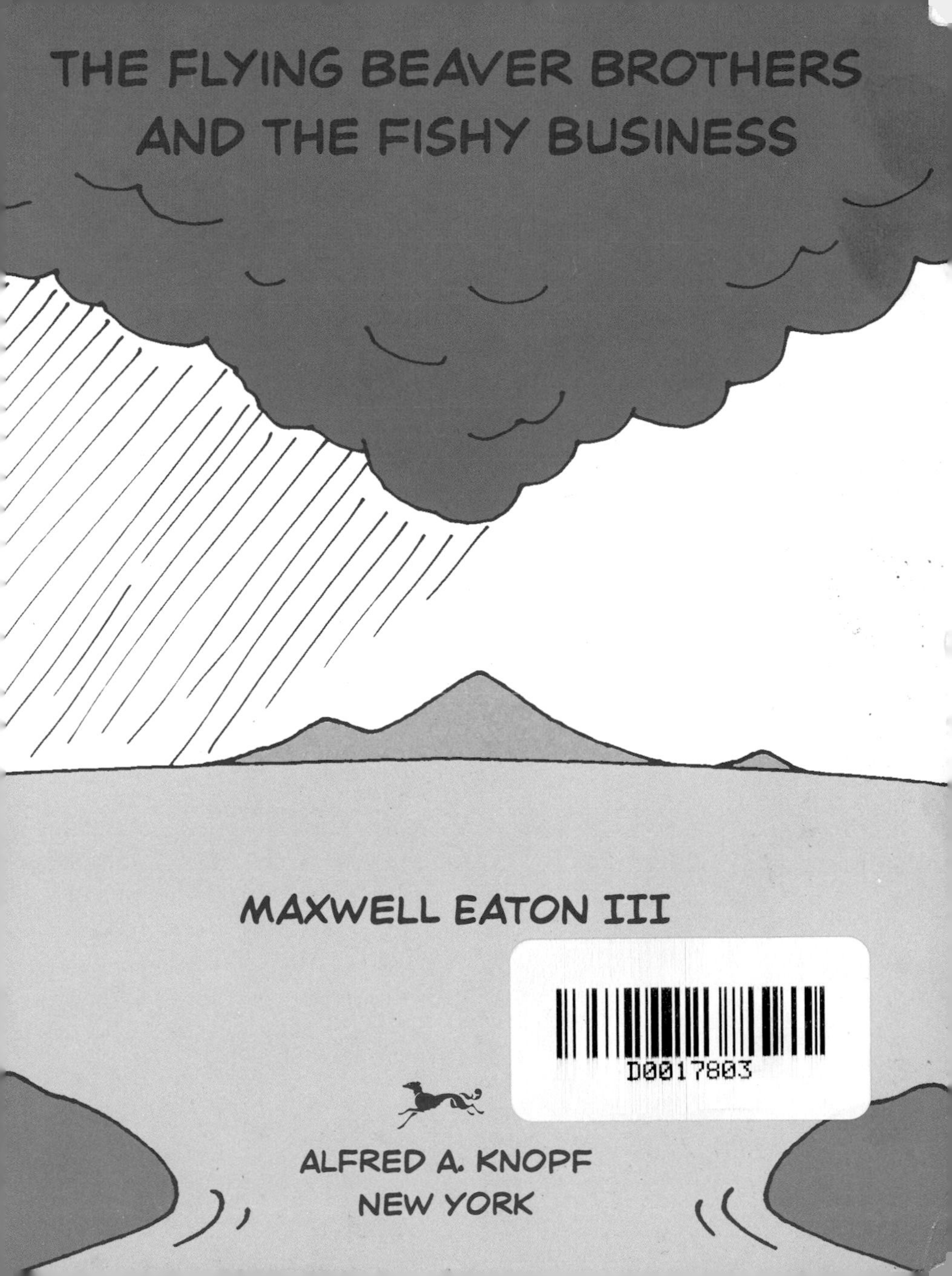

THE FLYING BEAVER BROTHERS AND THE FISHY BUSINESS

MAXWELL EATON III

ALFRED A. KNOPF
NEW YORK

For Kristin

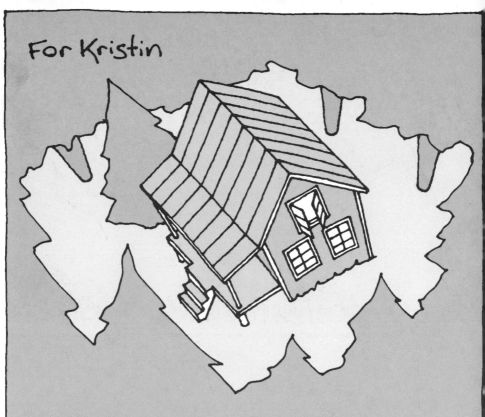

THIS IS A BORZOI BOOK PUBLISHED BY ALFRED A. KNOPF

This is a work of fiction. Names, characters, places, and incidents either are the product of the author's imagination or are used fictitiously. Any resemblance to actual persons, living or dead, events, or locales is entirely coincidental.

Copyright © 2012 by Maxwell Eaton III

All rights reserved. Published in the United States by Alfred A. Knopf, an imprint of Random House Children's Books, a division of Random House, Inc., New York. Knopf, Borzoi Books, and the colophon are registered trademarks of Random House, Inc.

Visit us on the Web! www.randomhouse.com/kids

Educators and librarians, for a variety of teaching tools, visit us at www.randomhouse.com/teachers

Library of Congress Cataloging-in-Publication Data

Eaton, Maxwell.

The flying beaver brothers and the fishy business / Maxwell Eaton III. — 1st ed.

p. cm.

Summary: Beavers Bub and Ace battle the Fish Stix corporation in an attempt to save their island's trees.

ISBN 978-0-375-86448-3 (pbk.) — ISBN 978-0-375-96448-0 (lib. bdg.)

[1. Graphic novels. 2. Beavers—Fiction. 3. Islands—Fiction. 4. Conservation of natural resources—Fiction.]

I. Title.

PZ7.7.E18Fm 2012   741.5'973—dc22   2011007925

The illustrations in this book were created using pen and ink with digital coloring.

MANUFACTURED IN MALAYSIA   January 2012   10 9 8 7 6 5 4   First Edition

Random House Children's Books supports the First Amendment and celebrates the right to read.

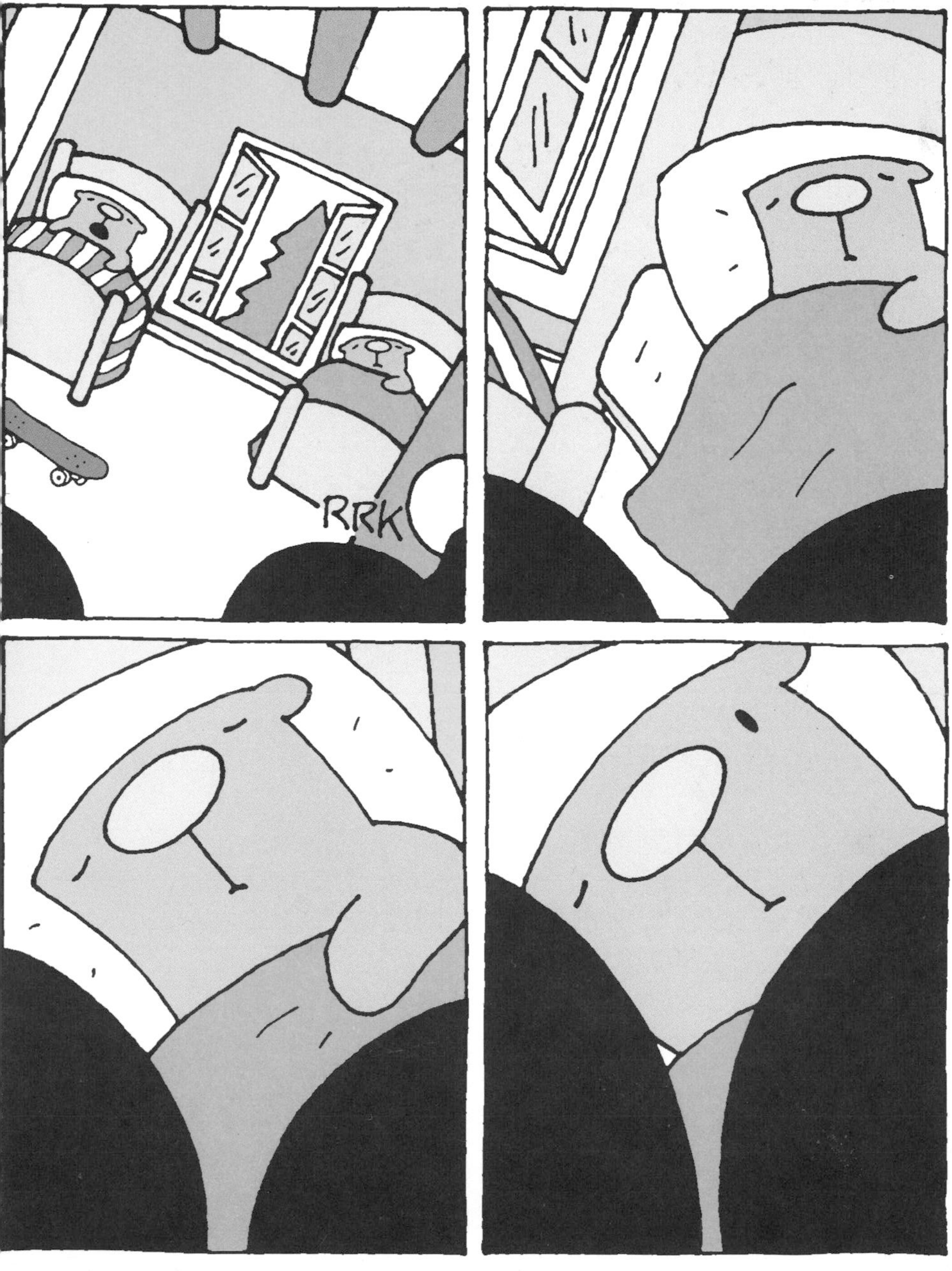
RRK

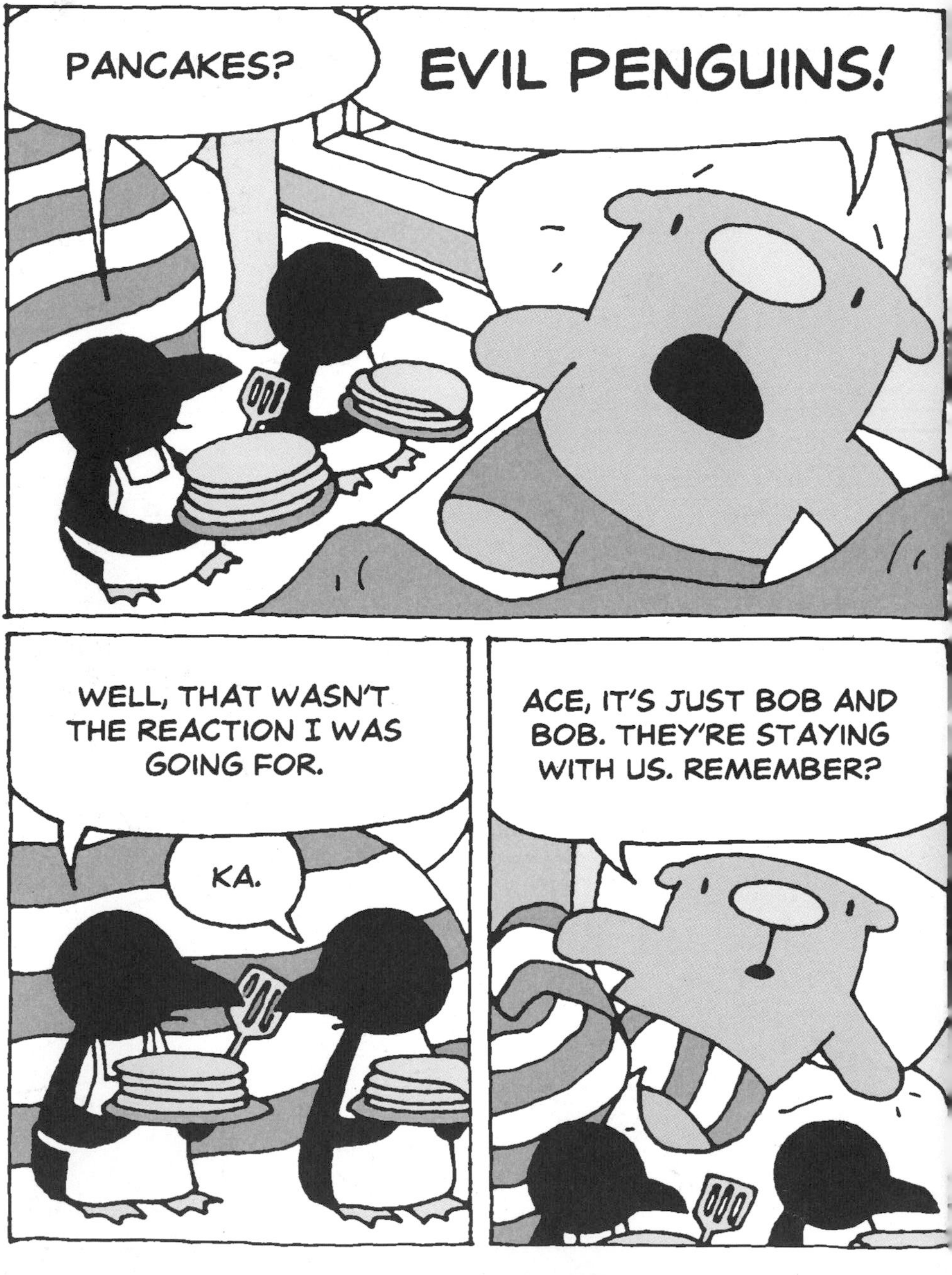
PANCAKES?
EVIL PENGUINS!
WELL, THAT WASN'T THE REACTION I WAS GOING FOR.
KA.
ACE, IT'S JUST BOB AND BOB. THEY'RE STAYING WITH US. REMEMBER?

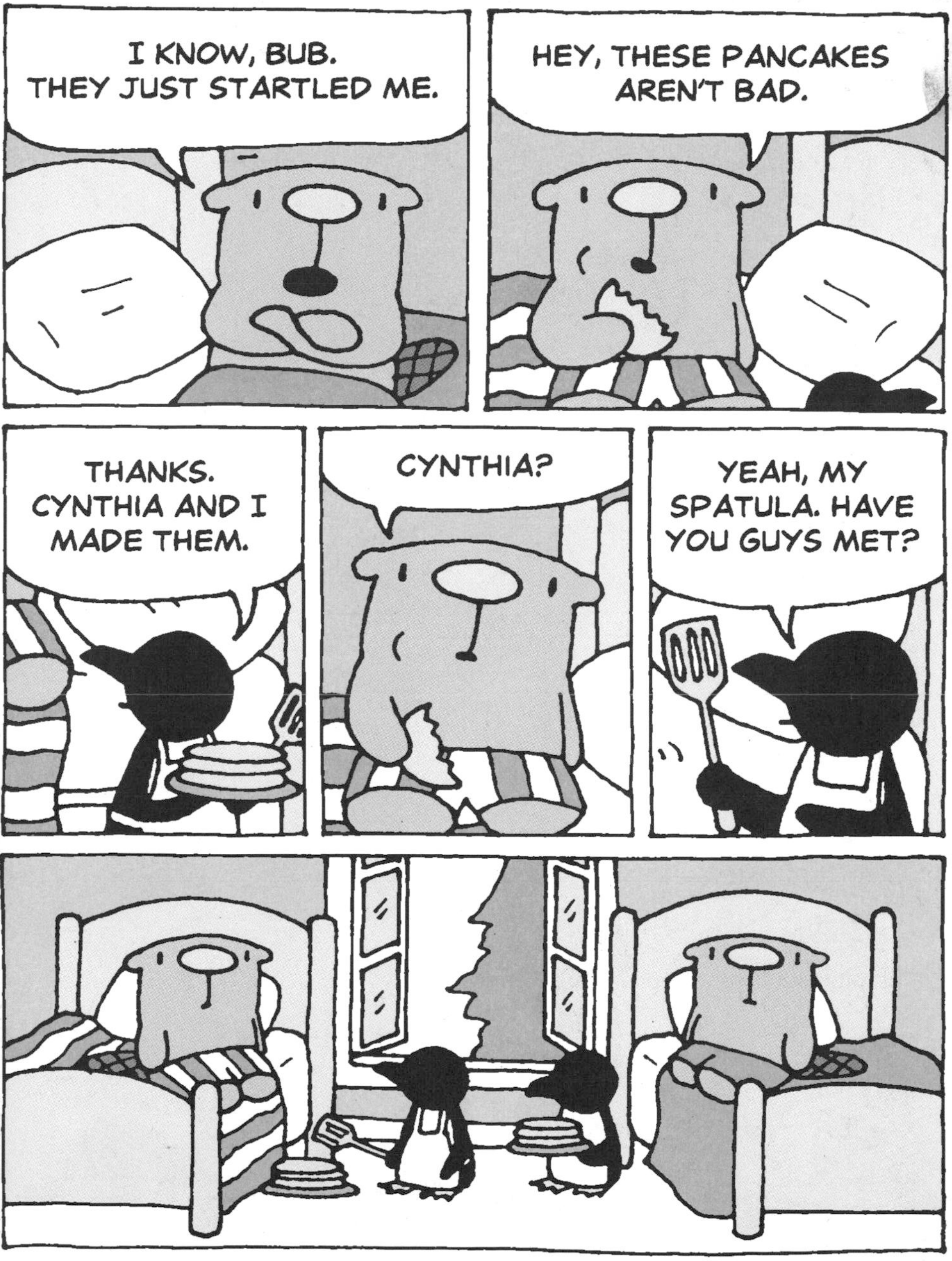
I KNOW, BUB.
THEY JUST STARTLED ME.
HEY, THESE PANCAKES AREN'T BAD.
THANKS. CYNTHIA AND I MADE THEM.
CYNTHIA?
YEAH, MY SPATULA. HAVE YOU GUYS MET?

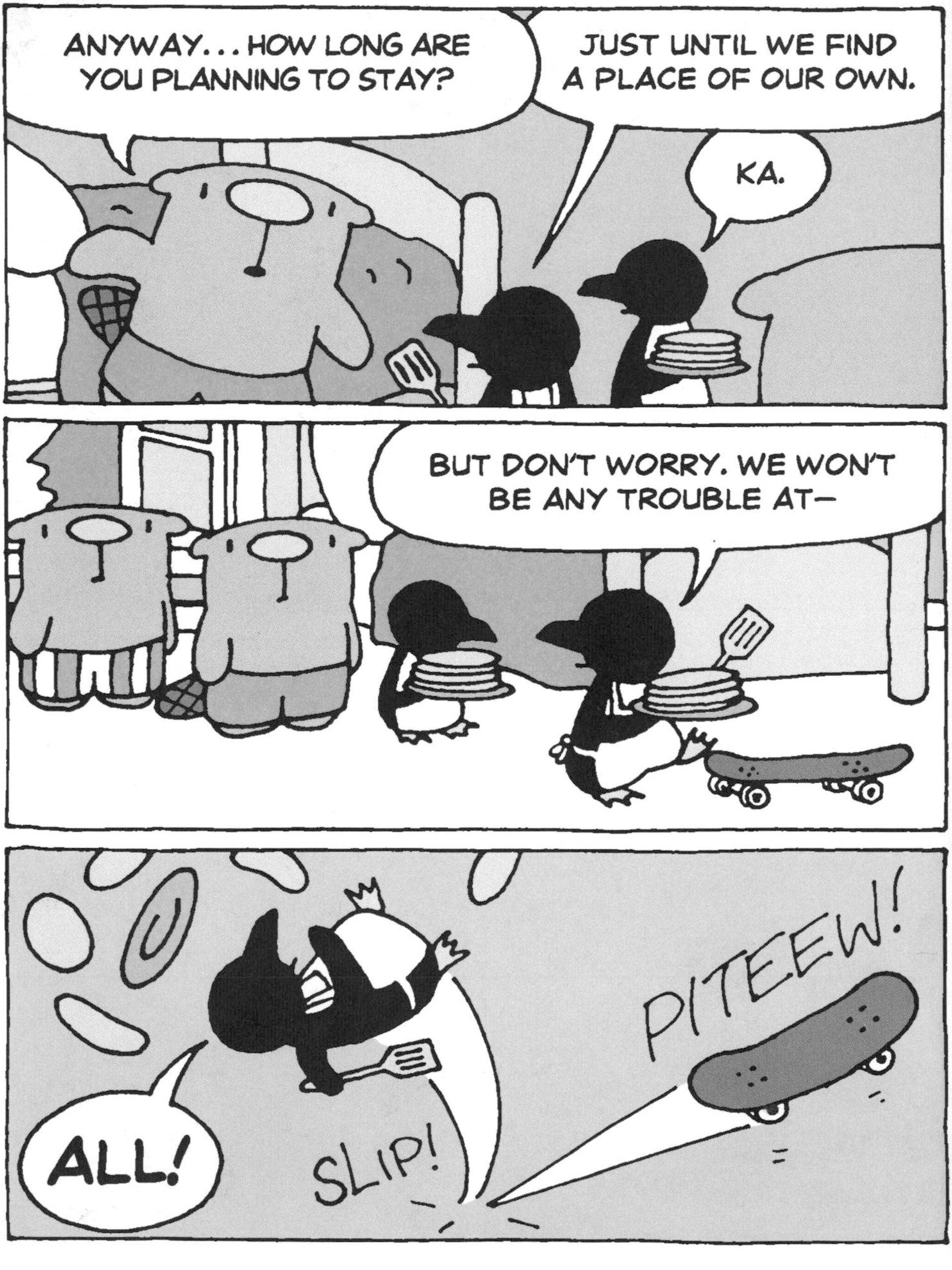
ANYWAY. . . HOW LONG ARE YOU PLANNING TO STAY?
JUST UNTIL WE FIND A PLACE OF OUR OWN.
KA.
BUT DON'T WORRY. WE WON'T BE ANY TROUBLE AT—
ALL!
SLIP!
PITEEW!

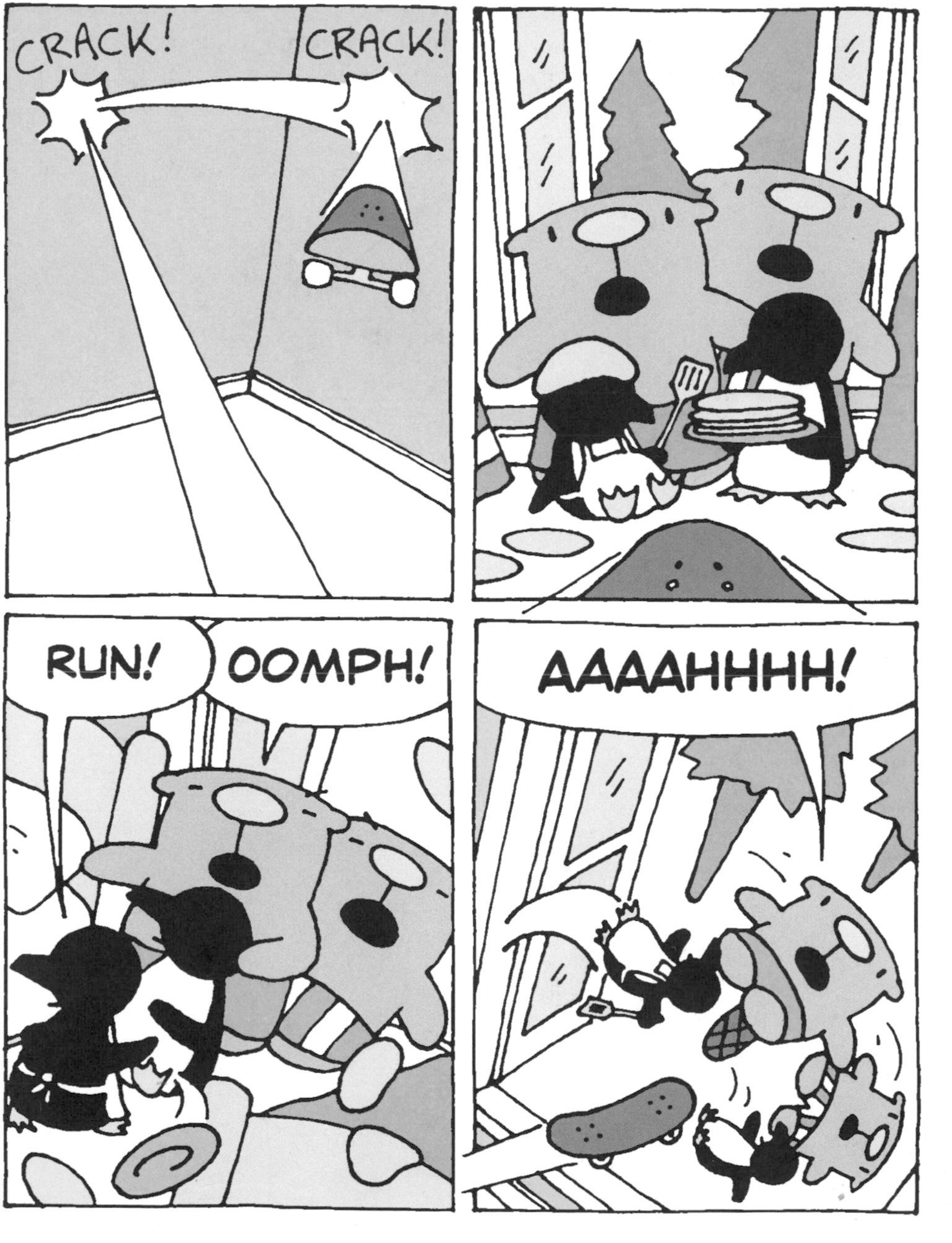
CRACK!
CRACK!
RUN!
OOMPH!
AAAAHHHH!

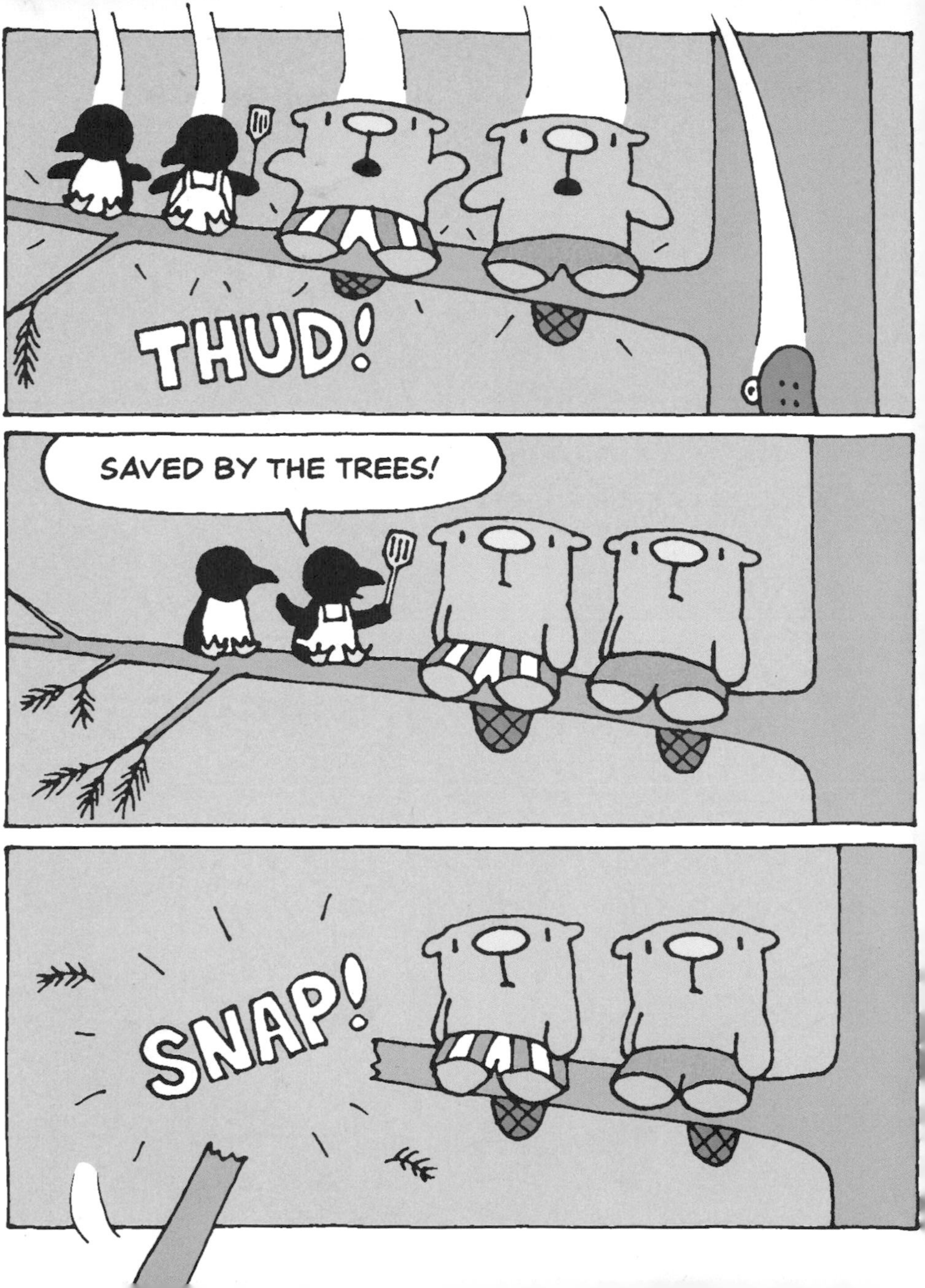
THUD!
SAVED BY THE TREES!
SNAP!

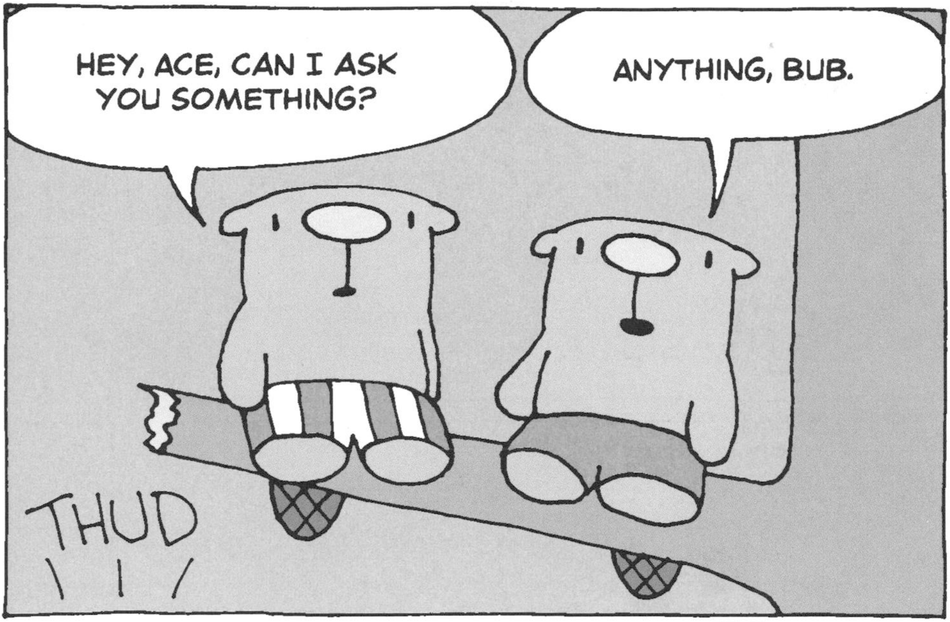
HEY, ACE, CAN I ASK YOU SOMETHING?
ANYTHING, BUB.
THUD

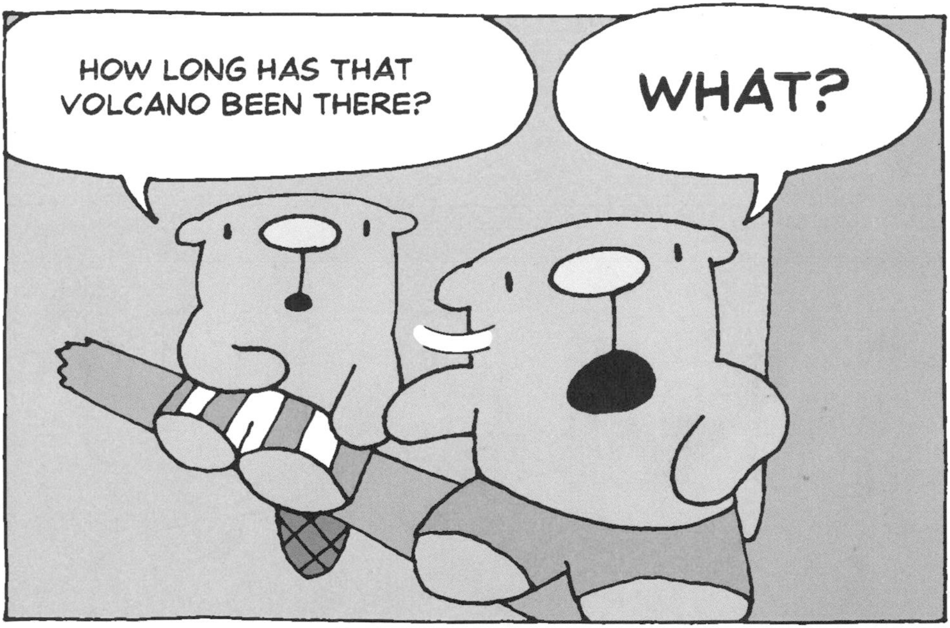
HOW LONG HAS THAT VOLCANO BEEN THERE?
WHAT?

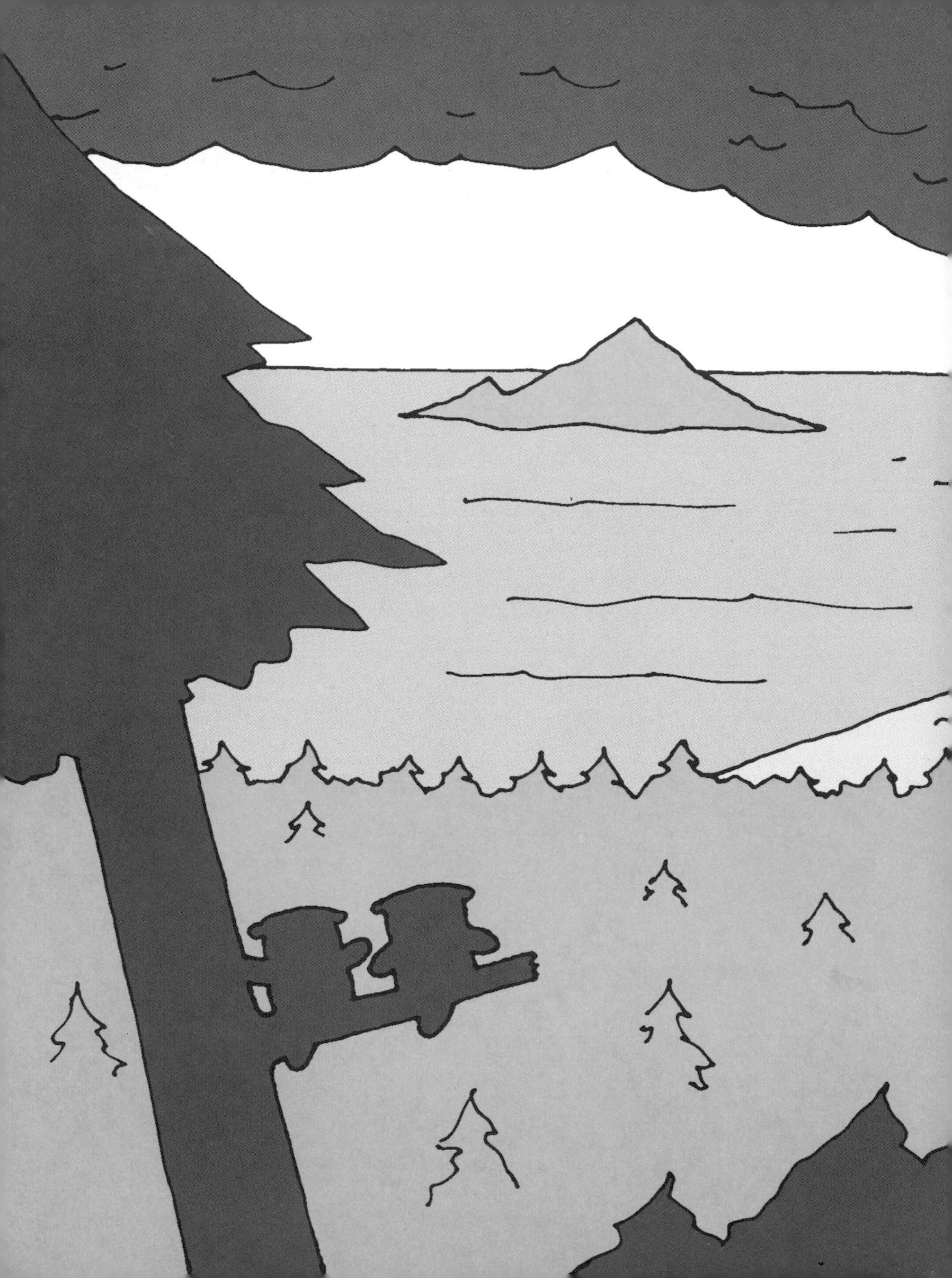

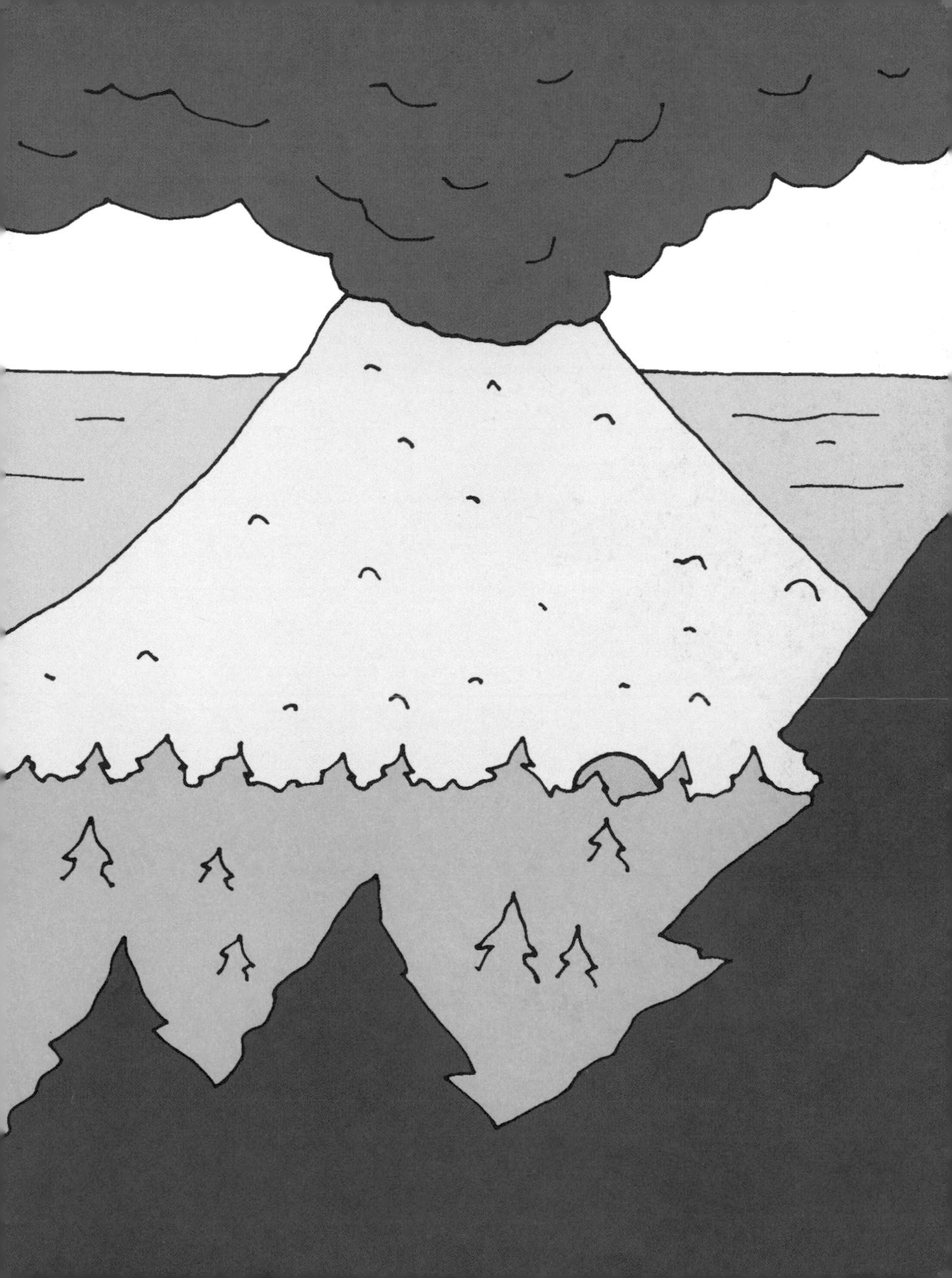

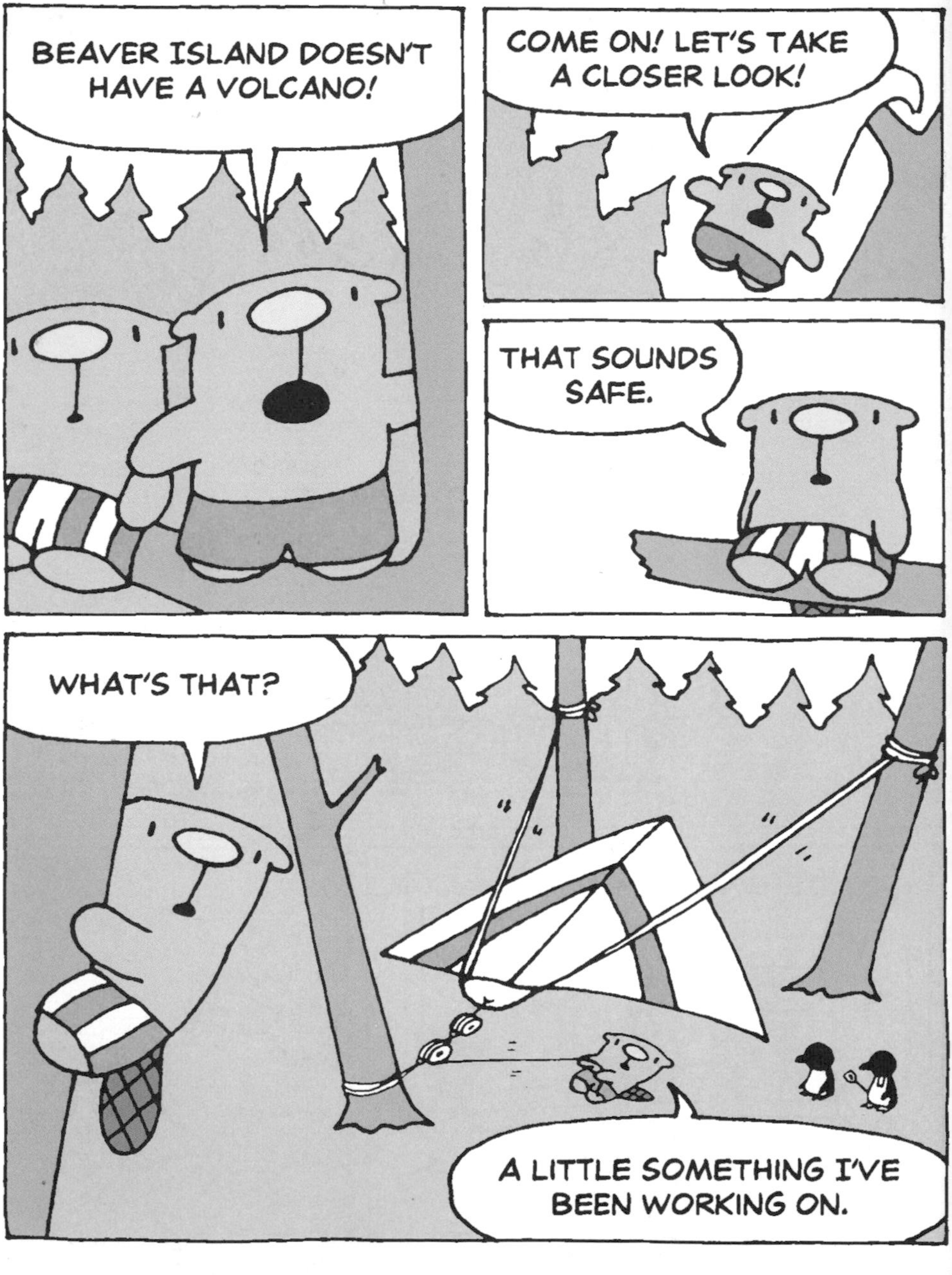

BEAVER ISLAND DOESN'T HAVE A VOLCANO!
COME ON! LET'S TAKE A CLOSER LOOK!
THAT SOUNDS SAFE.
WHAT'S THAT?
A LITTLE SOMETHING I'VE BEEN WORKING ON.

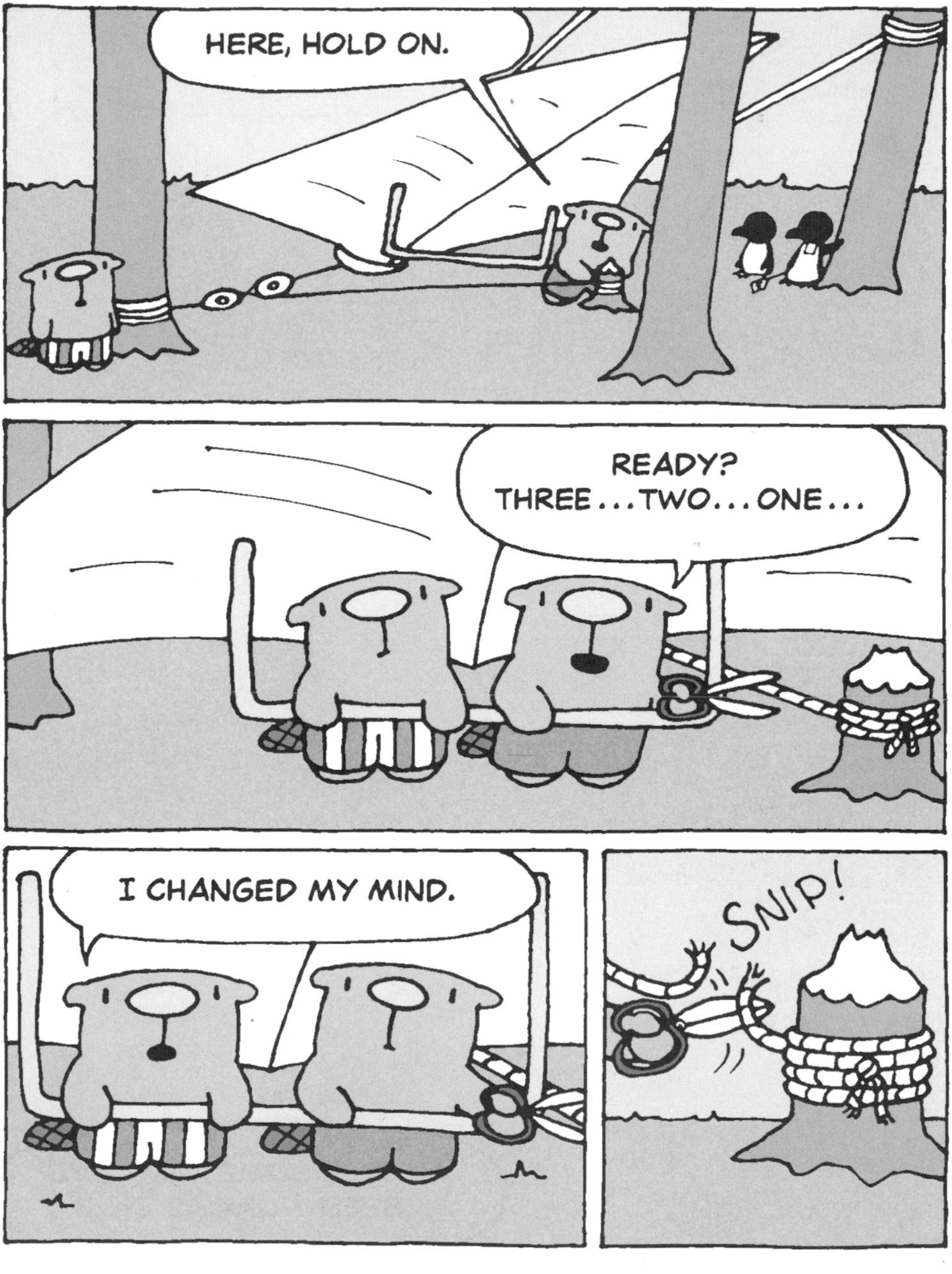
HERE, HOLD ON.
READY? THREE . . . TWO . . . ONE . . .
I CHANGED MY MIND.
SNIP!

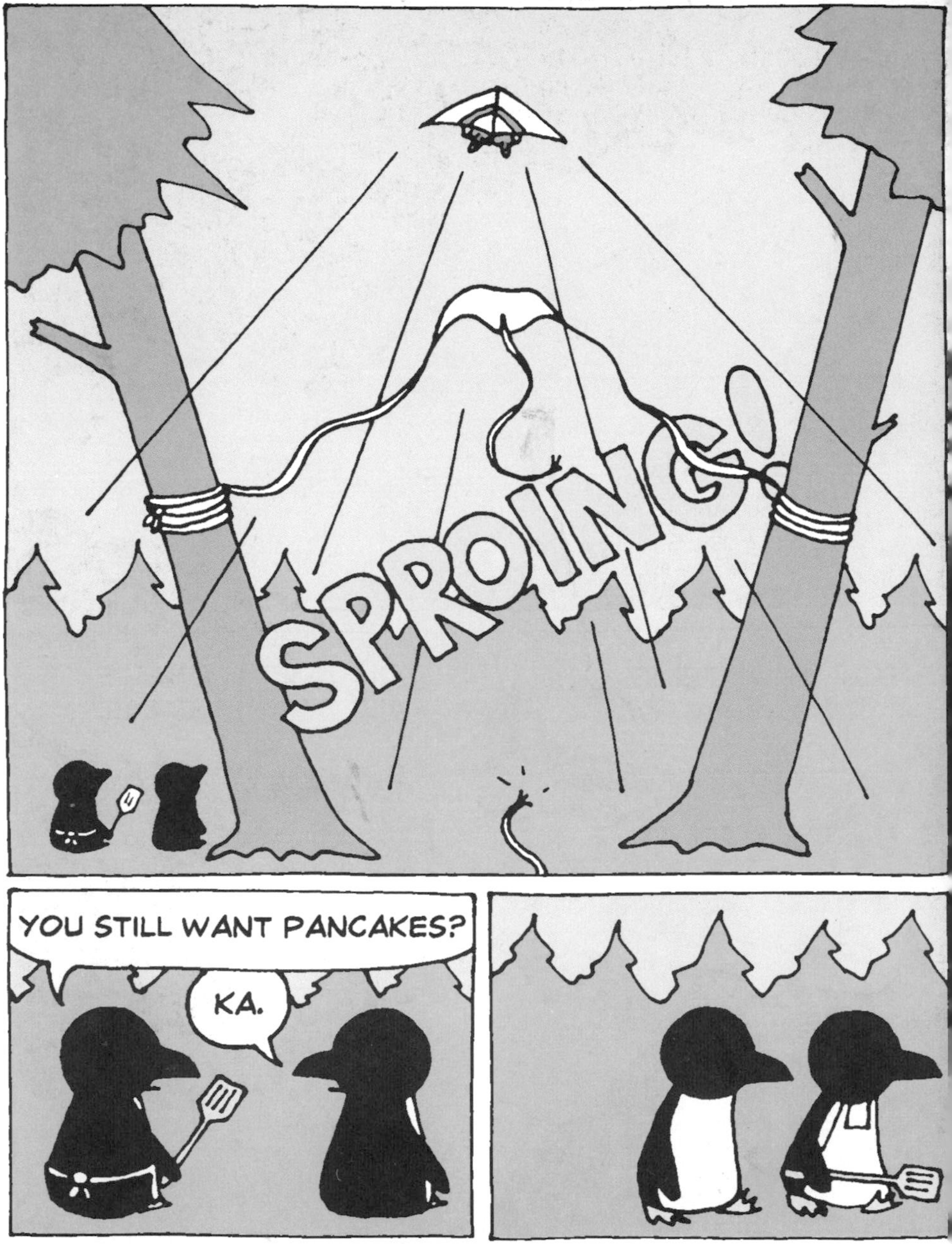
SPROING!
YOU STILL WANT PANCAKES?
KA.

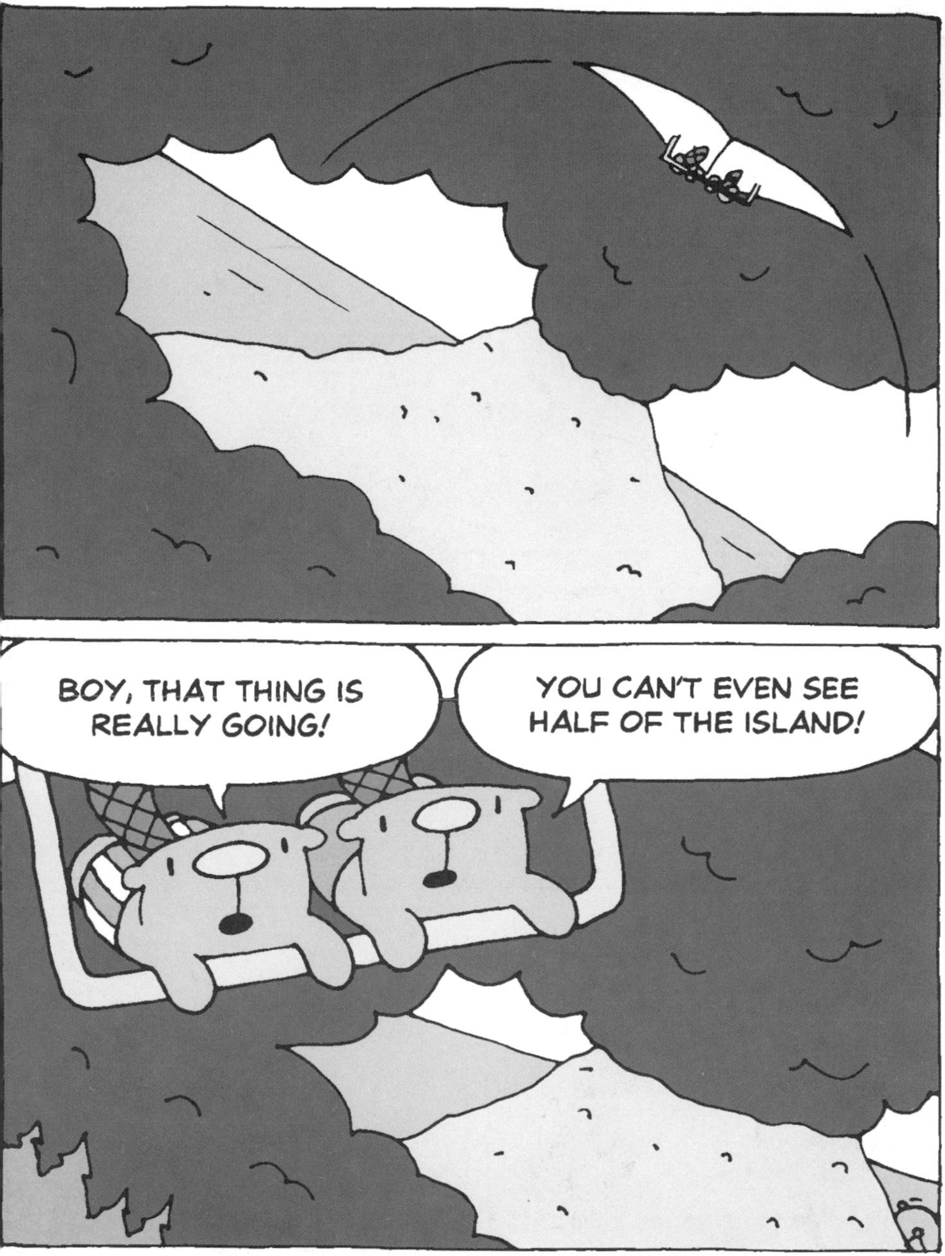
BOY, THAT THING IS REALLY GOING!
YOU CAN'T EVEN SEE HALF OF THE ISLAND!

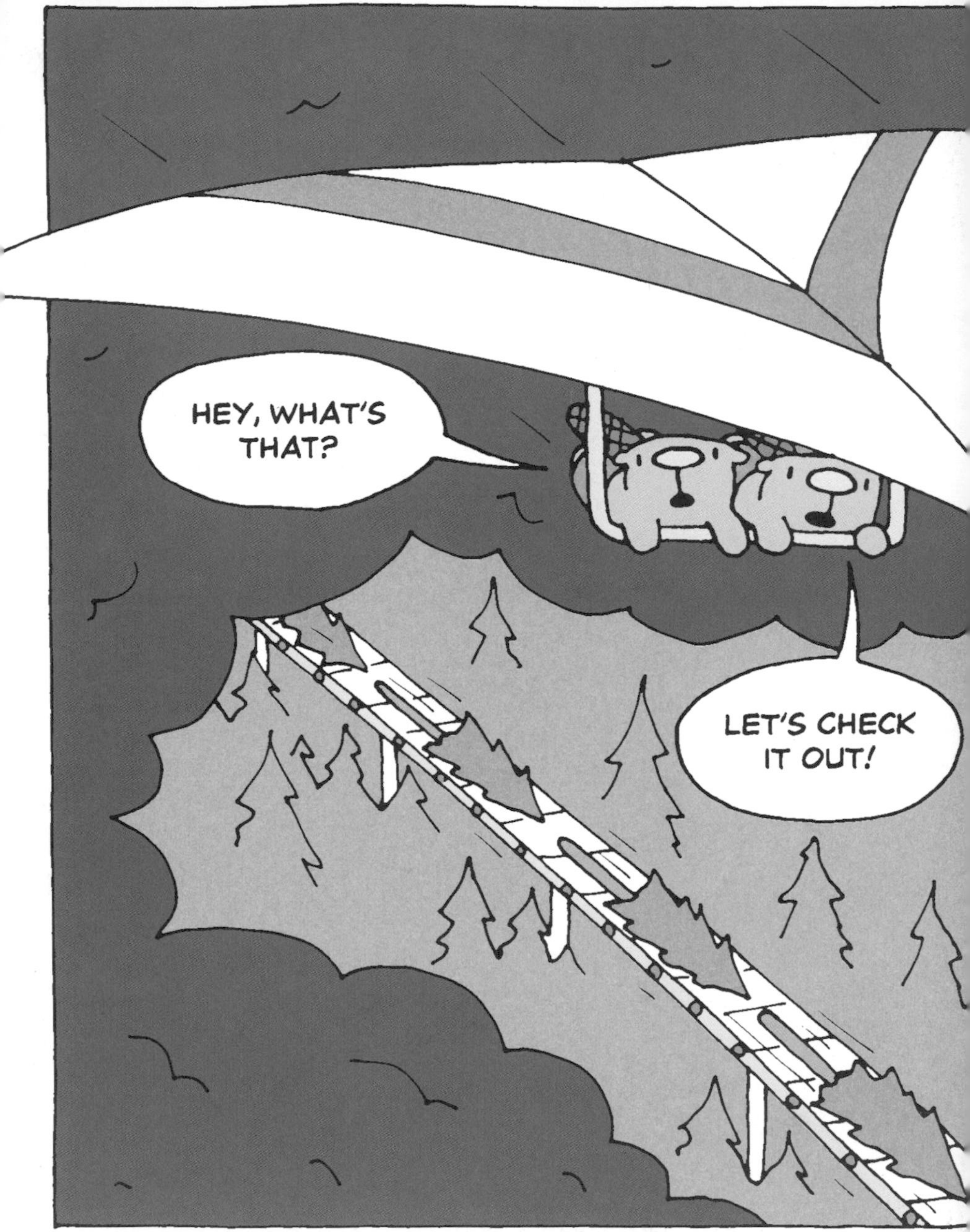
HEY, WHAT'S THAT?
LET'S CHECK IT OUT!

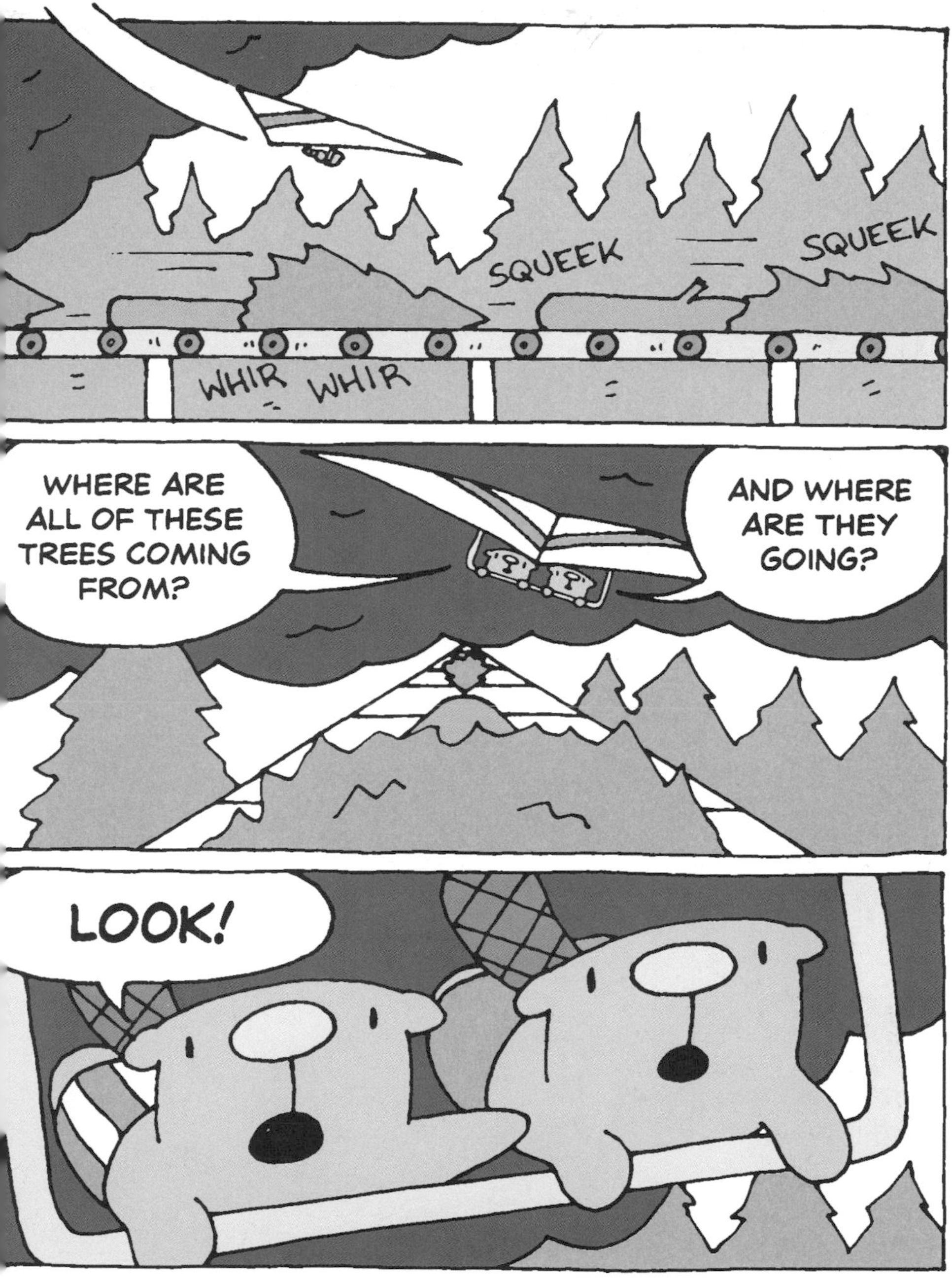
SQUEEK
SQUEEK
WHIR WHIR
WHERE ARE ALL OF THESE TREES COMING FROM?
AND WHERE ARE THEY GOING?
LOOK!

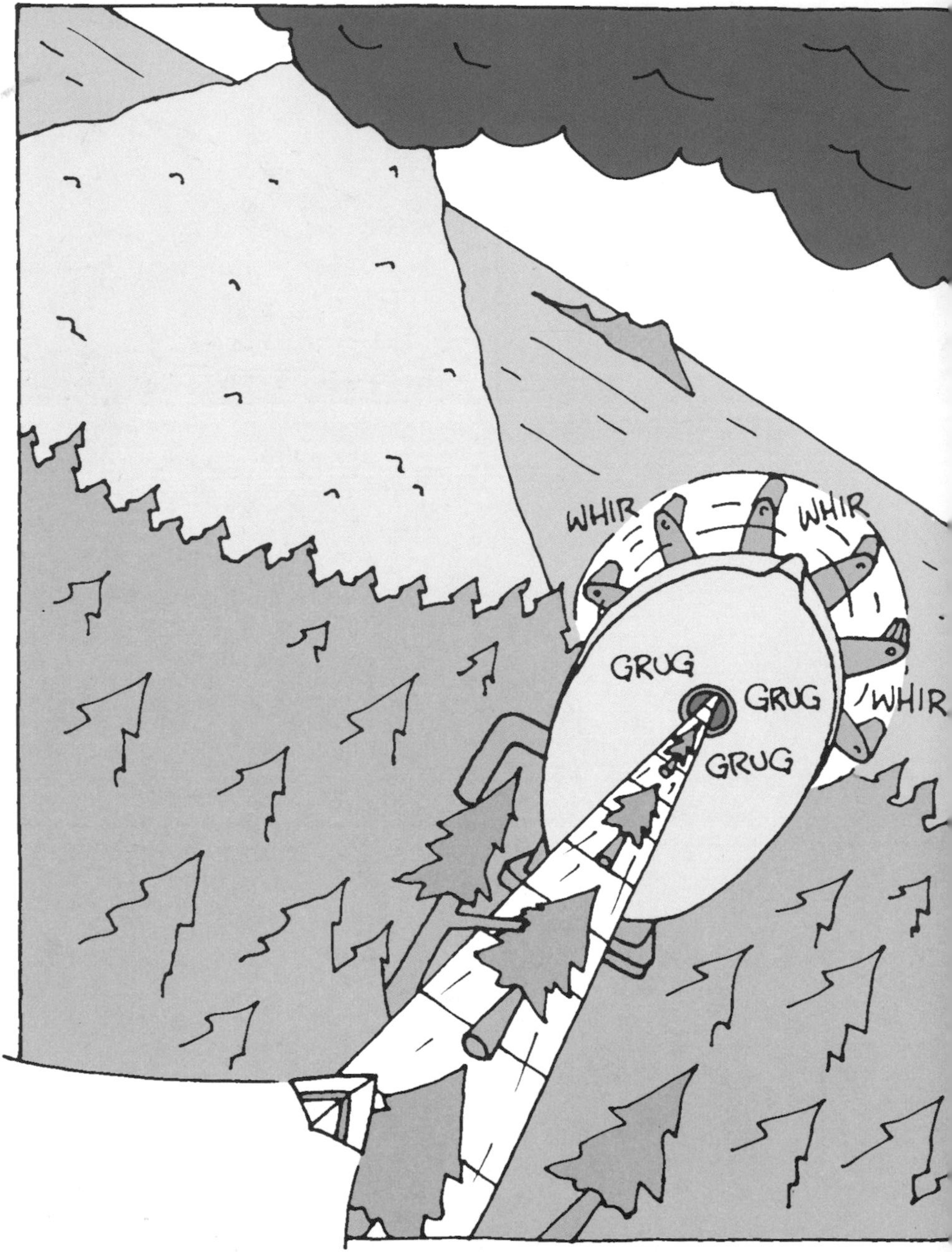
WHIR
WHIR
GRUG
GRUG
GRUG
WHIR

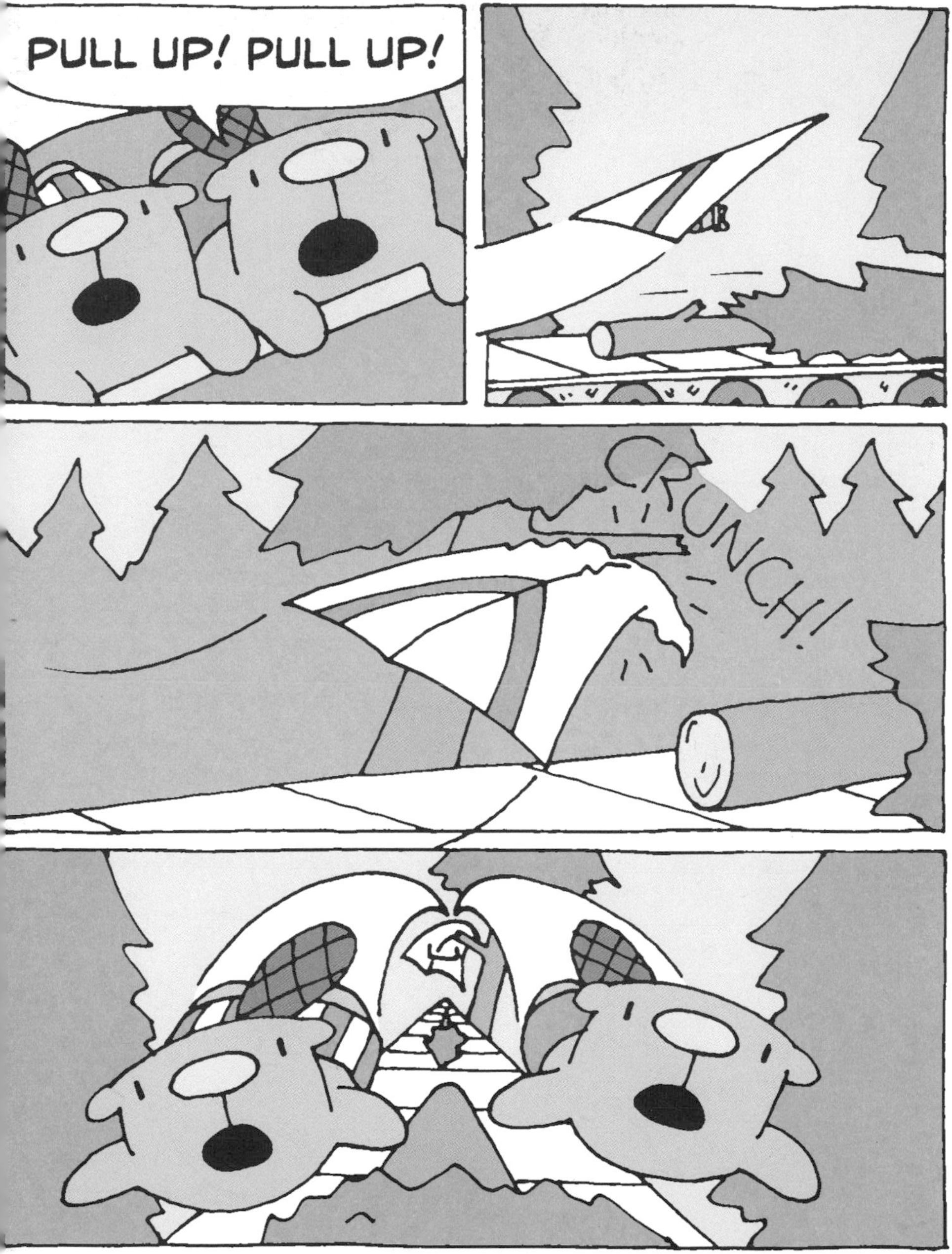
PULL UP! PULL UP!
CRUNCH!

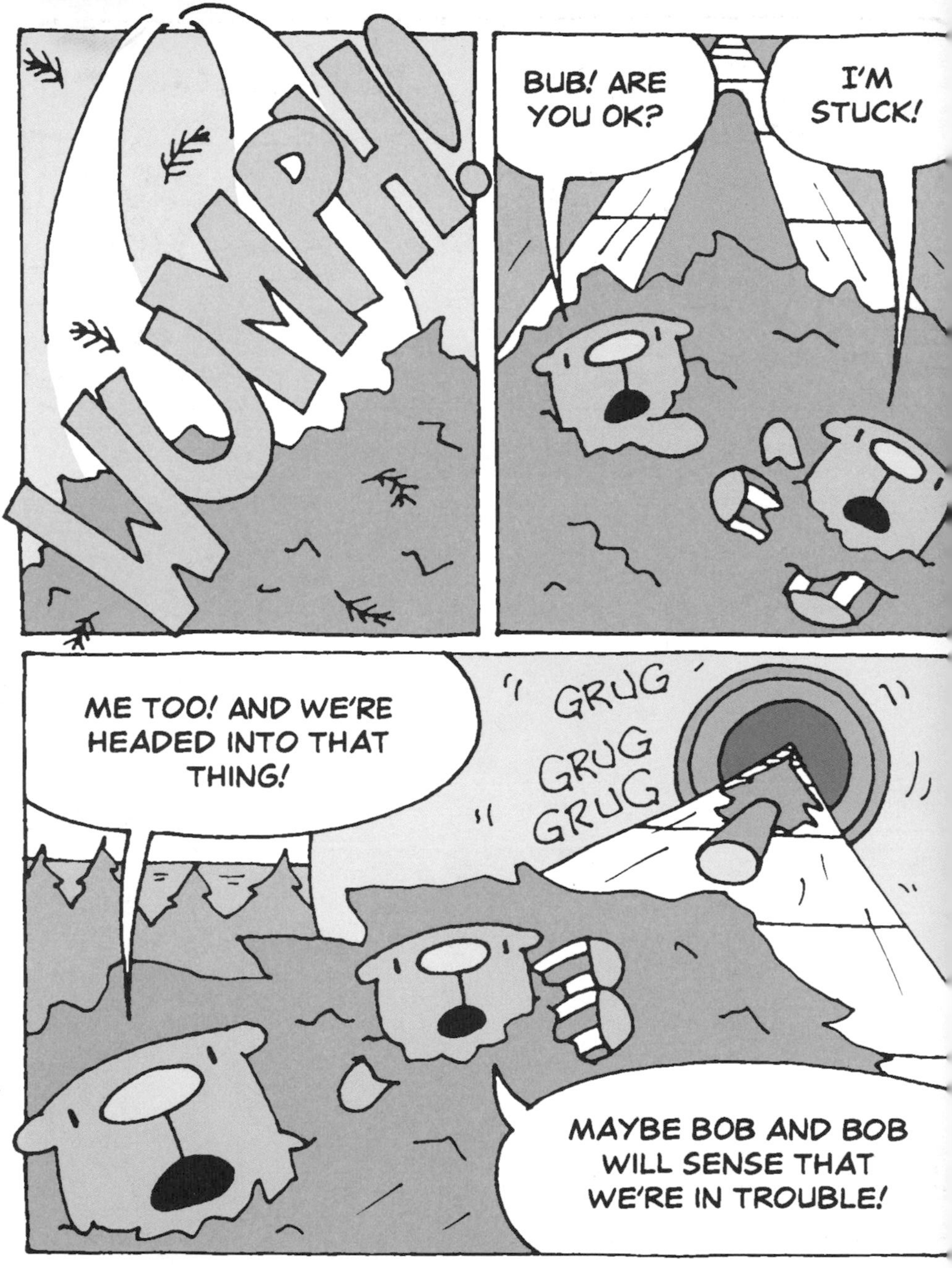
WUMPH!
BUB! ARE YOU OK?
I'M STUCK!
ME TOO! AND WE'RE HEADED INTO THAT THING!
GRUG GRUG GRUG
MAYBE BOB AND BOB WILL SENSE THAT WE'RE IN TROUBLE!

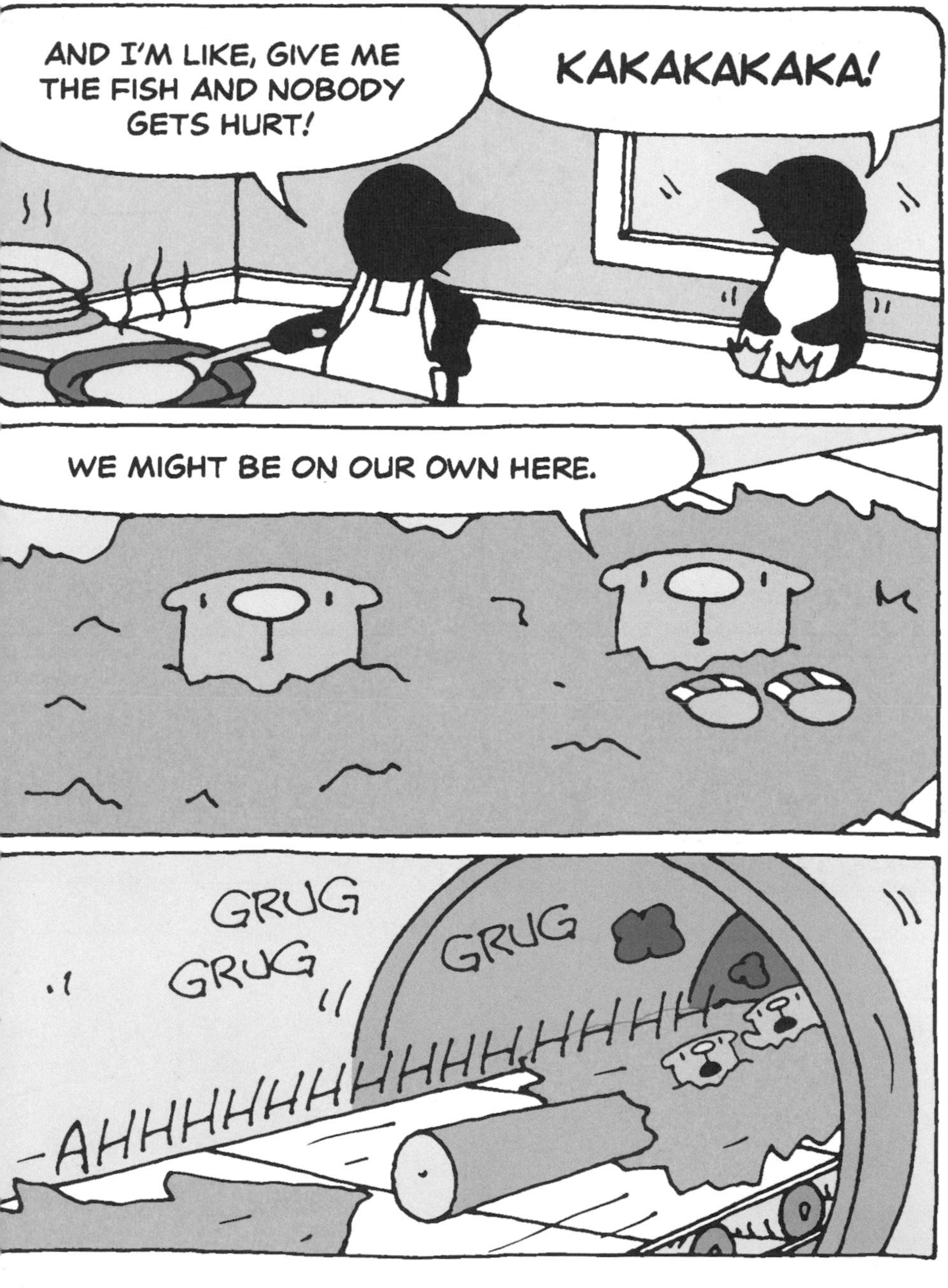
AND I'M LIKE, GIVE ME THE FISH AND NOBODY GETS HURT!
KAKAKAKAKA!
WE MIGHT BE ON OUR OWN HERE.
GRUG
GRUG
GRUG
AHHHHHHHHHHHHHHHHHHHH

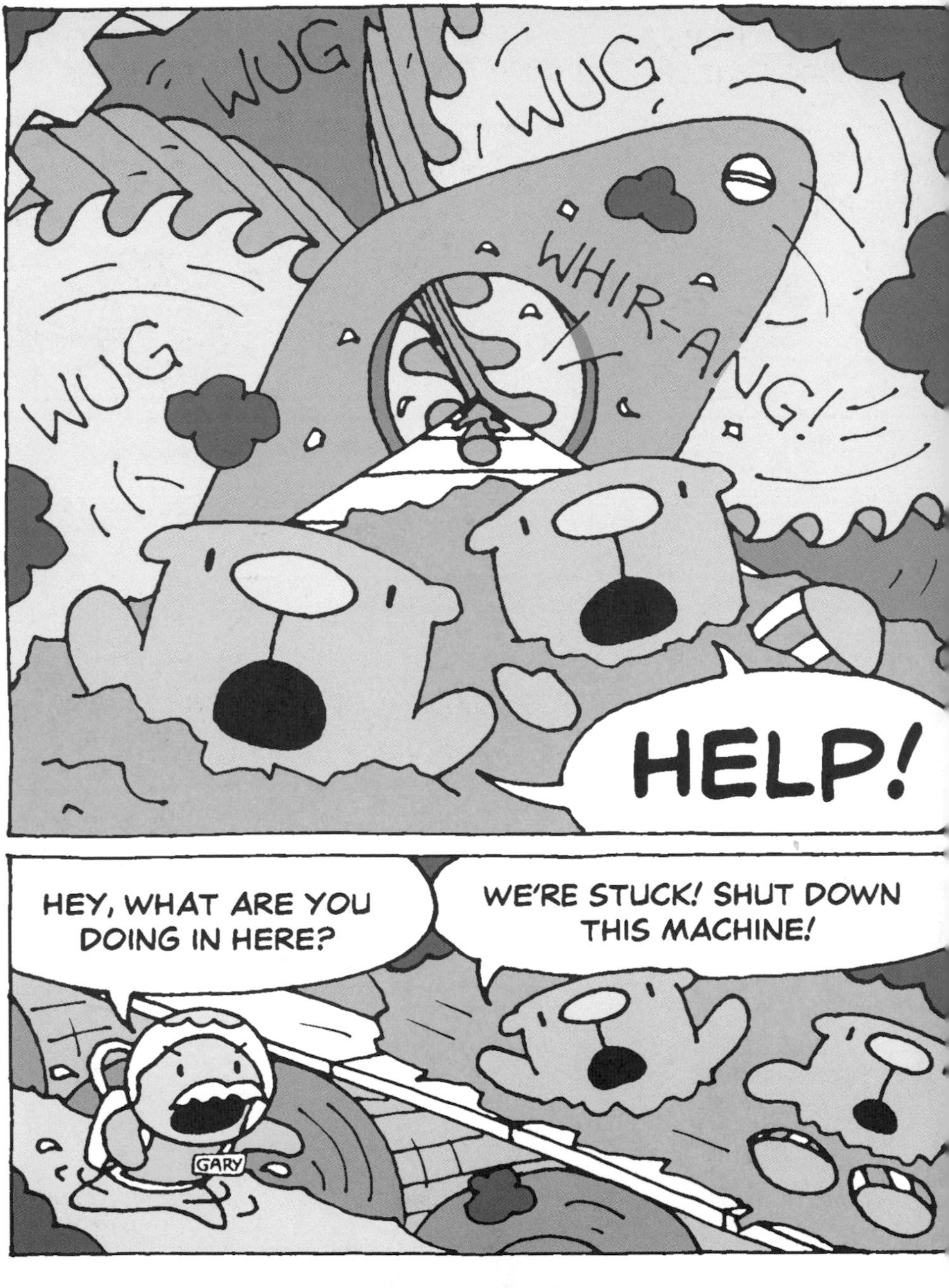
WUG
WUG
WUG
WHIR-ANG!
HELP!
HEY, WHAT ARE YOU DOING IN HERE?
WE'RE STUCK! SHUT DOWN THIS MACHINE!
GARY

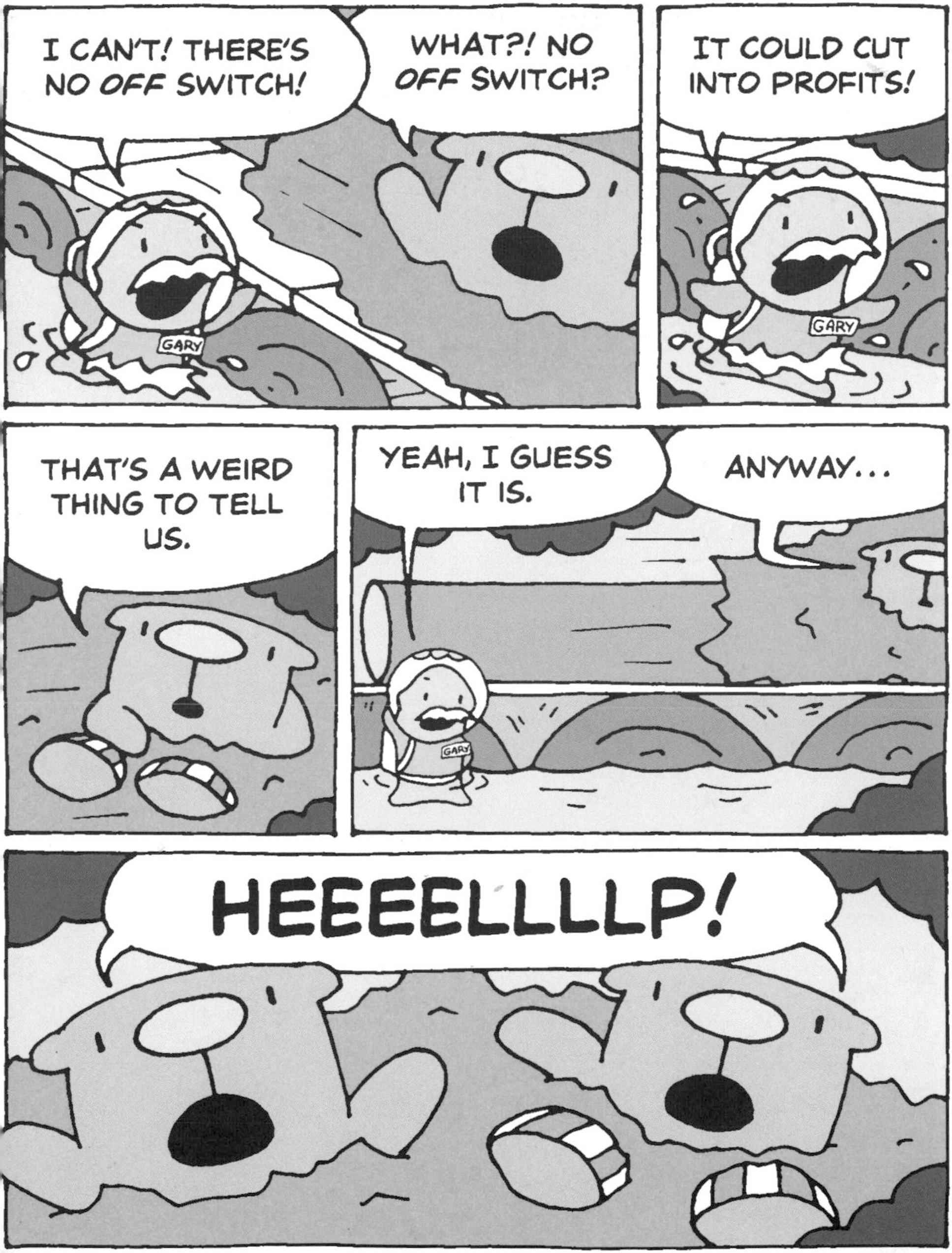
I CAN'T! THERE'S NO *OFF* SWITCH!
WHAT?! NO *OFF* SWITCH?
IT COULD CUT INTO PROFITS!
GARY
THAT'S A WEIRD THING TO TELL US.
YEAH, I GUESS IT IS.
ANYWAY...
GARY
HEEEEELLLLLP!

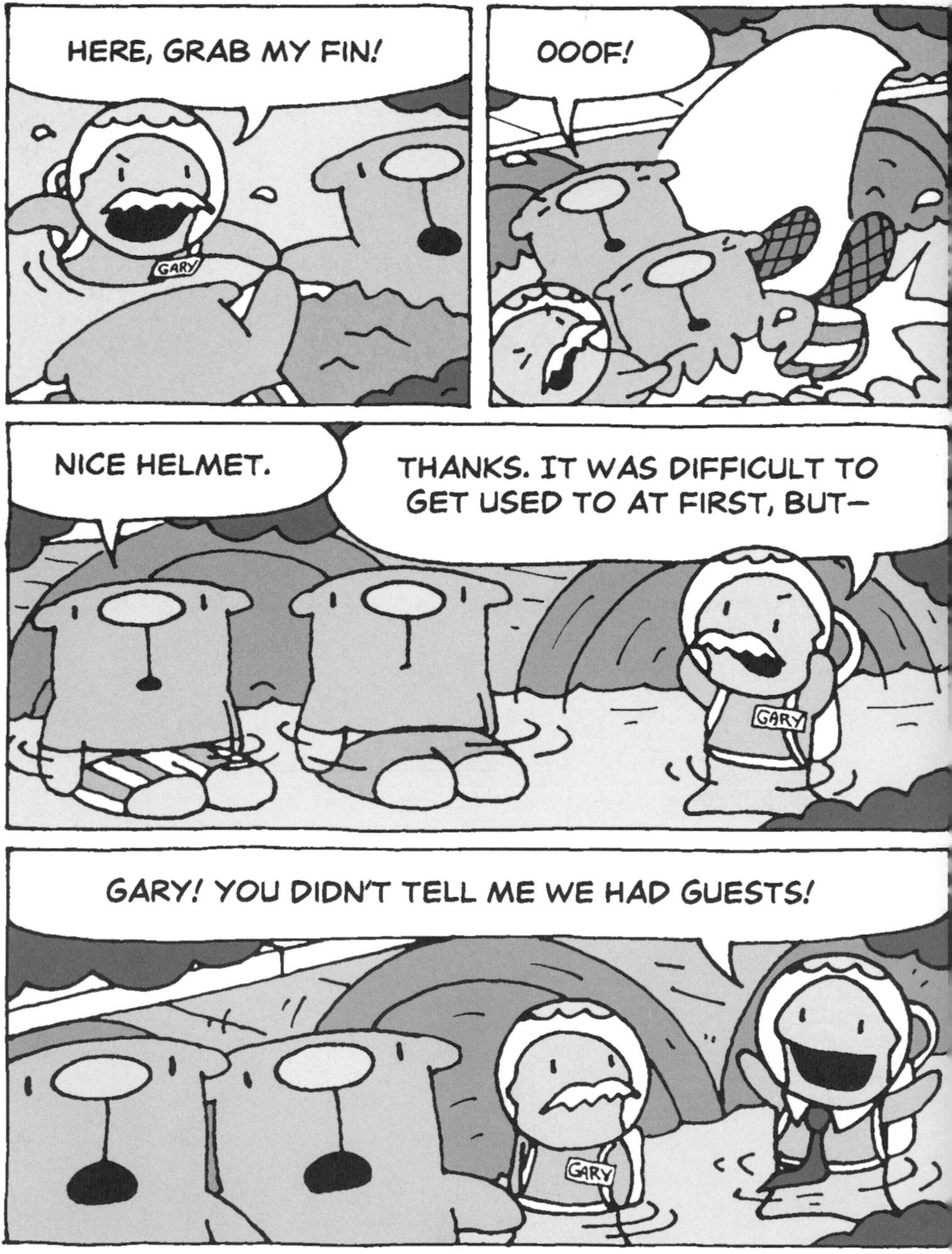
HERE, GRAB MY FIN!
GARY
OOOF!
NICE HELMET.
THANKS. IT WAS DIFFICULT TO GET USED TO AT FIRST, BUT—
GARY
GARY! YOU DIDN'T TELL ME WE HAD GUESTS!
GARY

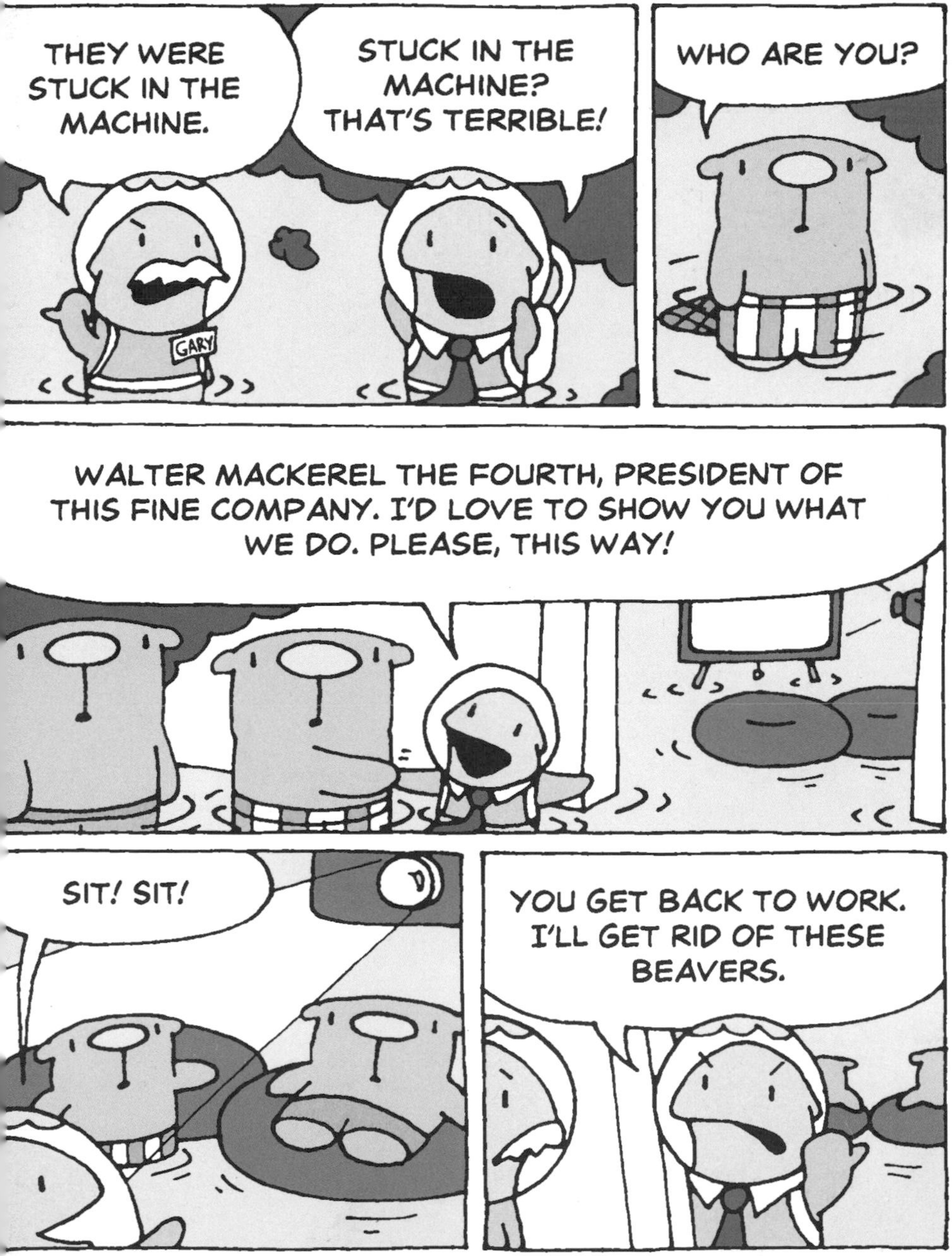

THEY WERE STUCK IN THE MACHINE.
STUCK IN THE MACHINE? THAT'S TERRIBLE!
GARY
WHO ARE YOU?
WALTER MACKEREL THE FOURTH, PRESIDENT OF THIS FINE COMPANY. I'D LOVE TO SHOW YOU WHAT WE DO. PLEASE, THIS WAY!
SIT! SIT!
YOU GET BACK TO WORK. I'LL GET RID OF THESE BEAVERS.

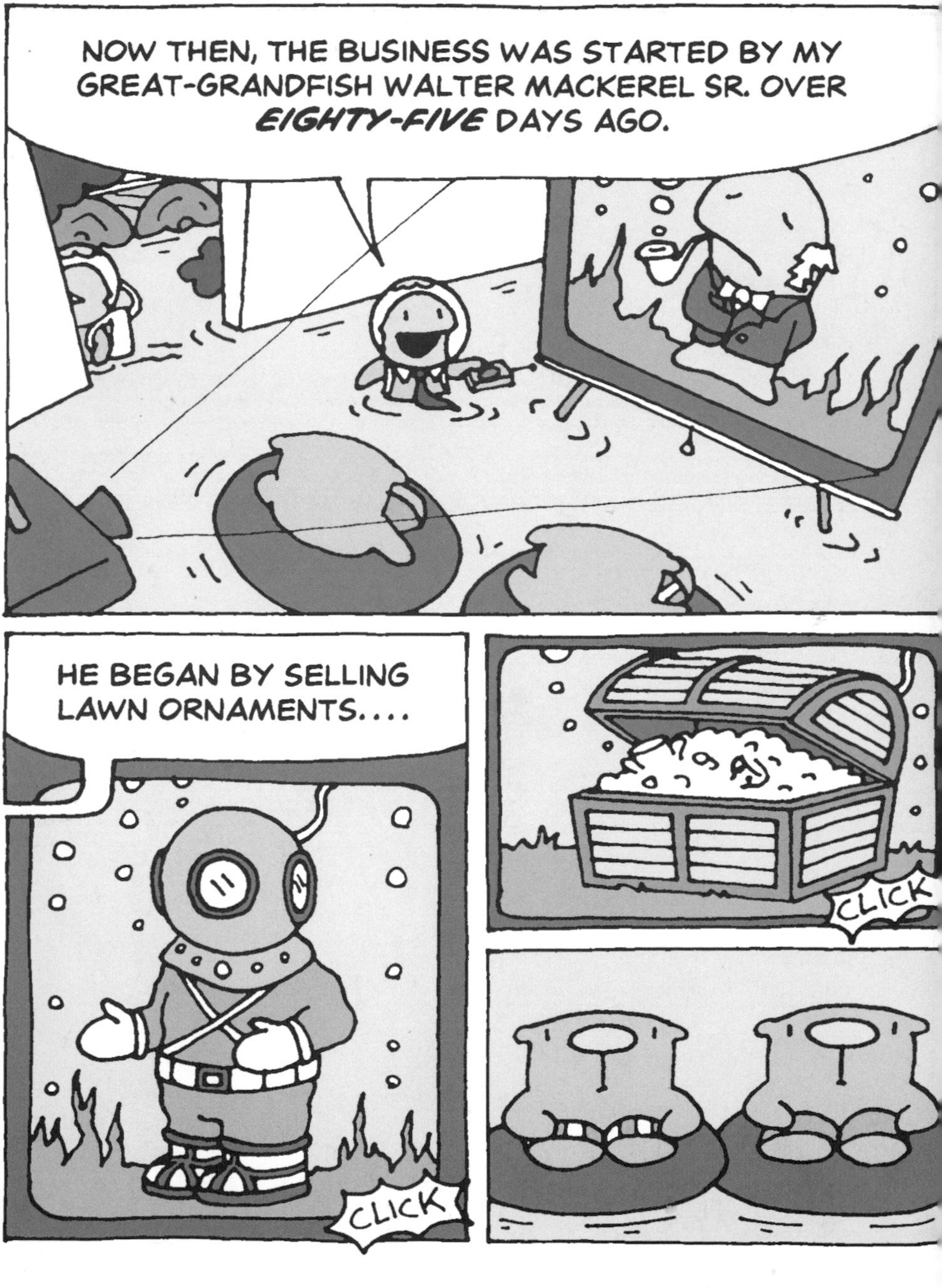
NOW THEN, THE BUSINESS WAS STARTED BY MY GREAT-GRANDFISH WALTER MACKEREL SR. OVER *EIGHTY-FIVE* DAYS AGO.
HE BEGAN BY SELLING LAWN ORNAMENTS....
CLICK
CLICK

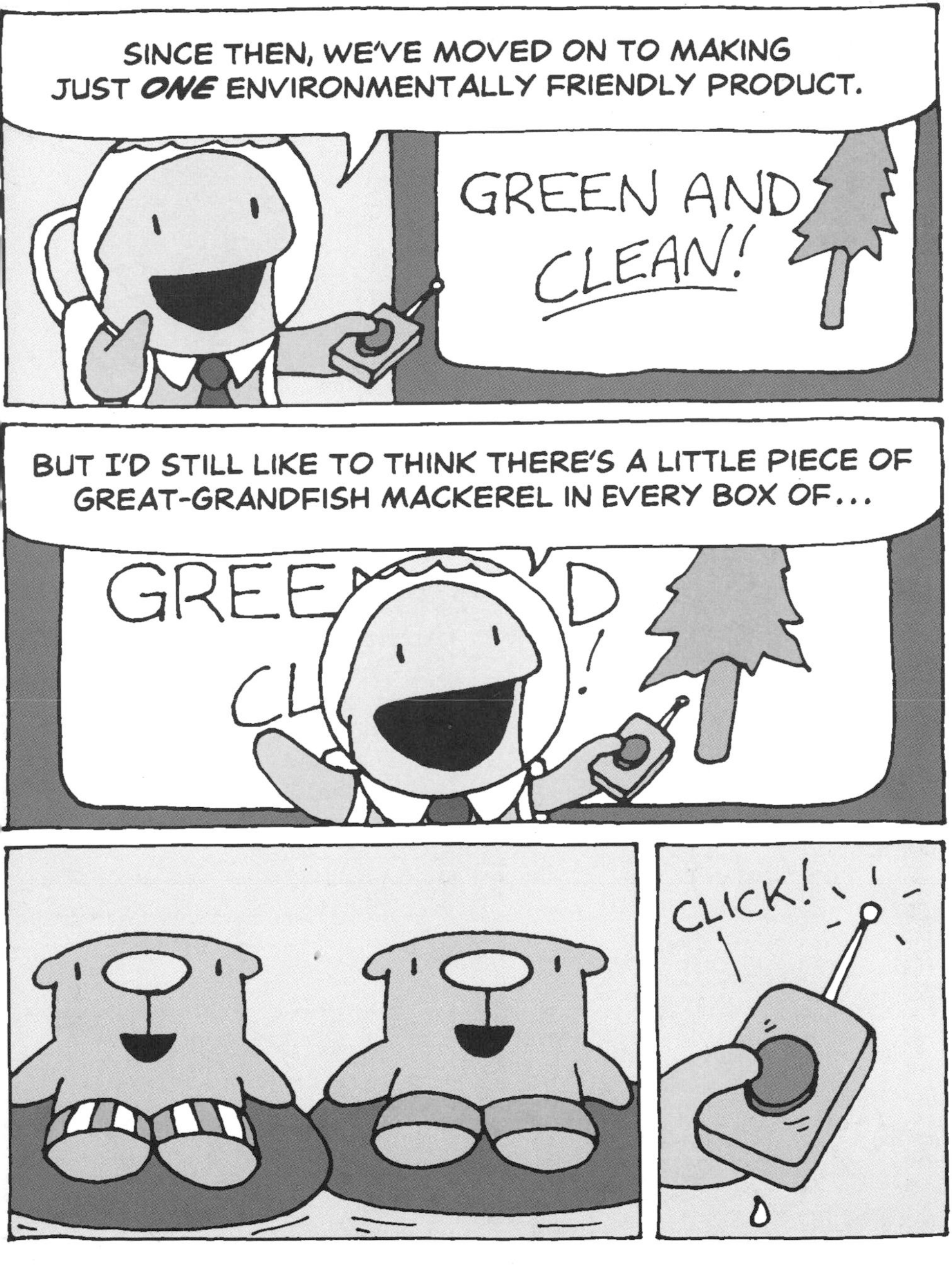
SINCE THEN, WE'VE MOVED ON TO MAKING JUST ***ONE*** ENVIRONMENTALLY FRIENDLY PRODUCT.
GREEN AND CLEAN!
BUT I'D STILL LIKE TO THINK THERE'S A LITTLE PIECE OF GREAT-GRANDFISH MACKEREL IN EVERY BOX OF...
CLICK!

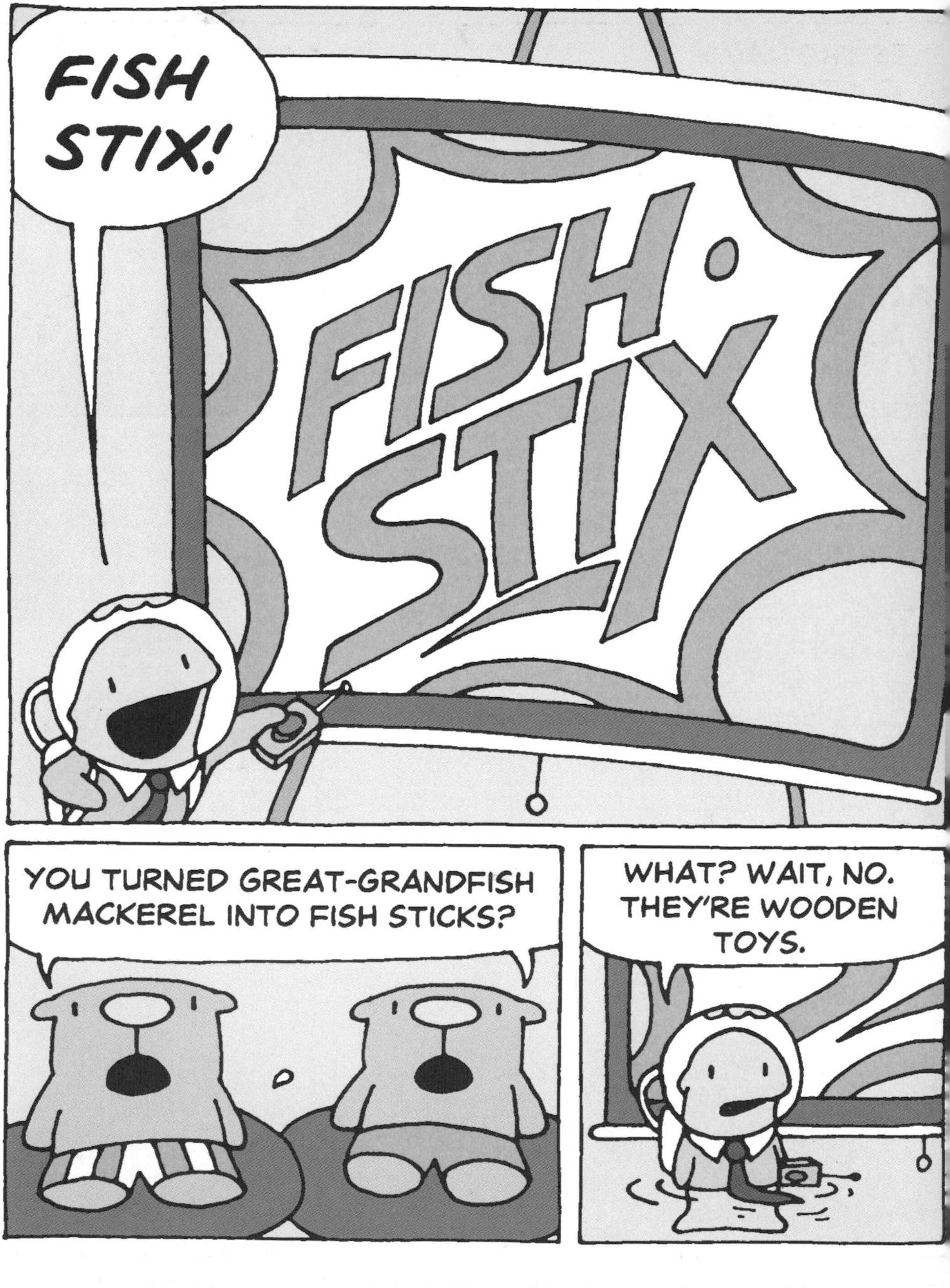
FISH STIX!
FISH STIX
YOU TURNED GREAT-GRANDFISH MACKEREL INTO FISH STICKS?
WHAT? WAIT, NO. THEY'RE WOODEN TOYS.

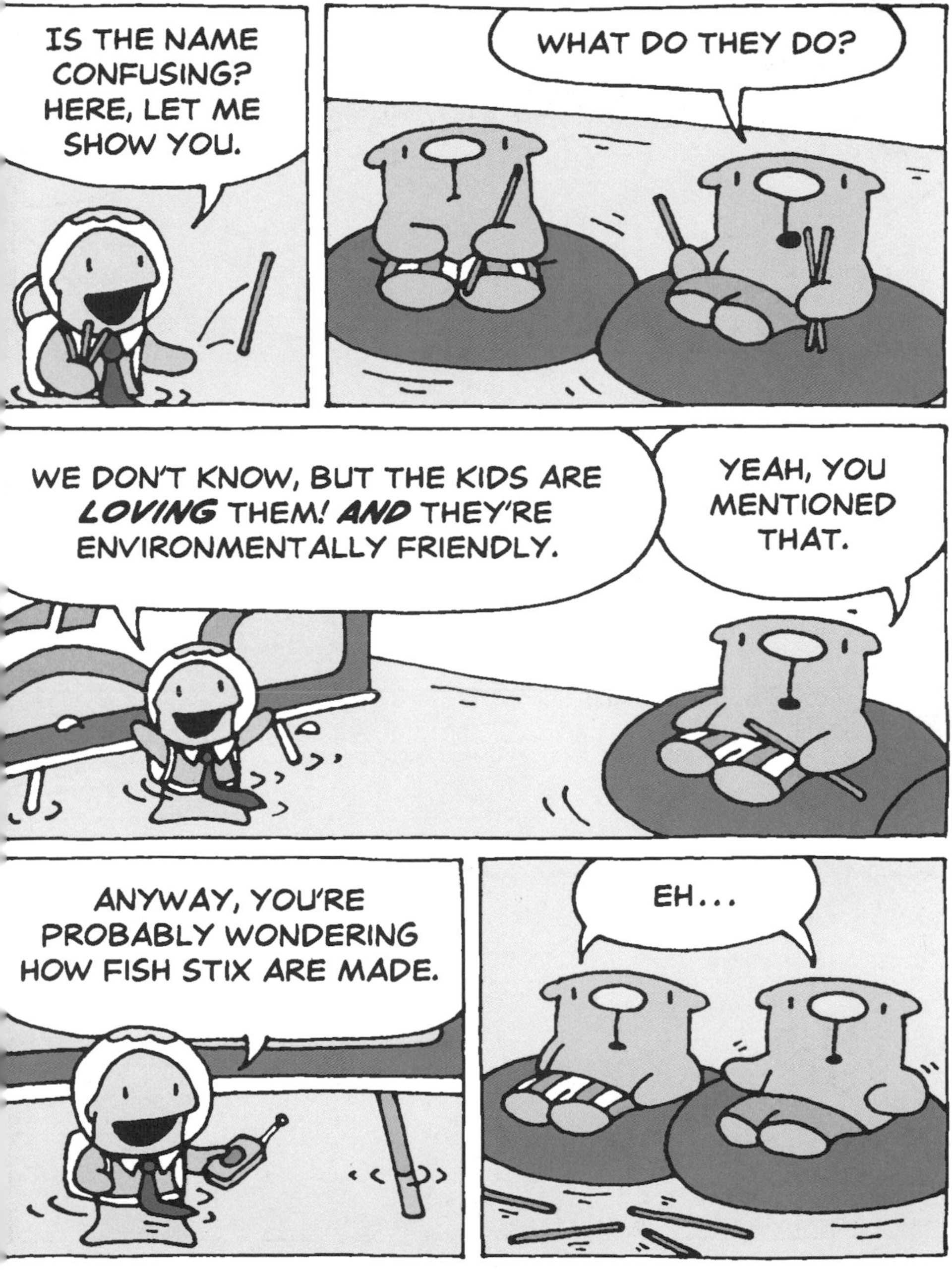
IS THE NAME CONFUSING? HERE, LET ME SHOW YOU.
WHAT DO THEY DO?
WE DON'T KNOW, BUT THE KIDS ARE *LOVING* THEM! ***AND*** THEY'RE ENVIRONMENTALLY FRIENDLY.
YEAH, YOU MENTIONED THAT.
ANYWAY, YOU'RE PROBABLY WONDERING HOW FISH STIX ARE MADE.
EH...

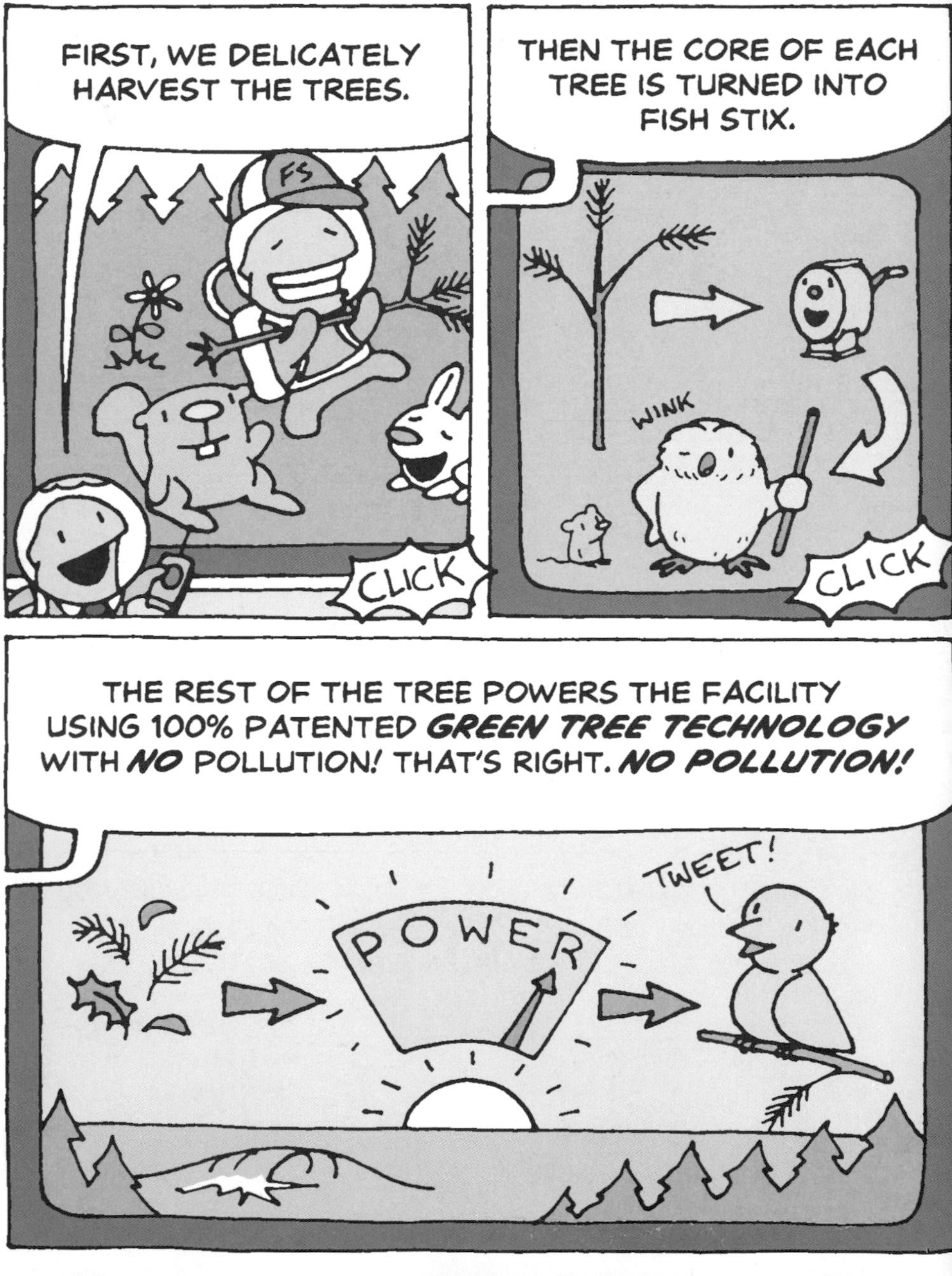
FIRST, WE DELICATELY HARVEST THE TREES.
FS
CLICK
THEN THE CORE OF EACH TREE IS TURNED INTO FISH STIX.
WINK
CLICK
THE REST OF THE TREE POWERS THE FACILITY USING 100% PATENTED GREEN TREE TECHNOLOGY WITH NO POLLUTION! THAT'S RIGHT. NO POLLUTION!
POWER
TWEET!

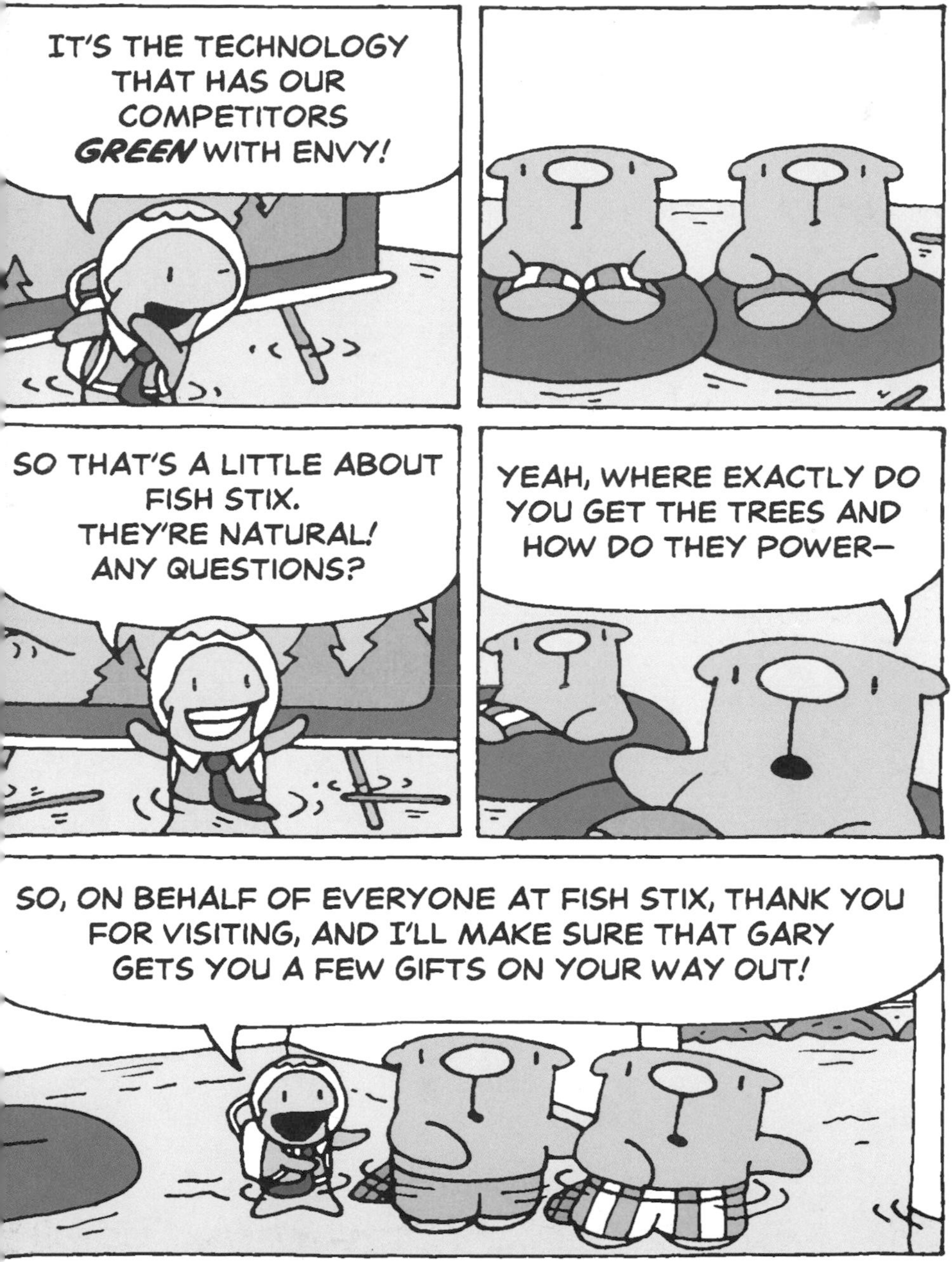
IT'S THE TECHNOLOGY THAT HAS OUR COMPETITORS *GREEN* WITH ENVY!
SO THAT'S A LITTLE ABOUT FISH STIX. THEY'RE NATURAL! ANY QUESTIONS?
YEAH, WHERE EXACTLY DO YOU GET THE TREES AND HOW DO THEY POWER–
SO, ON BEHALF OF EVERYONE AT FISH STIX, THANK YOU FOR VISITING, AND I'LL MAKE SURE THAT GARY GETS YOU A FEW GIFTS ON YOUR WAY OUT!

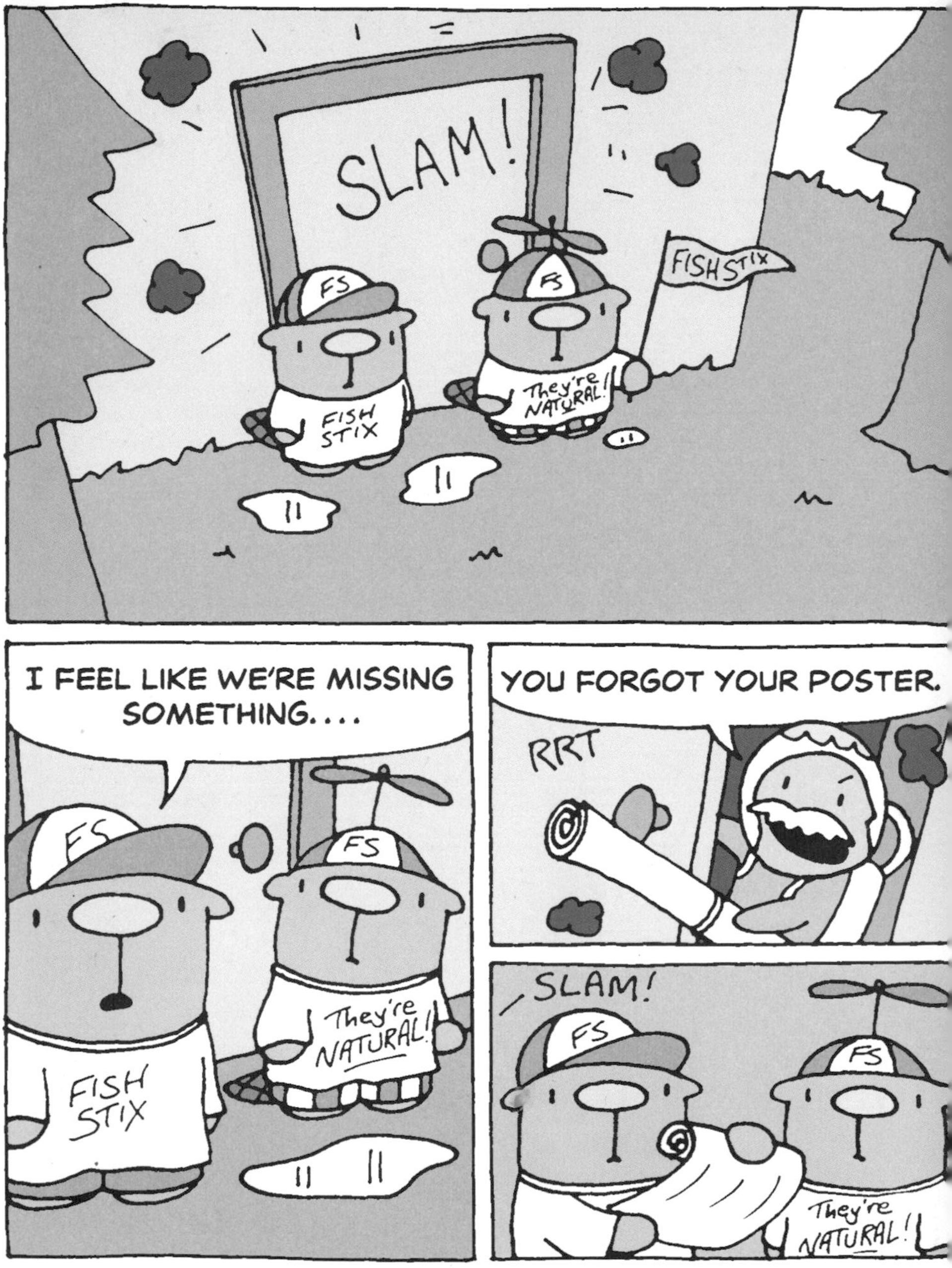
SLAM!
FS
FS
FISH STIX
They're NATURAL!
FISHSTIX
I FEEL LIKE WE'RE MISSING SOMETHING....
FS
FS
FISH STIX
They're NATURAL!
YOU FORGOT YOUR POSTER.
RRT
SLAM!
FS
FS
They're NATURAL!

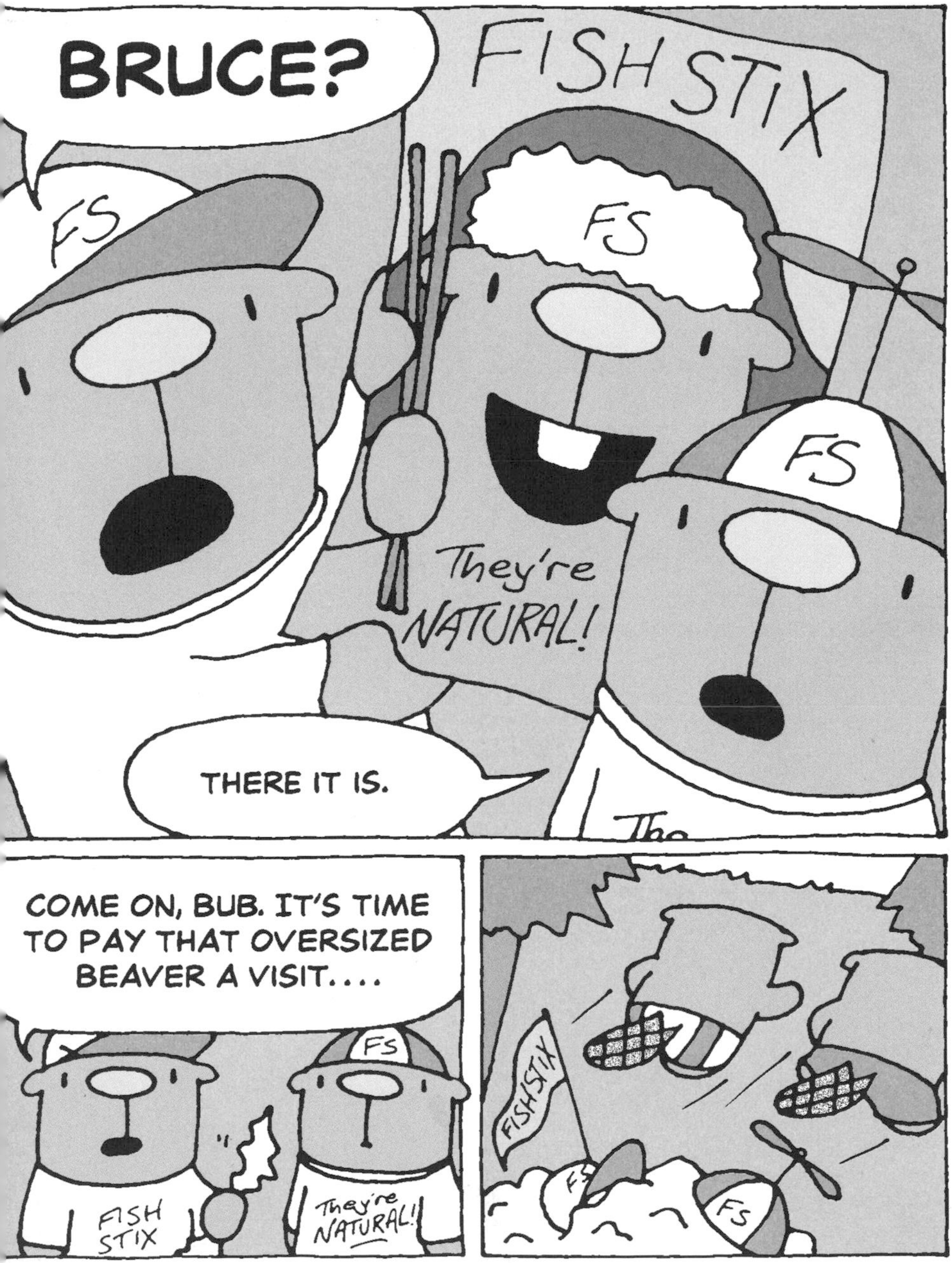
BRUCE?
FISH STIX
FS
FS
FS
They're NATURAL!
THERE IT IS.
COME ON, BUB. IT'S TIME TO PAY THAT OVERSIZED BEAVER A VISIT....
Fs
FISH STIX
They're NATURAL!
FISH STIX
FS
Fs

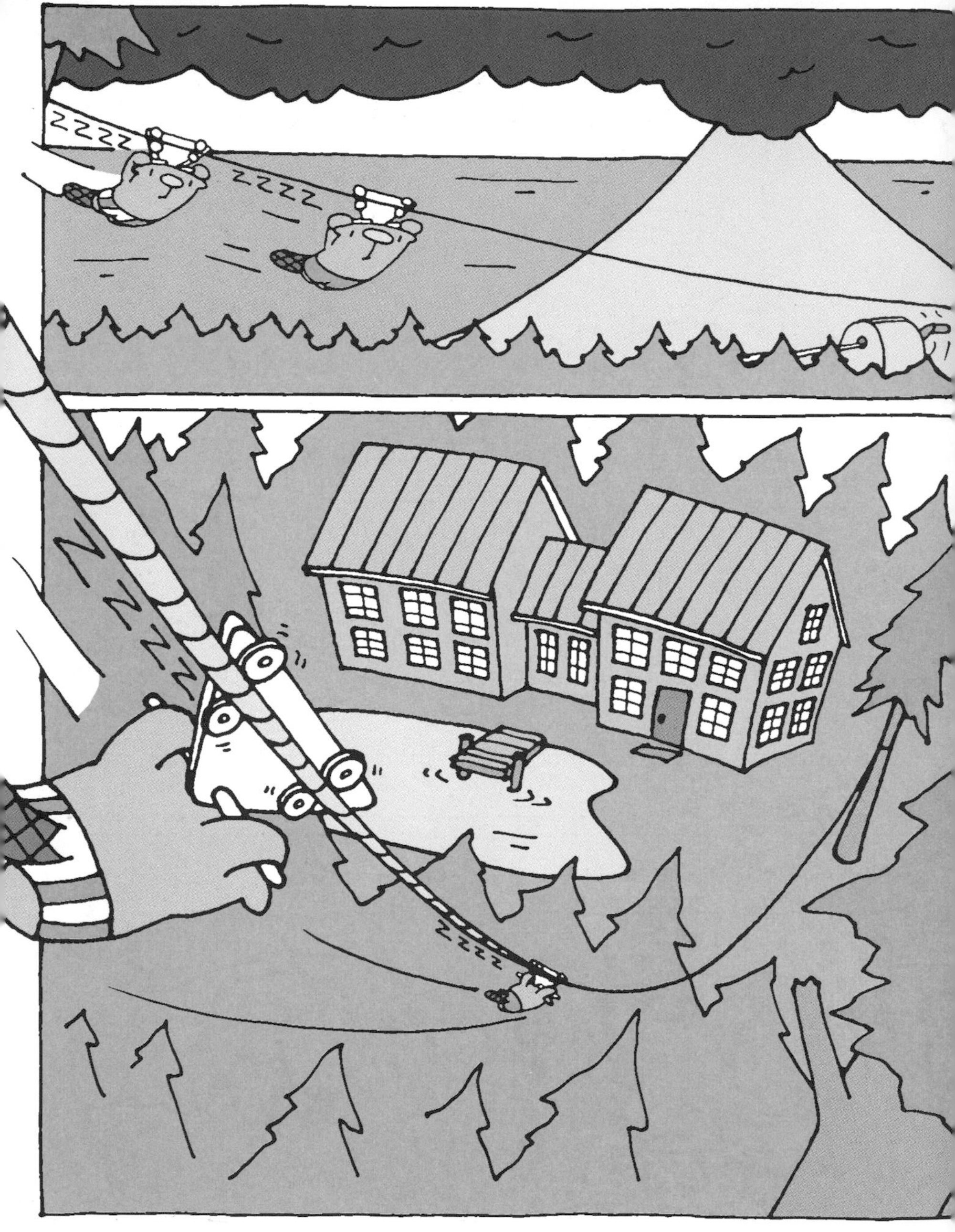
ZZZZ
ZZZZ
ZZZZ
ZZZZ

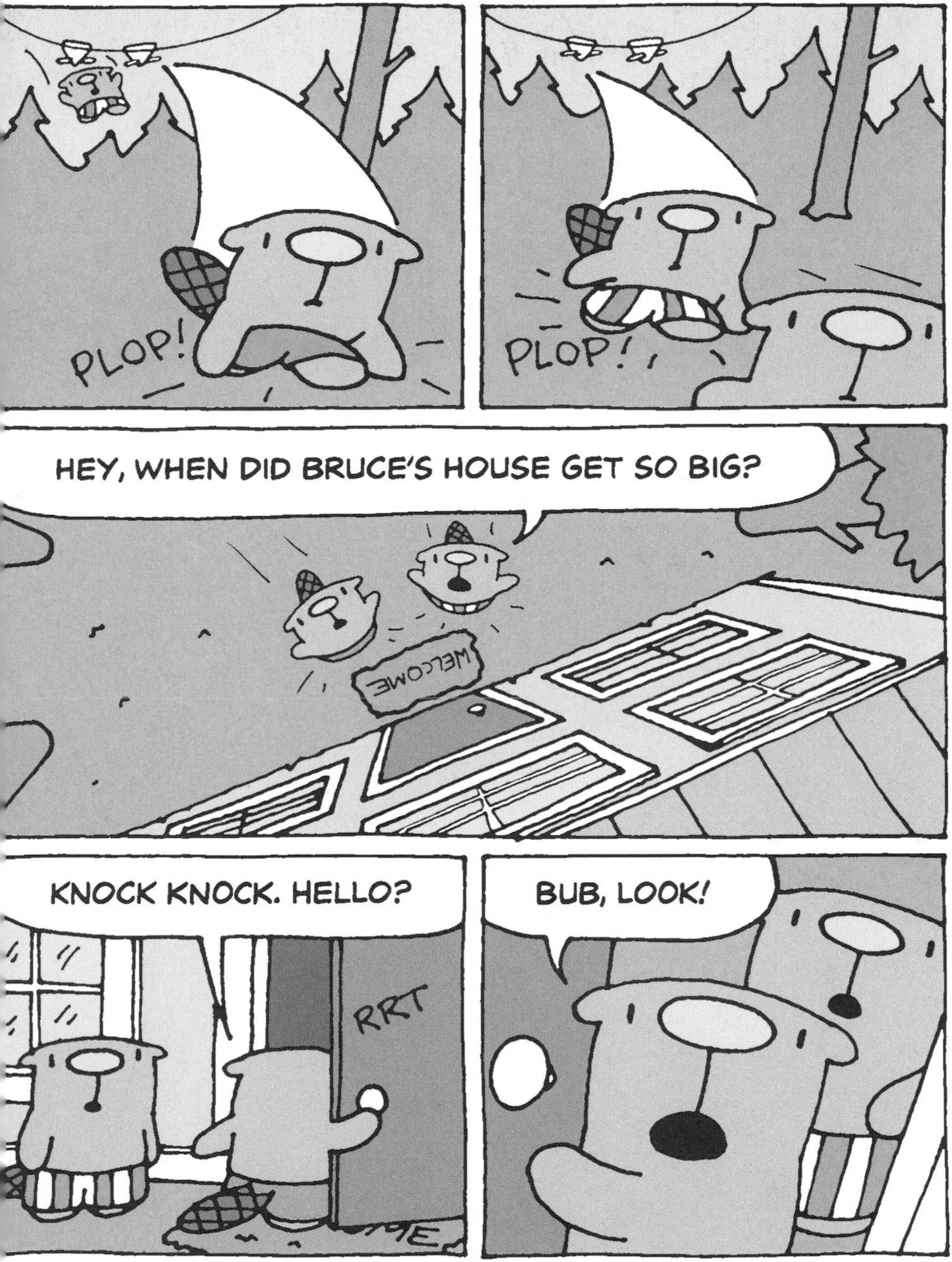
PLOP!
PLOP!
HEY, WHEN DID BRUCE'S HOUSE GET SO BIG?
WELCOME
KNOCK KNOCK. HELLO?
RRT
BUB, LOOK!

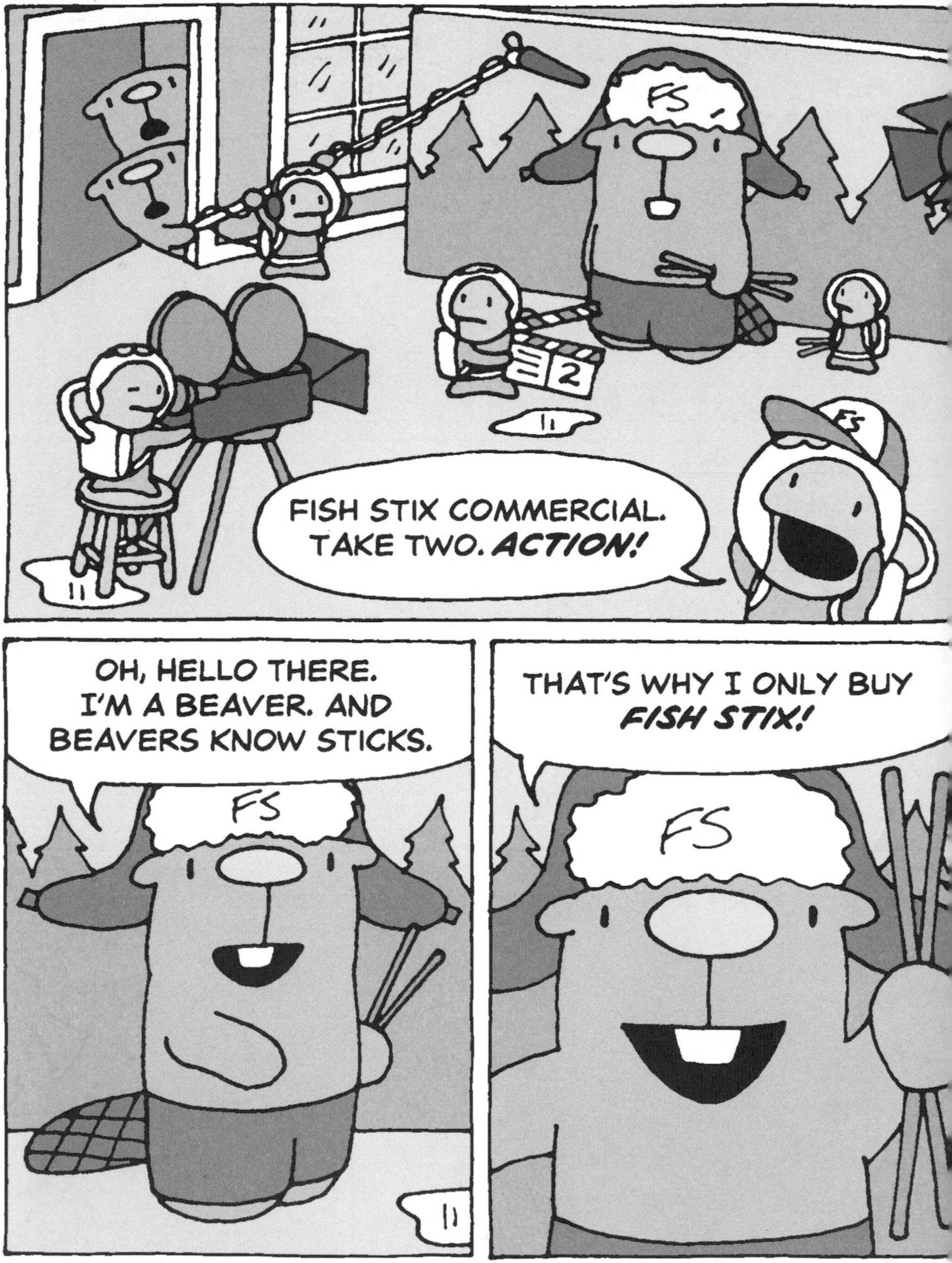
FISH STIX COMMERCIAL. TAKE TWO. ACTION!
OH, HELLO THERE. I'M A BEAVER. AND BEAVERS KNOW STICKS.
THAT'S WHY I ONLY BUY FISH STIX!

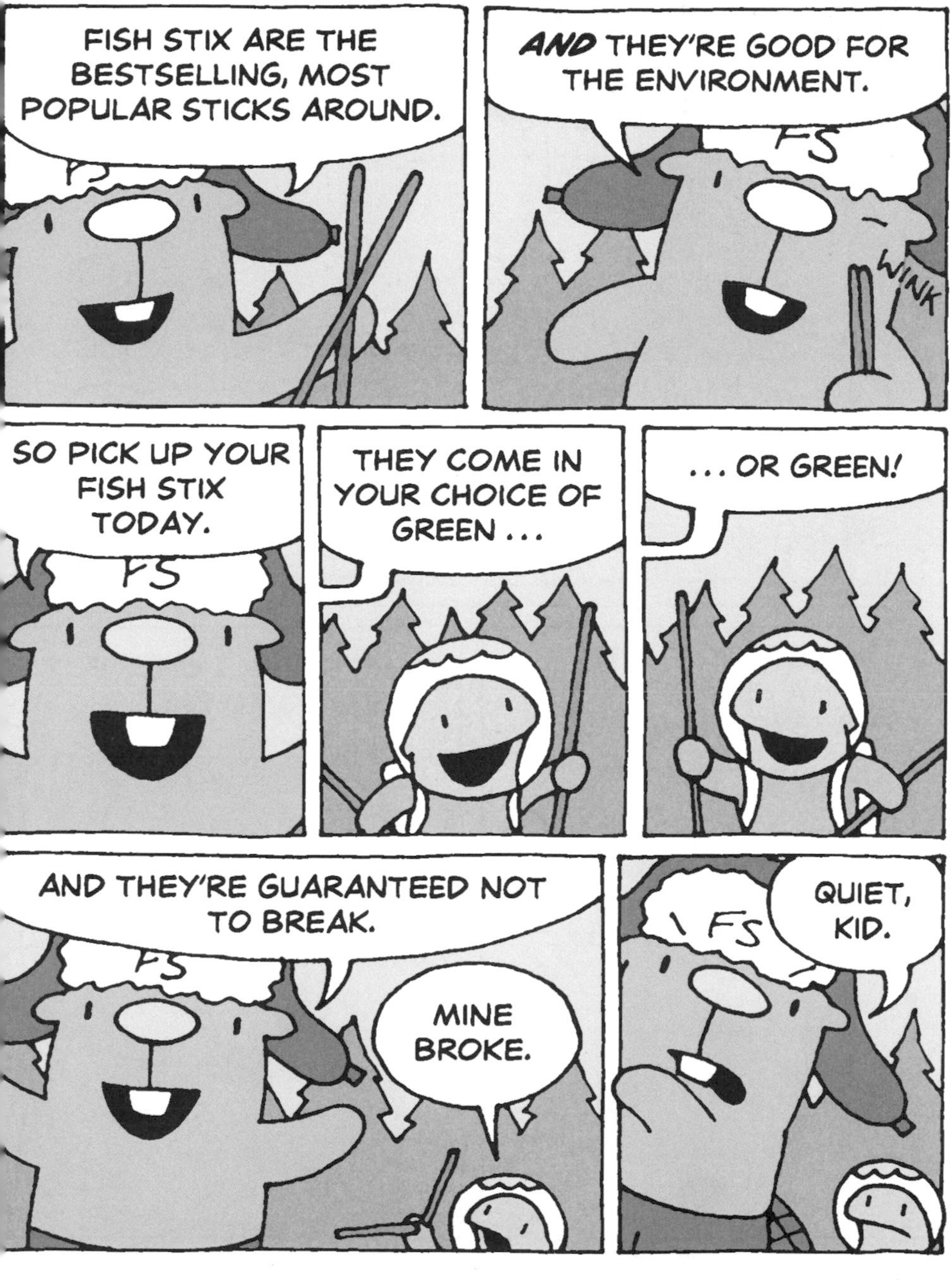
FISH STIX ARE THE BESTSELLING, MOST POPULAR STICKS AROUND.
FS
AND THEY'RE GOOD FOR THE ENVIRONMENT.
FS
WINK
SO PICK UP YOUR FISH STIX TODAY.
FS
THEY COME IN YOUR CHOICE OF GREEN . . .
. . . OR GREEN!
AND THEY'RE GUARANTEED NOT TO BREAK.
FS
MINE BROKE.
FS
QUIET, KID.

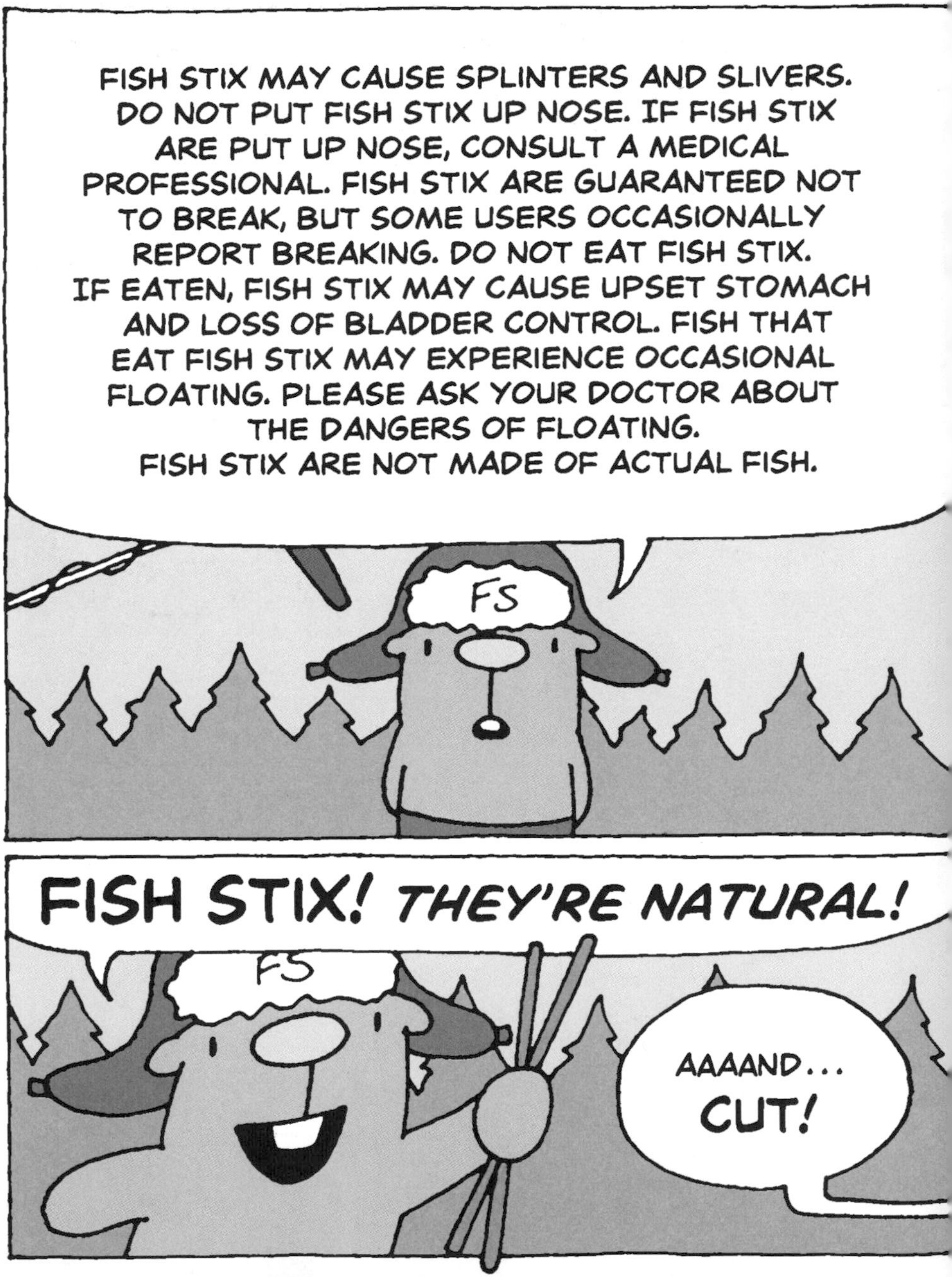
FISH STIX MAY CAUSE SPLINTERS AND SLIVERS. DO NOT PUT FISH STIX UP NOSE. IF FISH STIX ARE PUT UP NOSE, CONSULT A MEDICAL PROFESSIONAL. FISH STIX ARE GUARANTEED NOT TO BREAK, BUT SOME USERS OCCASIONALLY REPORT BREAKING. DO NOT EAT FISH STIX. IF EATEN, FISH STIX MAY CAUSE UPSET STOMACH AND LOSS OF BLADDER CONTROL. FISH THAT EAT FISH STIX MAY EXPERIENCE OCCASIONAL FLOATING. PLEASE ASK YOUR DOCTOR ABOUT THE DANGERS OF FLOATING. FISH STIX ARE NOT MADE OF ACTUAL FISH.
FS
FISH STIX! *THEY'RE NATURAL!*
FS
AAAAND... CUT!

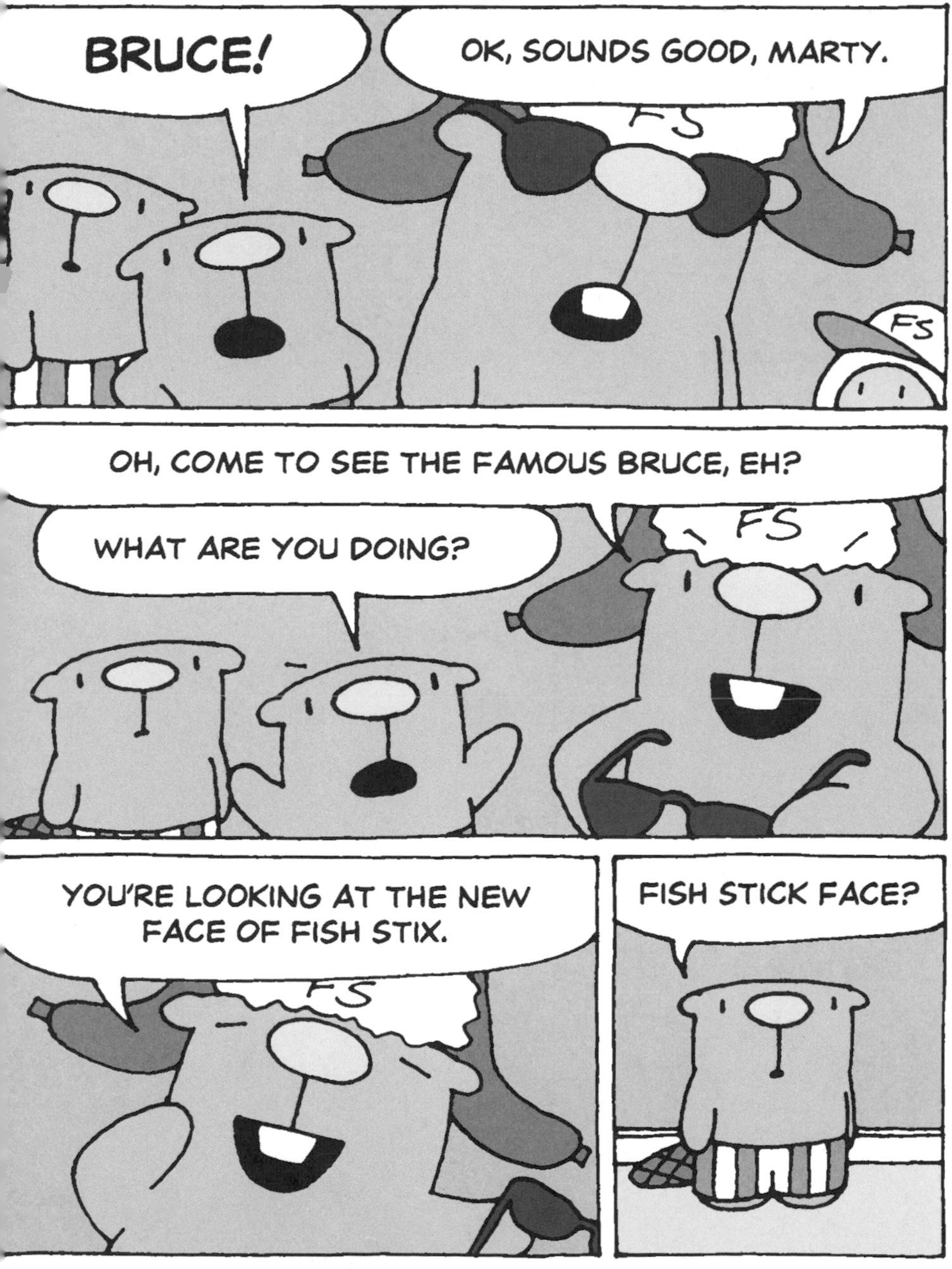
BRUCE!
OK, SOUNDS GOOD, MARTY.
FS
FS
OH, COME TO SEE THE FAMOUS BRUCE, EH?
WHAT ARE YOU DOING?
FS
YOU'RE LOOKING AT THE NEW FACE OF FISH STIX.
FS
FISH STICK FACE?

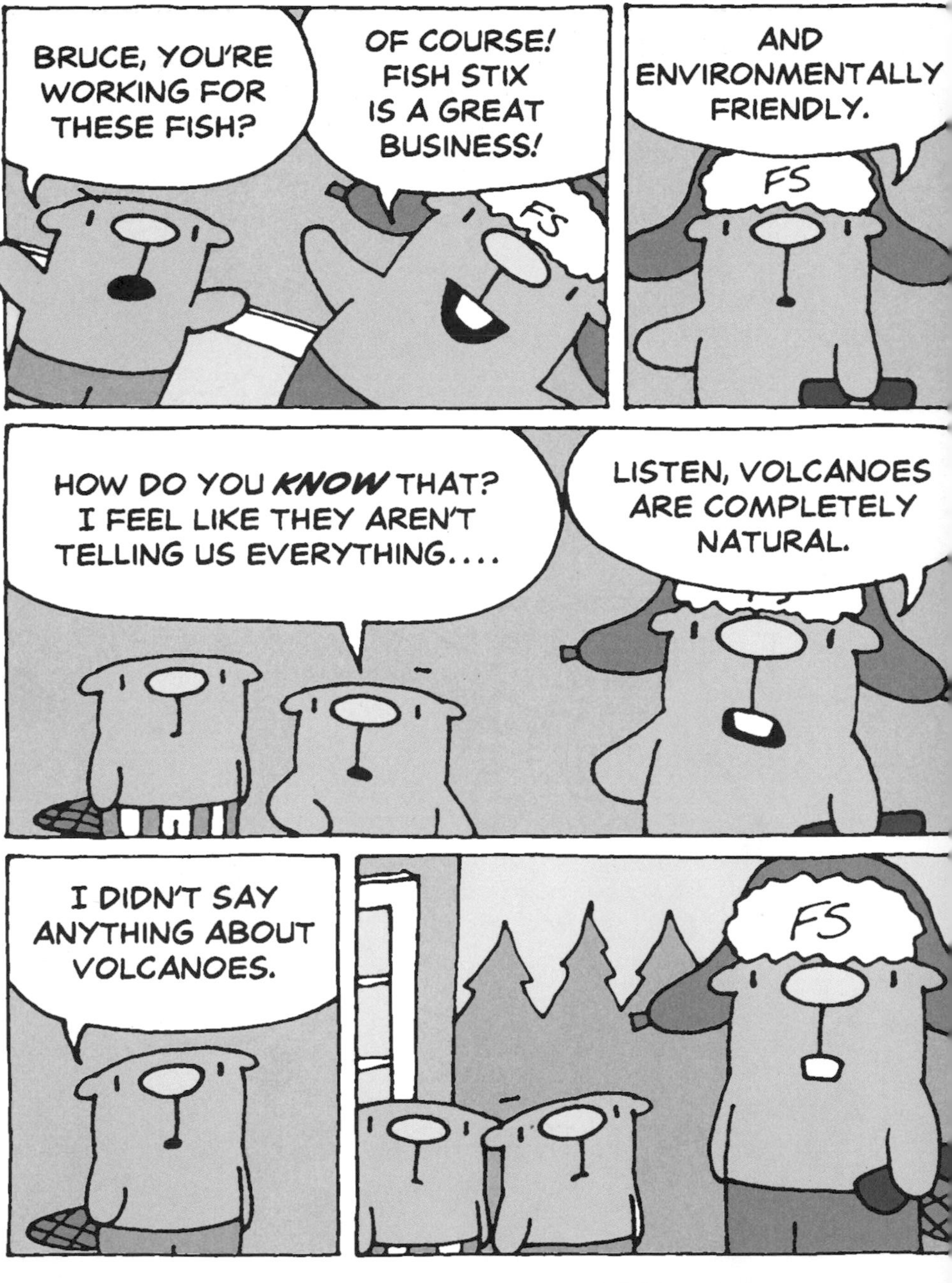
BRUCE, YOU'RE WORKING FOR THESE FISH?
OF COURSE! FISH STIX IS A GREAT BUSINESS!
FS
AND ENVIRONMENTALLY FRIENDLY.
FS
HOW DO YOU *KNOW* THAT? I FEEL LIKE THEY AREN'T TELLING US EVERYTHING....
LISTEN, VOLCANOES ARE COMPLETELY NATURAL.
I DIDN'T SAY ANYTHING ABOUT VOLCANOES.
FS

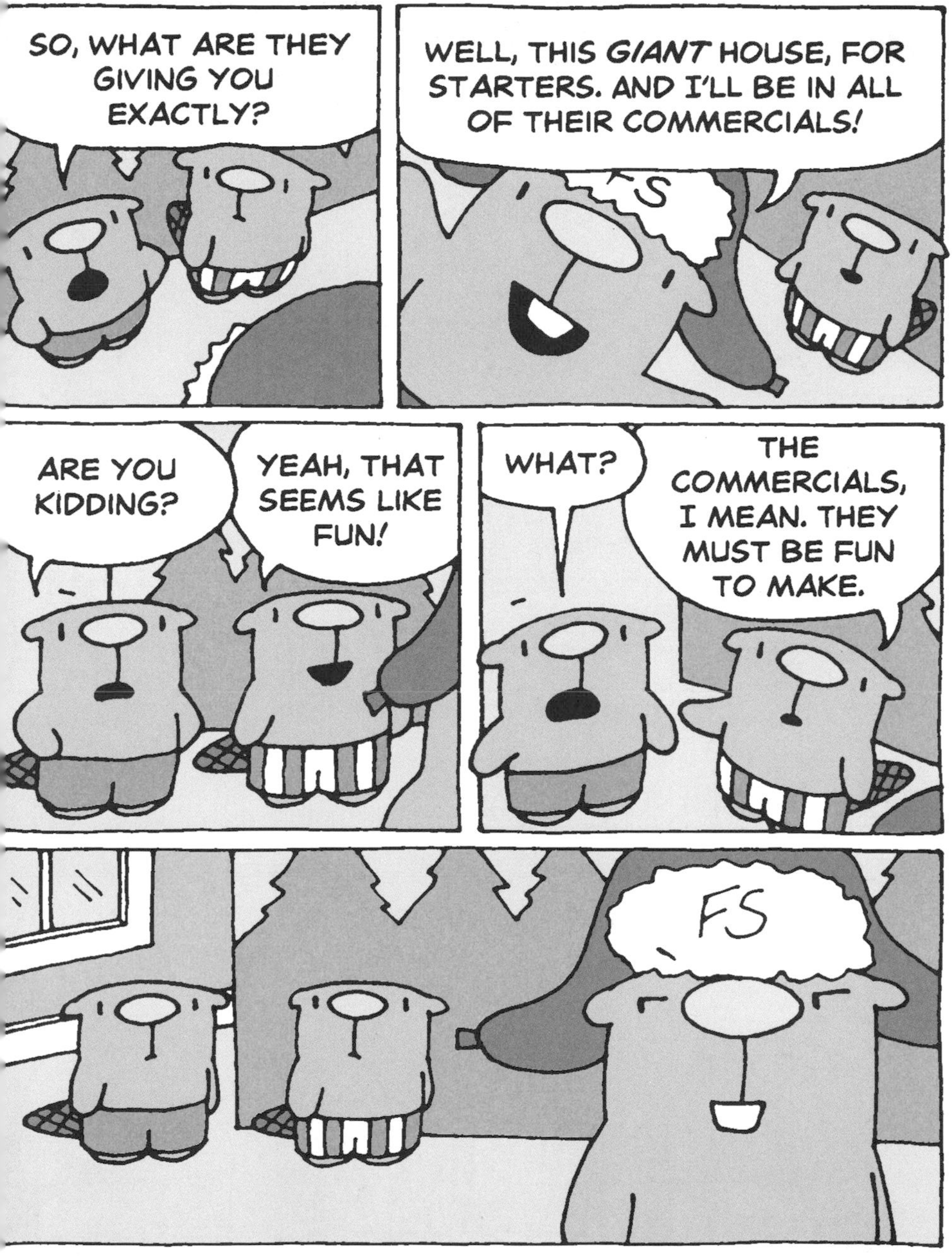
SO, WHAT ARE THEY GIVING YOU EXACTLY?
WELL, THIS *GIANT* HOUSE, FOR STARTERS. AND I'LL BE IN ALL OF THEIR COMMERCIALS!
FS
ARE YOU KIDDING?
YEAH, THAT SEEMS LIKE FUN!
WHAT?
THE COMMERCIALS, I MEAN. THEY MUST BE FUN TO MAKE.
FS

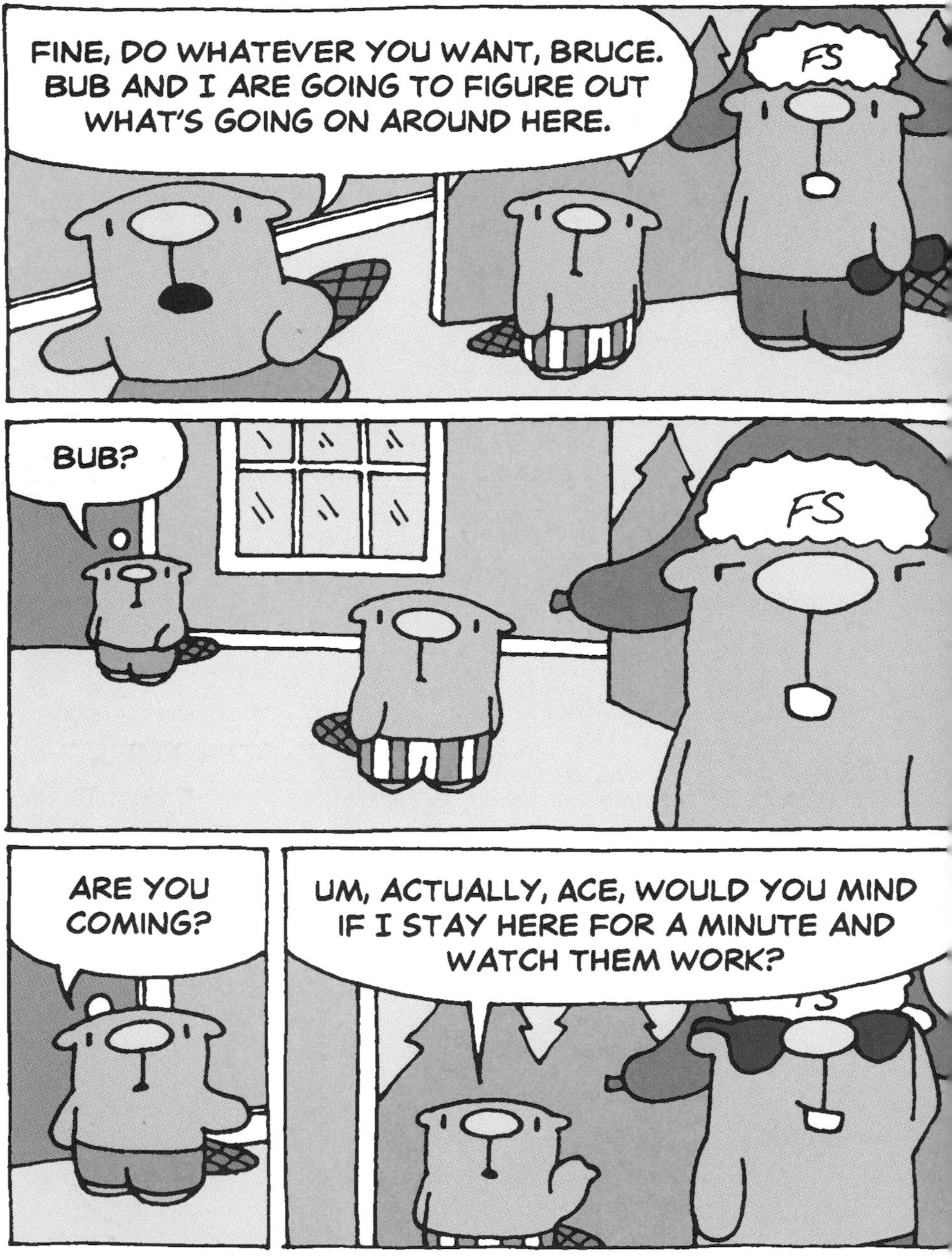
FINE, DO WHATEVER YOU WANT, BRUCE. BUB AND I ARE GOING TO FIGURE OUT WHAT'S GOING ON AROUND HERE.
FS
BUB?
FS
ARE YOU COMING?
UM, ACTUALLY, ACE, WOULD YOU MIND IF I STAY HERE FOR A MINUTE AND WATCH THEM WORK?

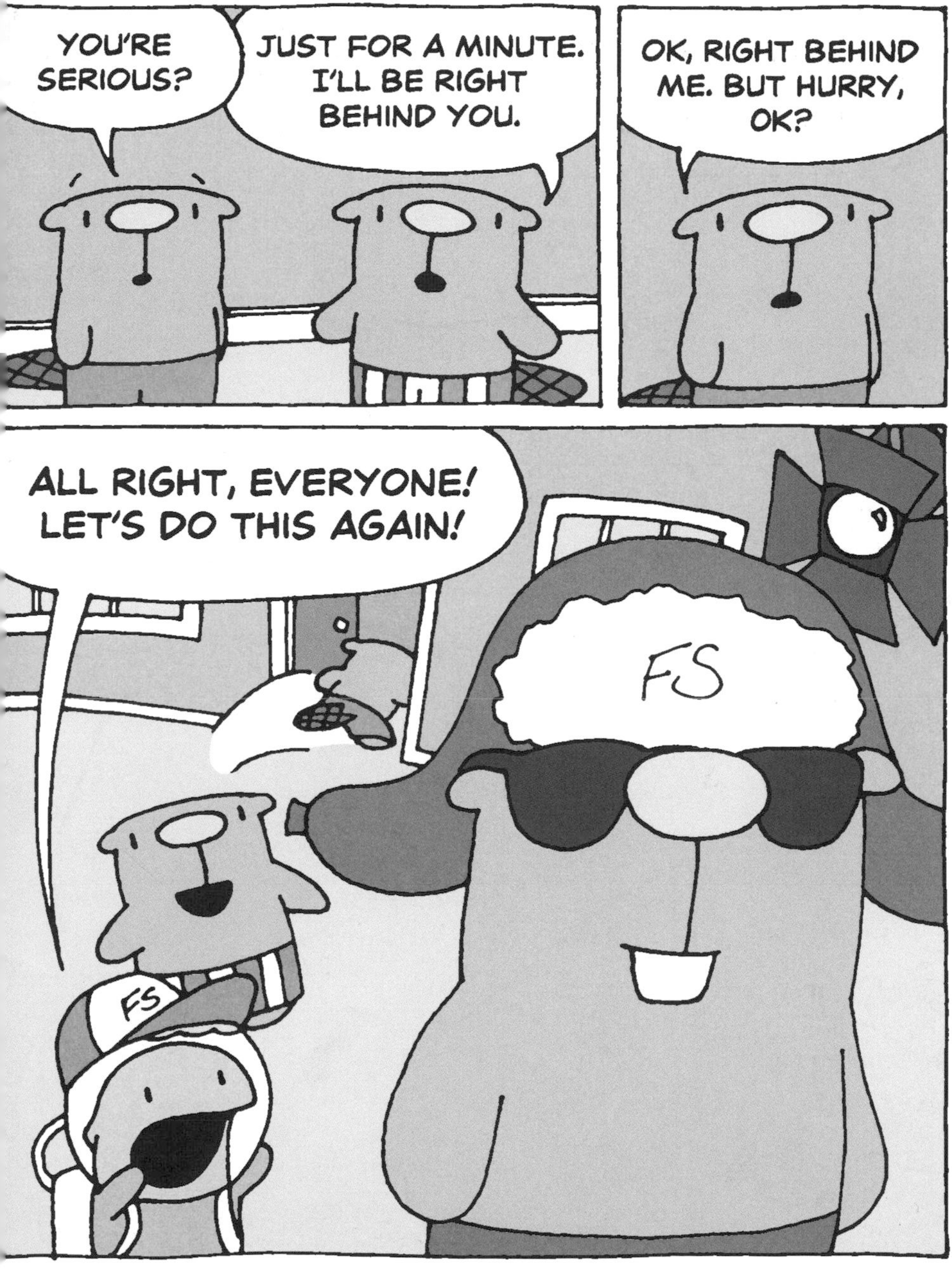
YOU'RE SERIOUS?
JUST FOR A MINUTE. I'LL BE RIGHT BEHIND YOU.
OK, RIGHT BEHIND ME. BUT HURRY, OK?
ALL RIGHT, EVERYONE! LET'S DO THIS AGAIN!
FS
FS

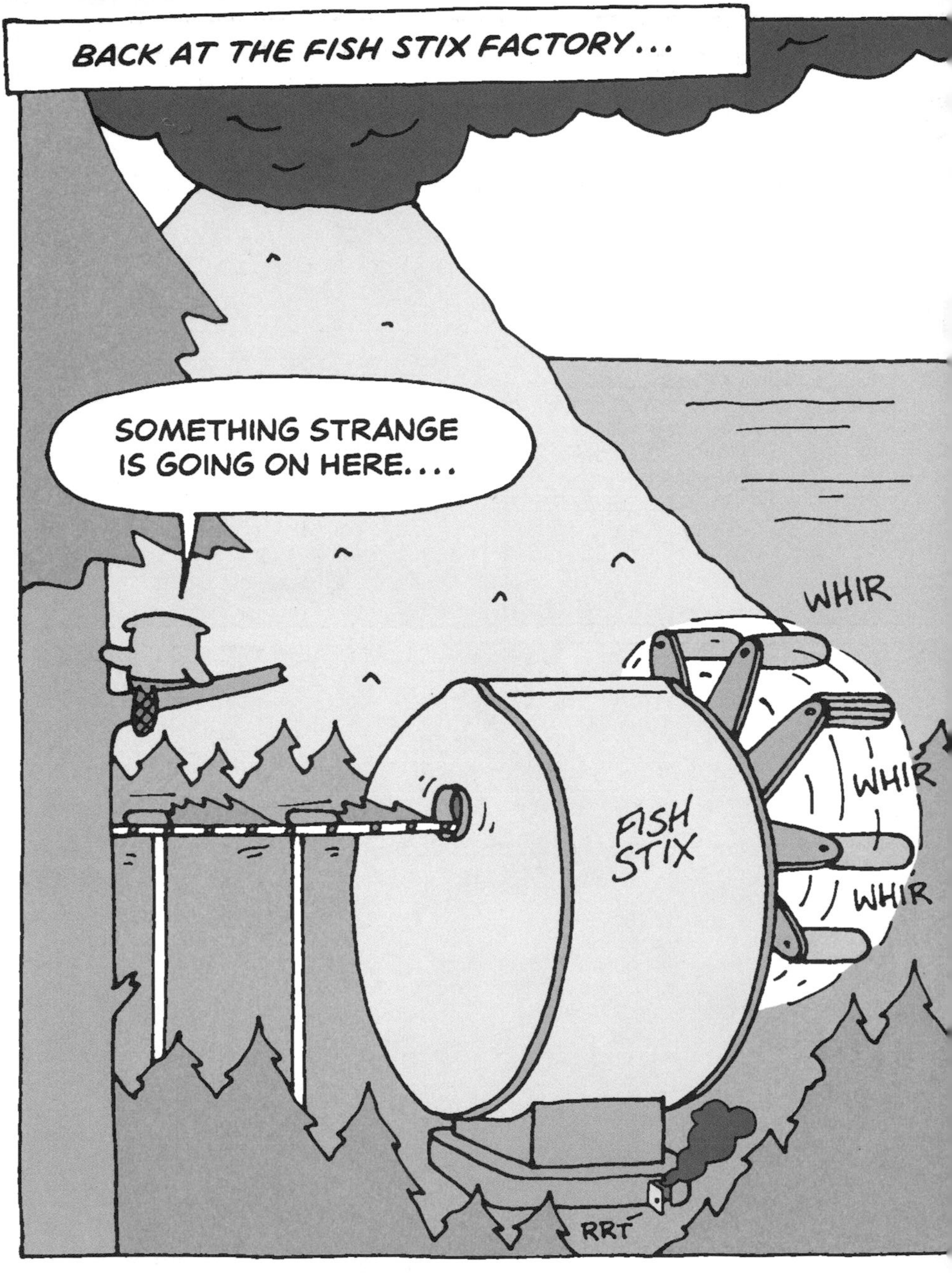
BACK AT THE FISH STIX FACTORY...
SOMETHING STRANGE IS GOING ON HERE....
WHIR
WHIR
WHIR
FISH STIX
RRT

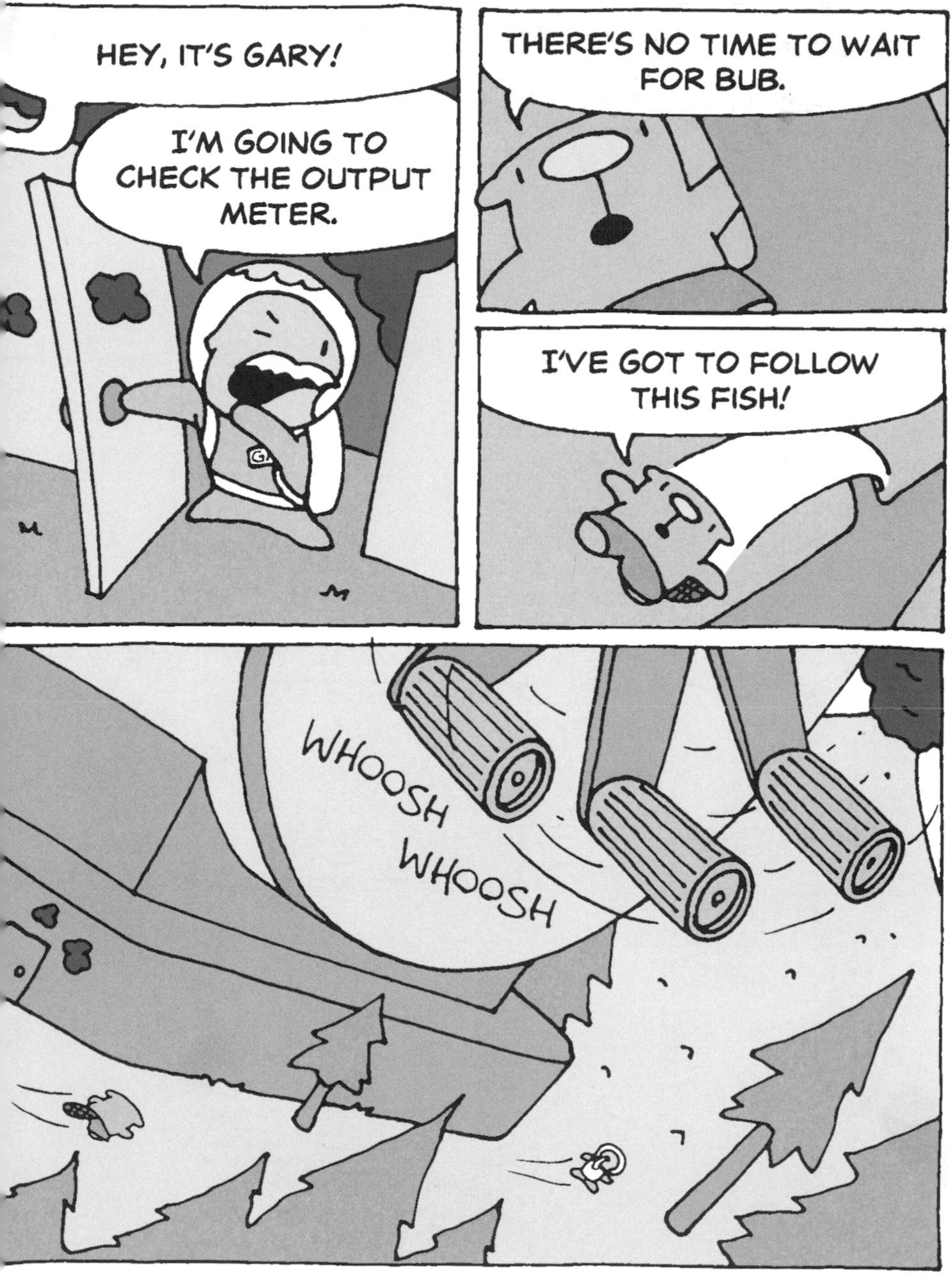
HEY, IT'S GARY!
I'M GOING TO CHECK THE OUTPUT METER.
THERE'S NO TIME TO WAIT FOR BUB.
I'VE GOT TO FOLLOW THIS FISH!
WHOOSH
WHOOSH

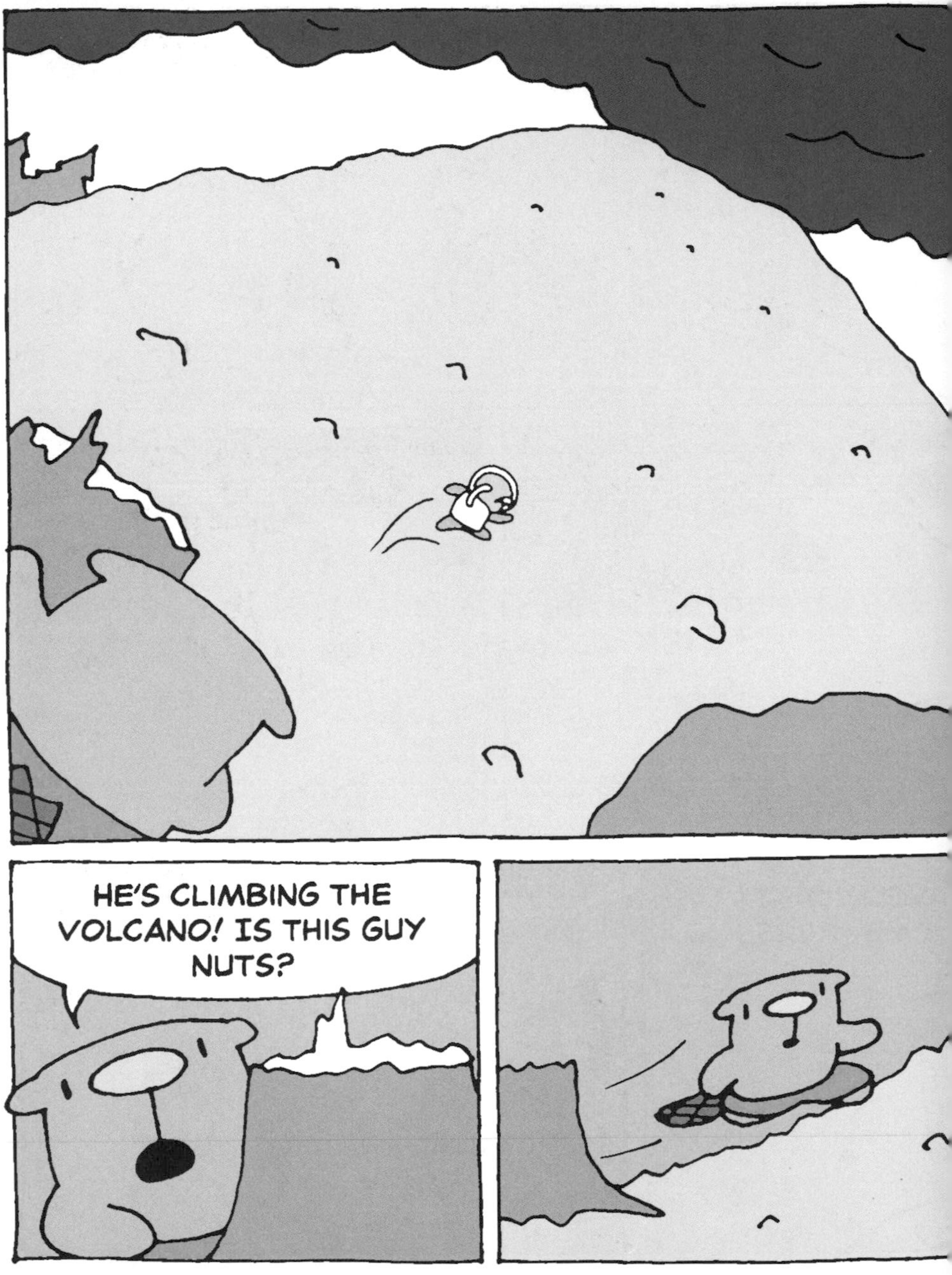
HE'S CLIMBING THE VOLCANO! IS THIS GUY NUTS?

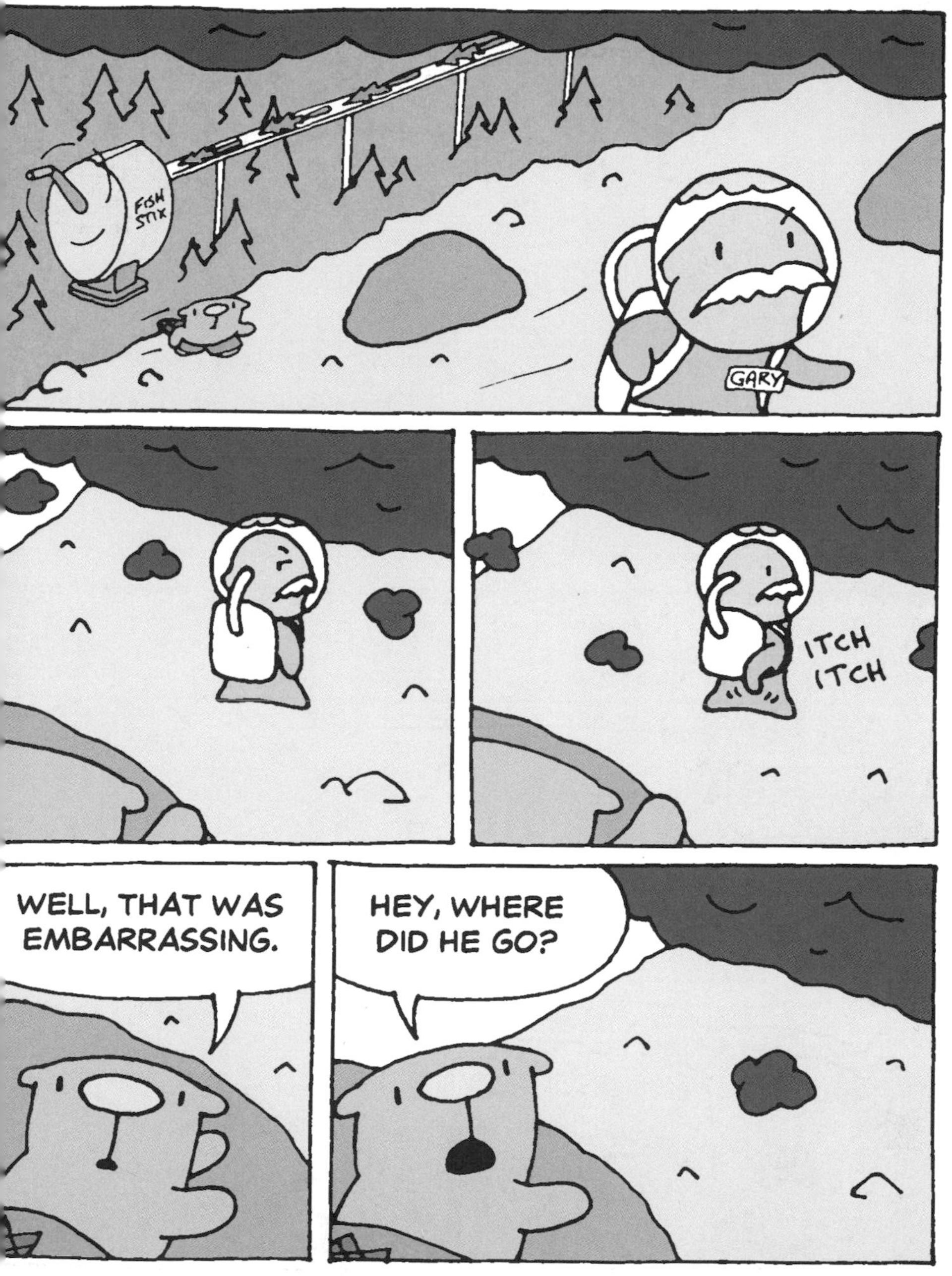
FISH STIX
GARY
ITCH ITCH
WELL, THAT WAS EMBARRASSING.
HEY, WHERE DID HE GO?

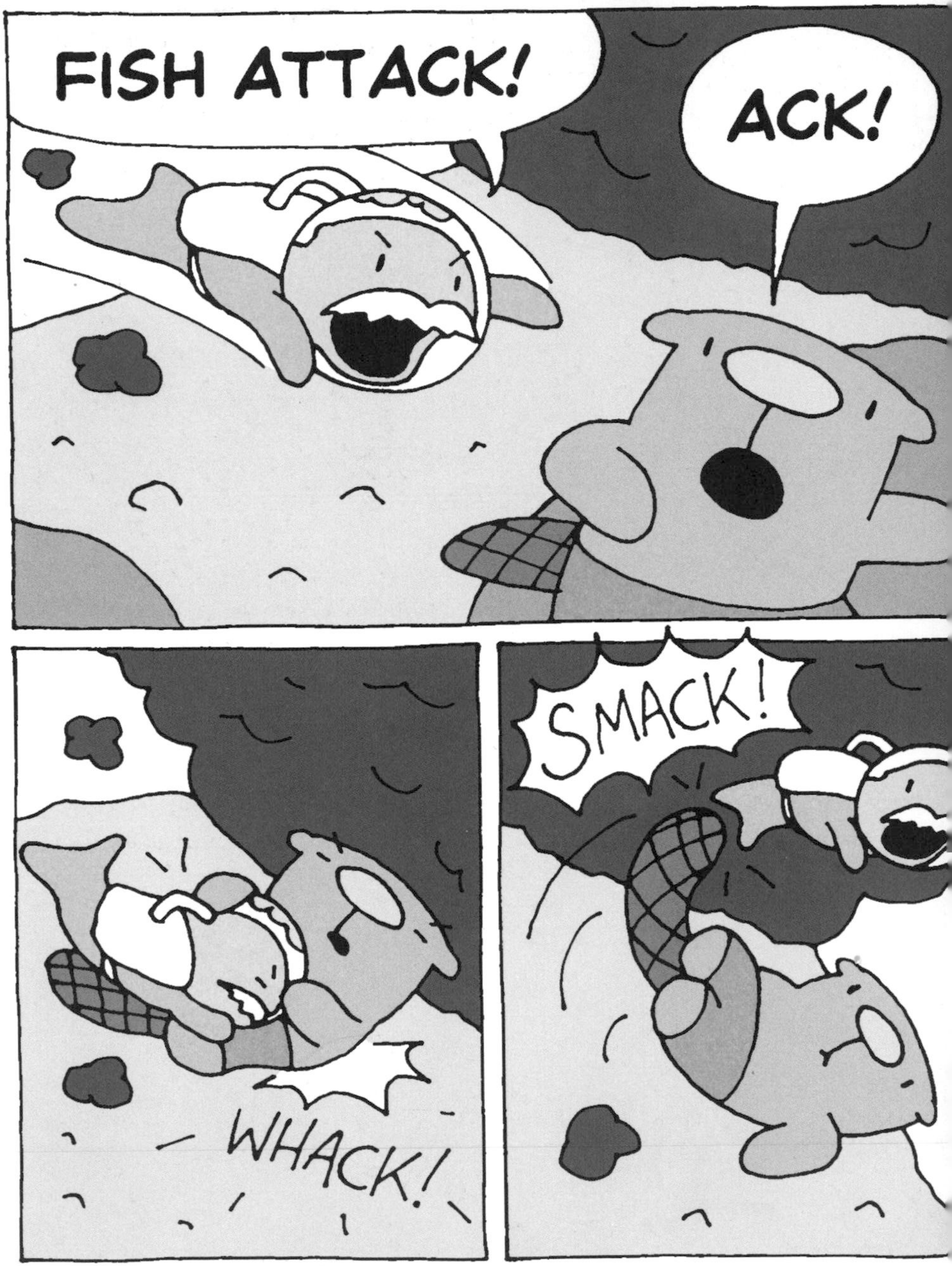
FISH ATTACK!
ACK!
WHACK!
SMACK!

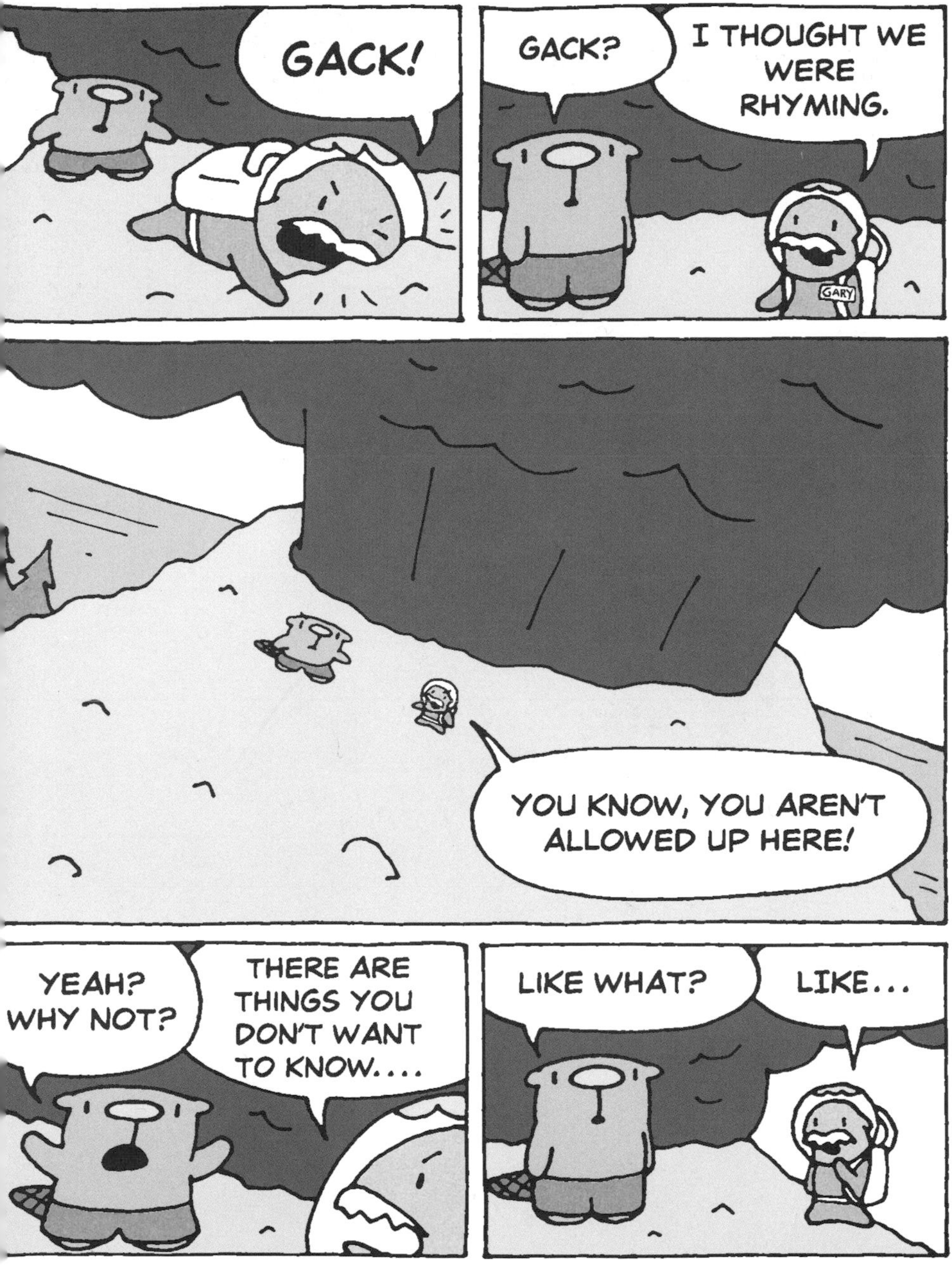
GACK!
GACK?
I THOUGHT WE WERE RHYMING.
GARY
YOU KNOW, YOU AREN'T ALLOWED UP HERE!
YEAH? WHY NOT?
THERE ARE THINGS YOU DON'T WANT TO KNOW....
LIKE WHAT?
LIKE...

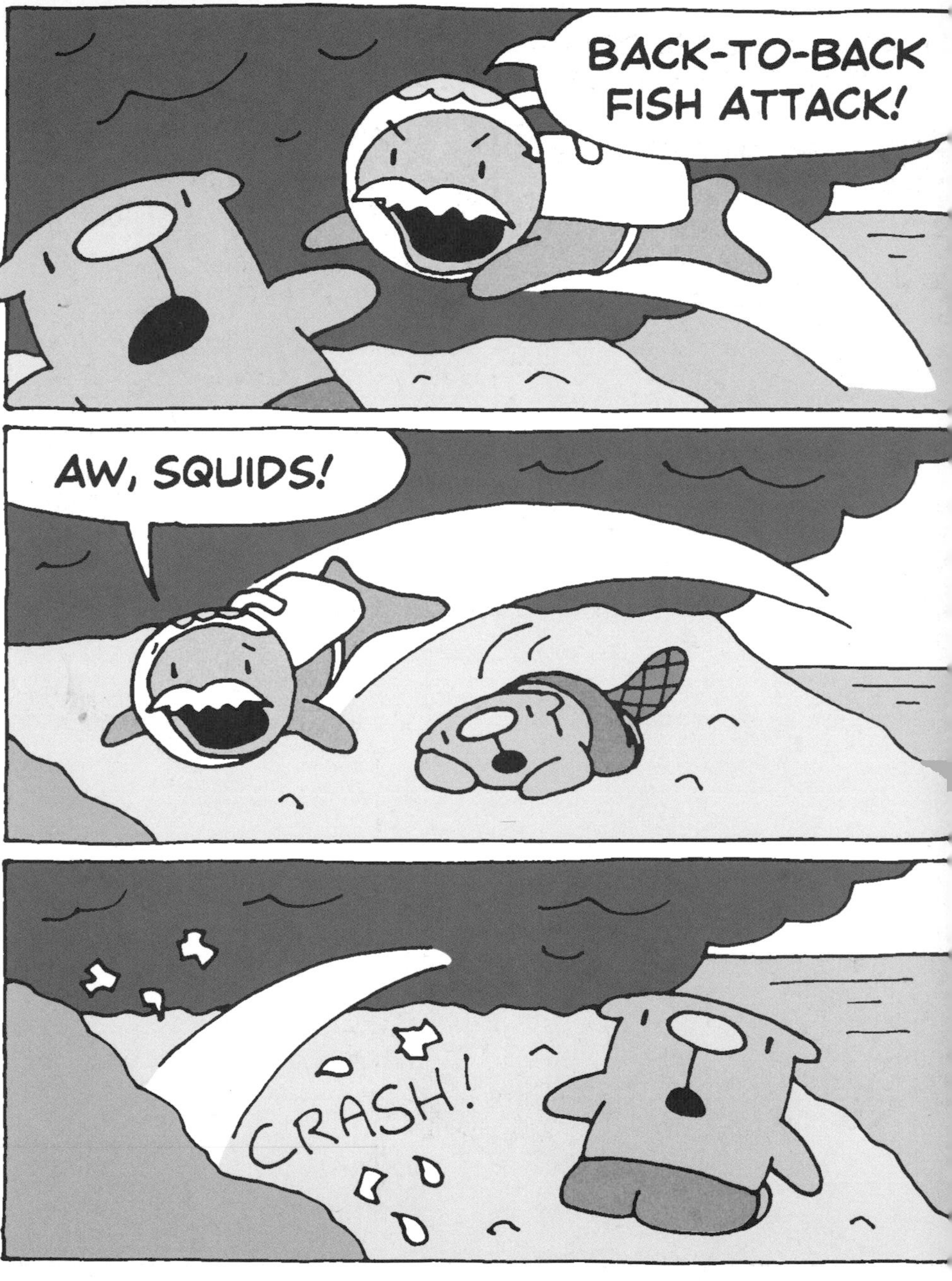
BACK-TO-BACK FISH ATTACK!
AW, SQUIDS!
CRASH!

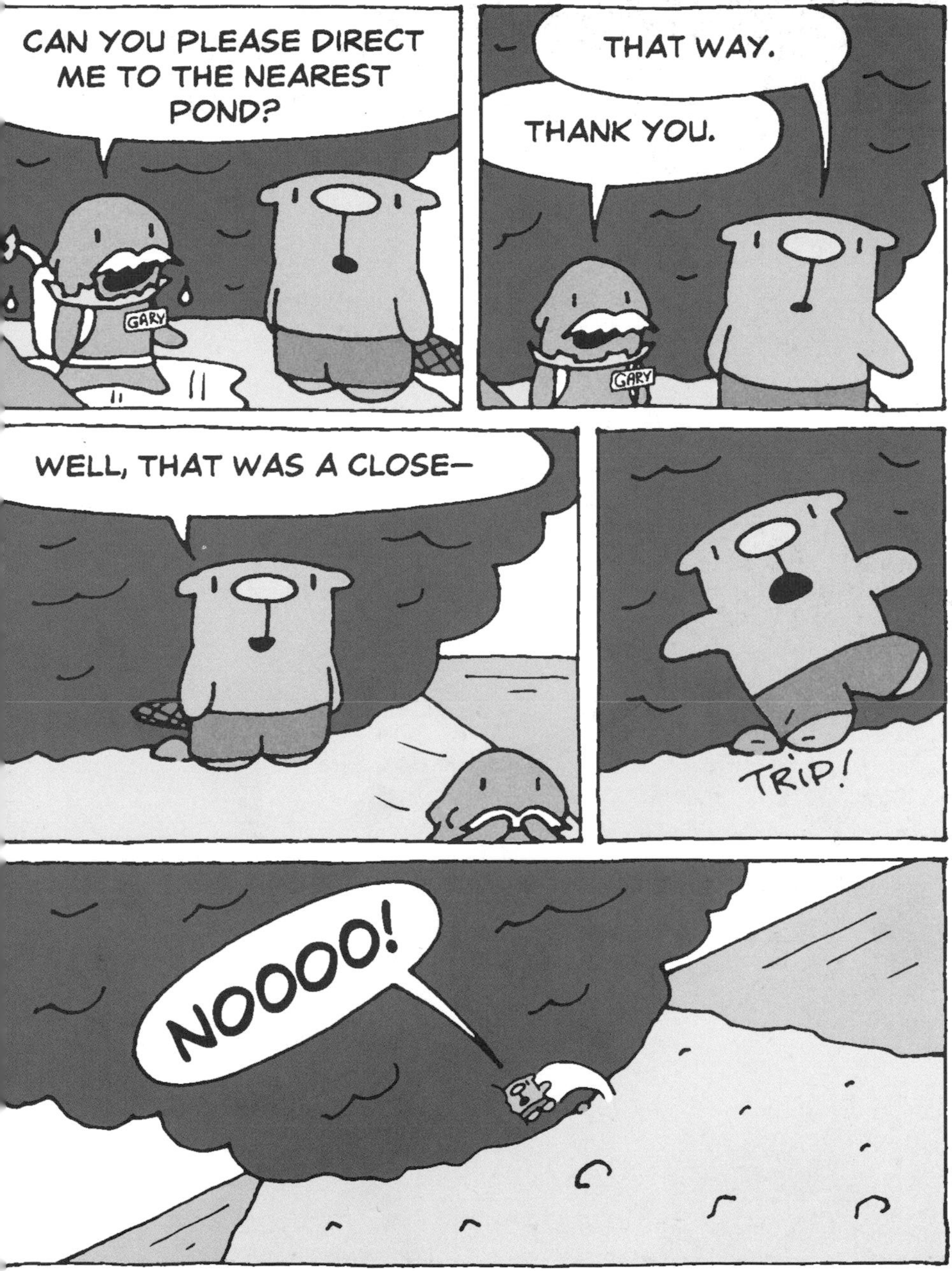
CAN YOU PLEASE DIRECT ME TO THE NEAREST POND?
GARY
THAT WAY.
THANK YOU.
GARY
WELL, THAT WAS A CLOSE—
TRIP!
NOOOO!

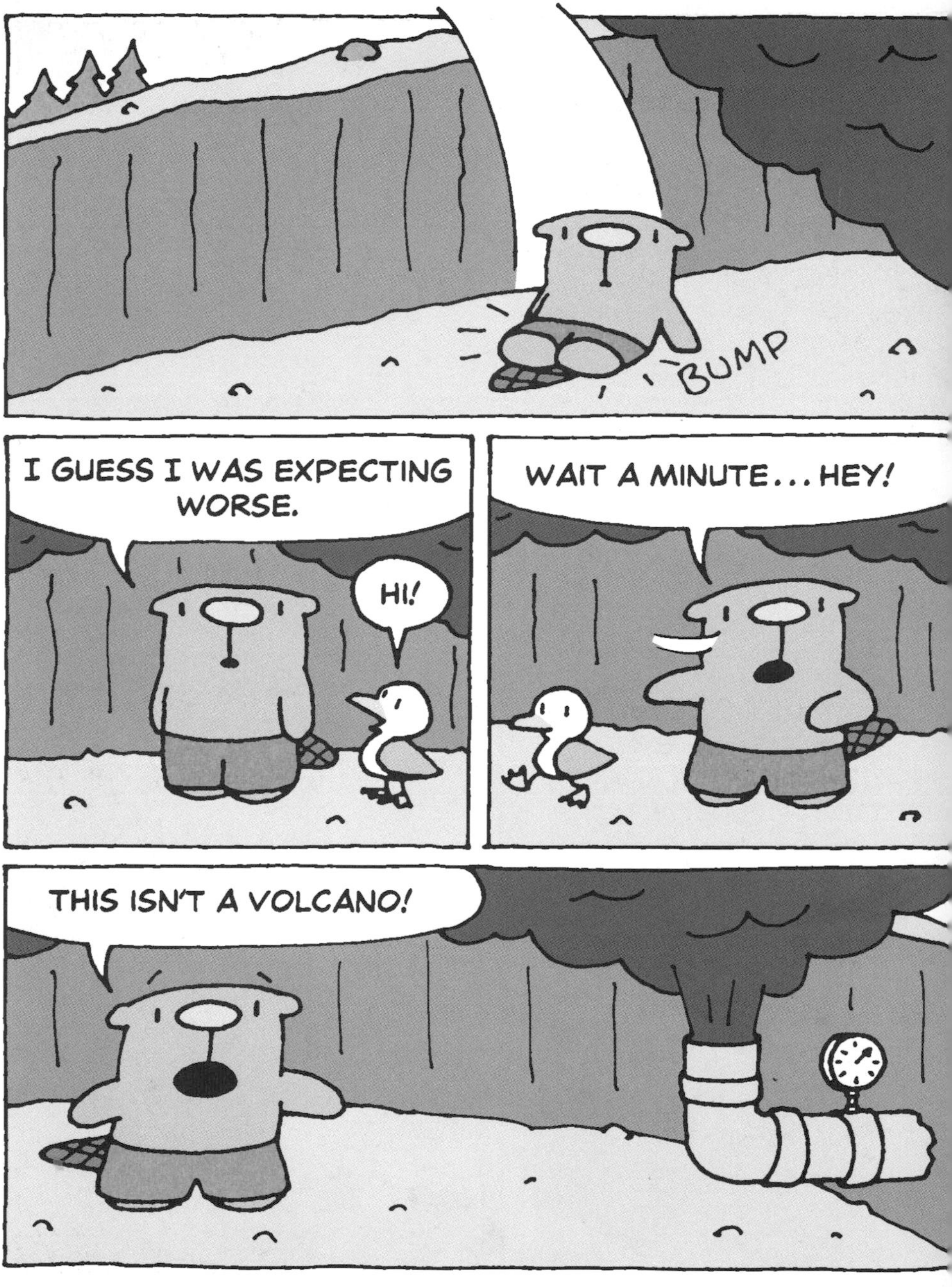
BUMP
I GUESS I WAS EXPECTING WORSE.
HI!
WAIT A MINUTE... HEY!
THIS ISN'T A VOLCANO!

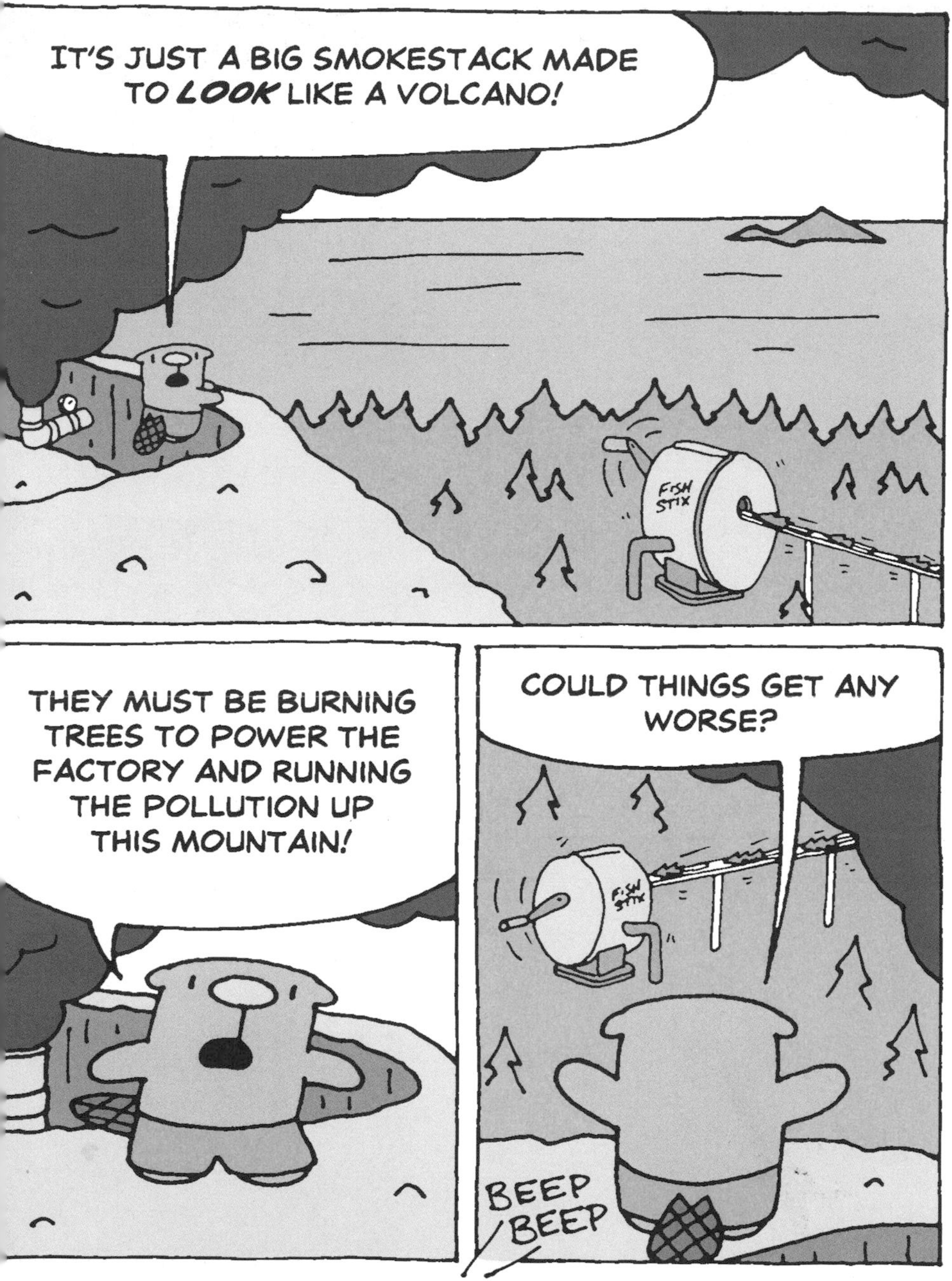
IT'S JUST A BIG SMOKESTACK MADE TO *LOOK* LIKE A VOLCANO!
FISH STIX
THEY MUST BE BURNING TREES TO POWER THE FACTORY AND RUNNING THE POLLUTION UP THIS MOUNTAIN!
COULD THINGS GET ANY WORSE?
FISH STIX
BEEP BEEP

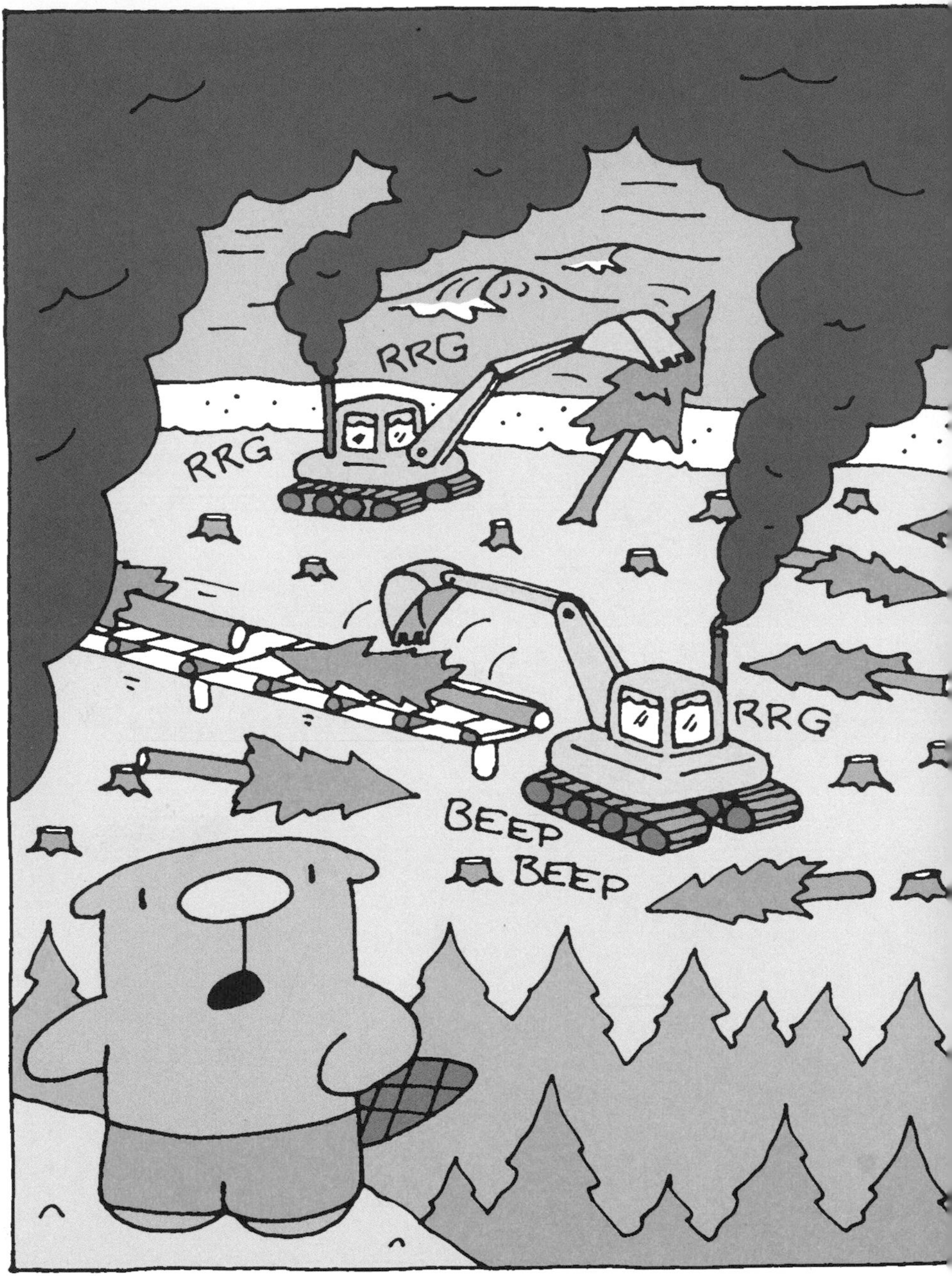
RRG
RRG
RRG
BEEP
BEEP

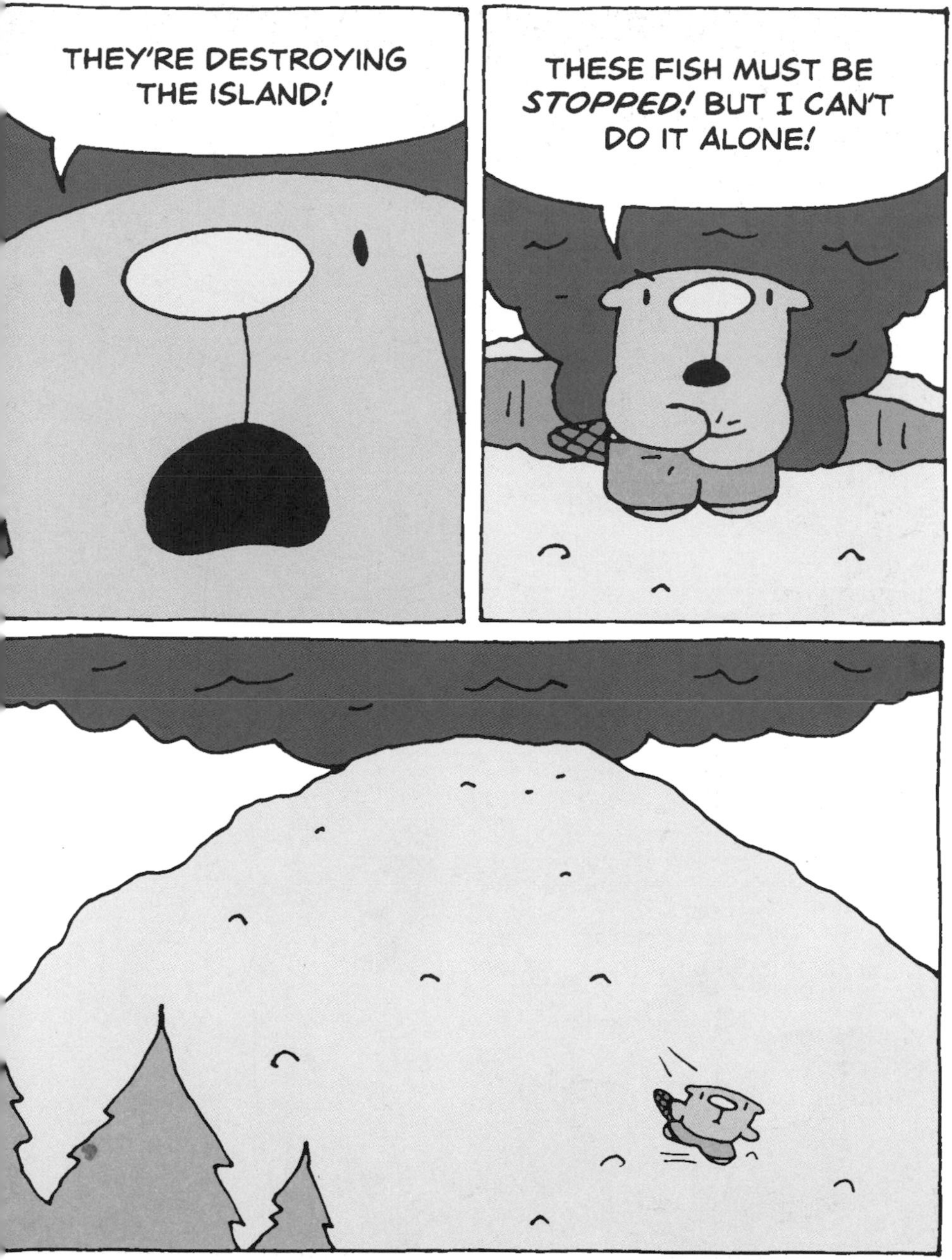
THEY'RE DESTROYING THE ISLAND!
THESE FISH MUST BE *STOPPED!* BUT I CAN'T DO IT ALONE!

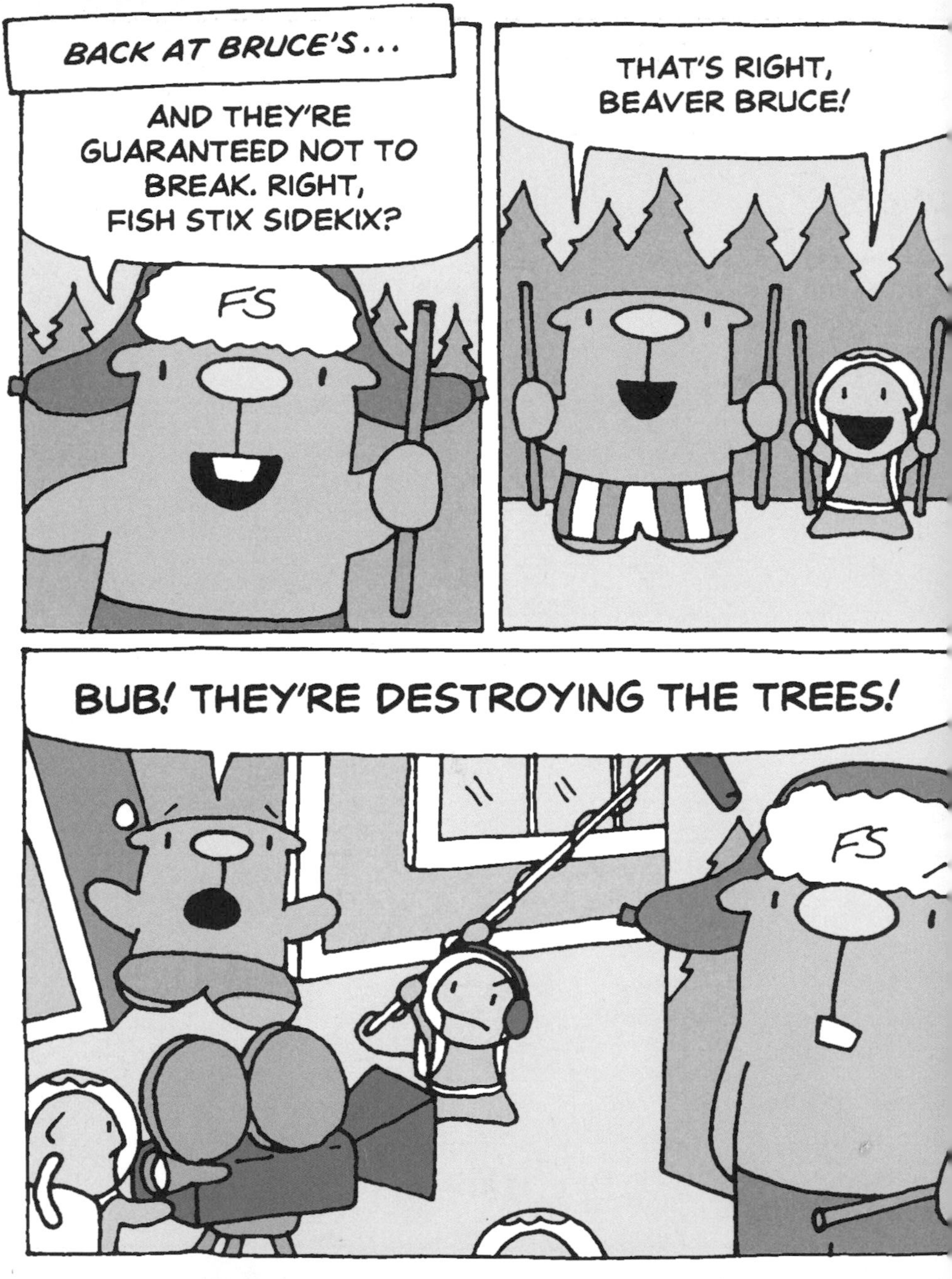
BACK AT BRUCE'S...
AND THEY'RE GUARANTEED NOT TO BREAK. RIGHT, FISH STIX SIDEKIX?
FS
THAT'S RIGHT, BEAVER BRUCE!
BUB! THEY'RE DESTROYING THE TREES!
FS

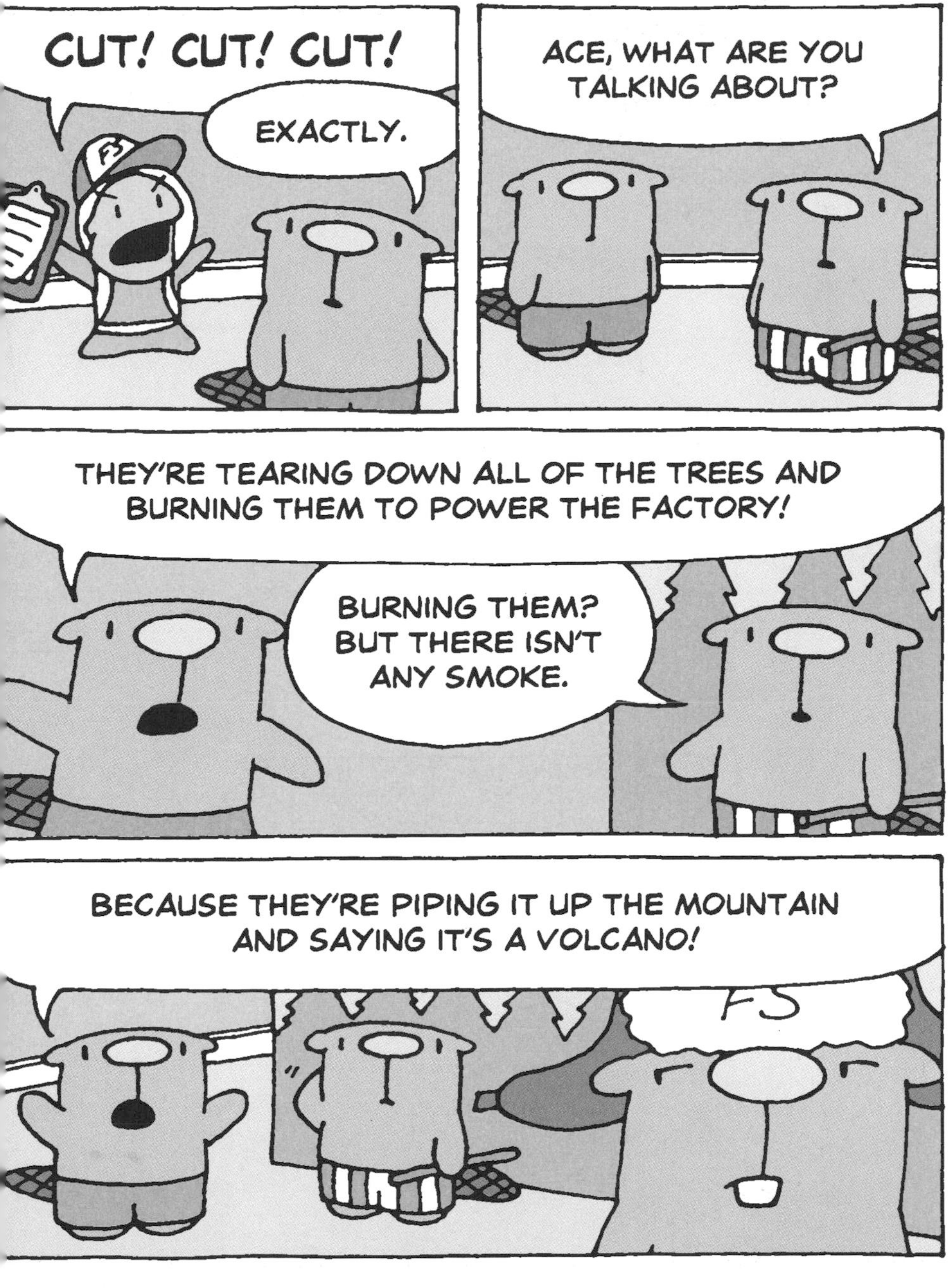
CUT! CUT! CUT!
EXACTLY.
ACE, WHAT ARE YOU TALKING ABOUT?
THEY'RE TEARING DOWN ALL OF THE TREES AND BURNING THEM TO POWER THE FACTORY!
BURNING THEM? BUT THERE ISN'T ANY SMOKE.
BECAUSE THEY'RE PIPING IT UP THE MOUNTAIN AND SAYING IT'S A VOLCANO!
FS

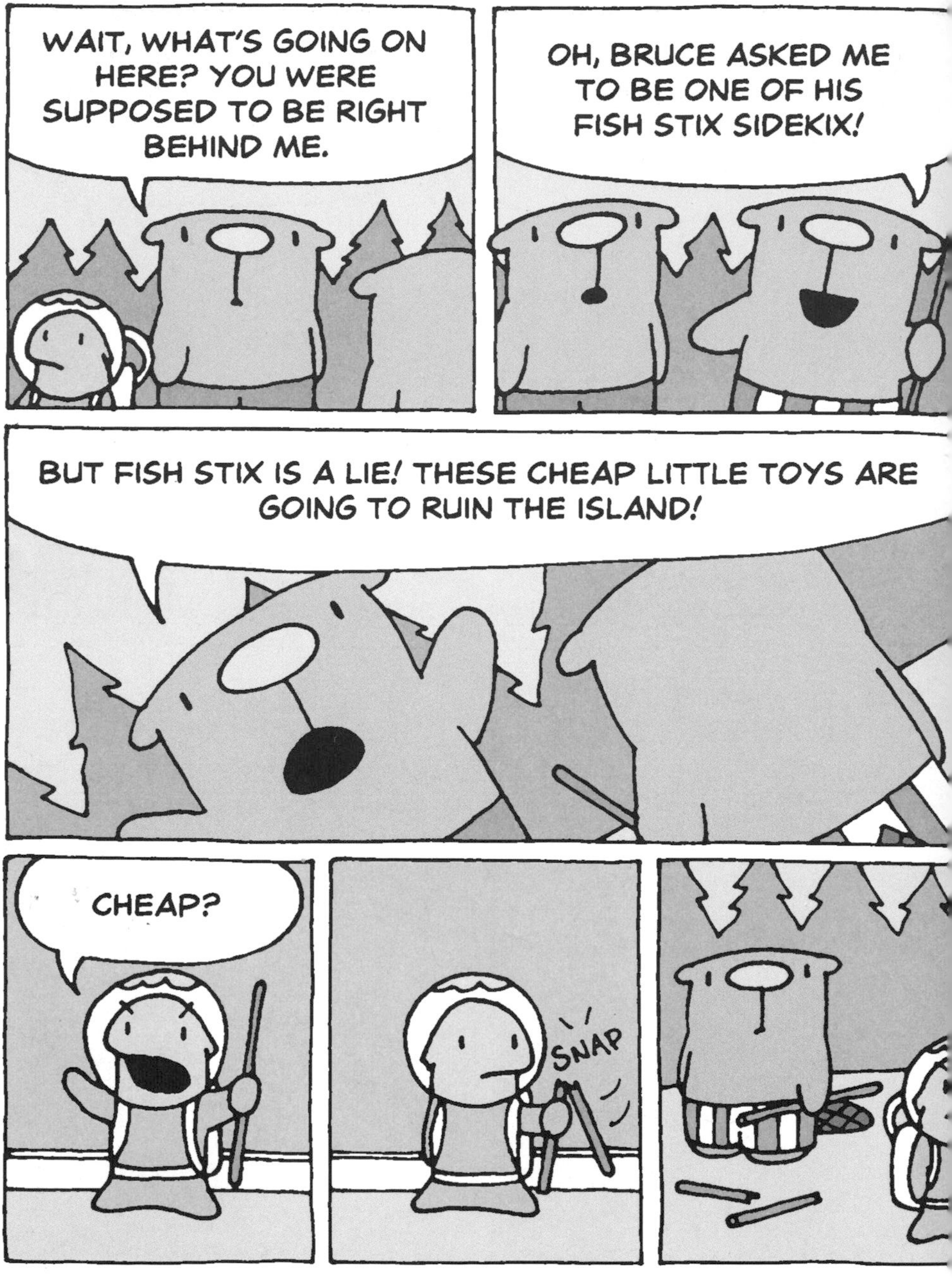
WAIT, WHAT'S GOING ON HERE? YOU WERE SUPPOSED TO BE RIGHT BEHIND ME.
OH, BRUCE ASKED ME TO BE ONE OF HIS FISH STIX SIDEKIX!
BUT FISH STIX IS A LIE! THESE CHEAP LITTLE TOYS ARE GOING TO RUIN THE ISLAND!
CHEAP?
SNAP

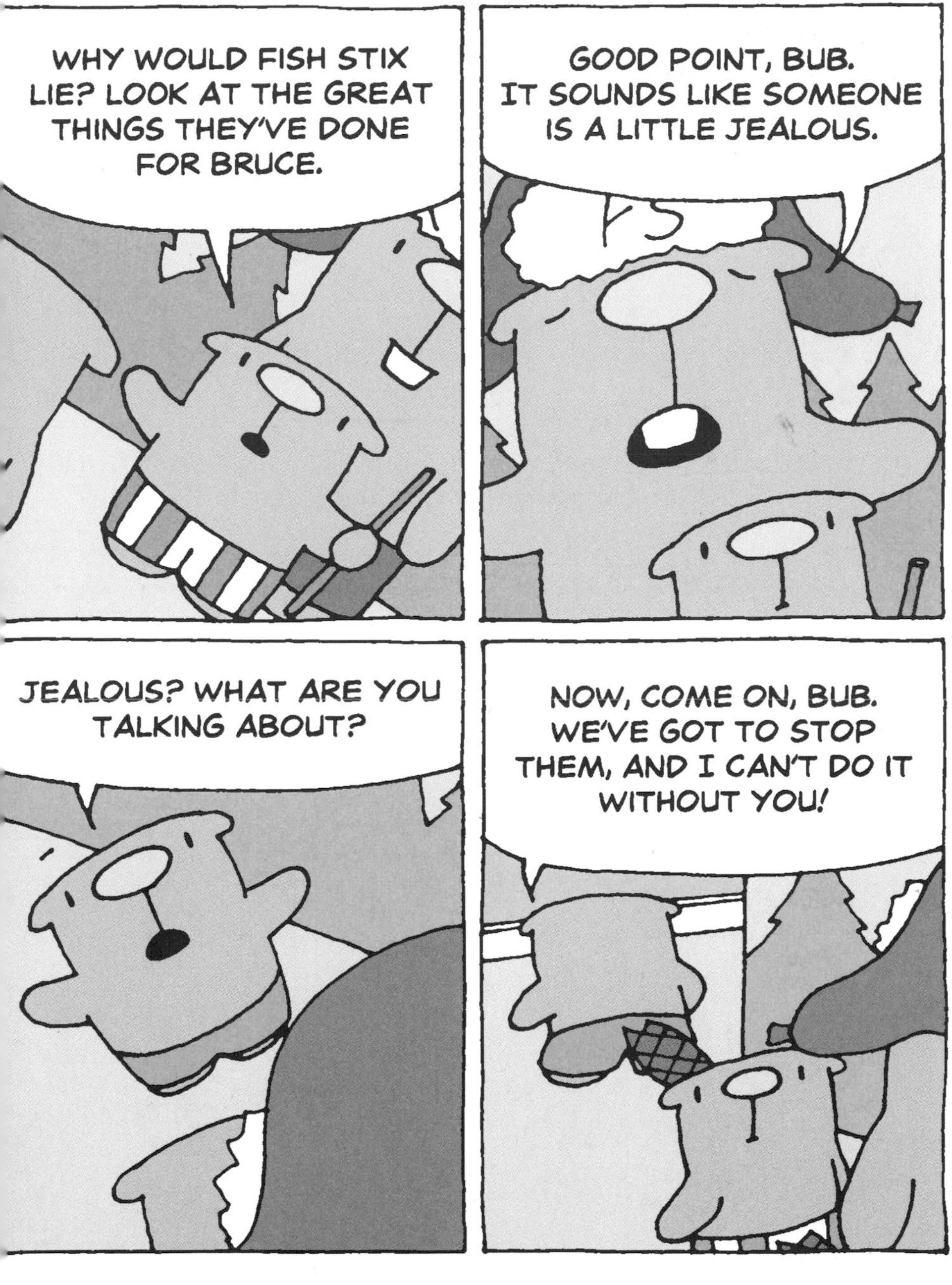
WHY WOULD FISH STIX LIE? LOOK AT THE GREAT THINGS THEY'VE DONE FOR BRUCE.
GOOD POINT, BUB. IT SOUNDS LIKE SOMEONE IS A LITTLE JEALOUS.
JEALOUS? WHAT ARE YOU TALKING ABOUT?
NOW, COME ON, BUB. WE'VE GOT TO STOP THEM, AND I CAN'T DO IT WITHOUT YOU!

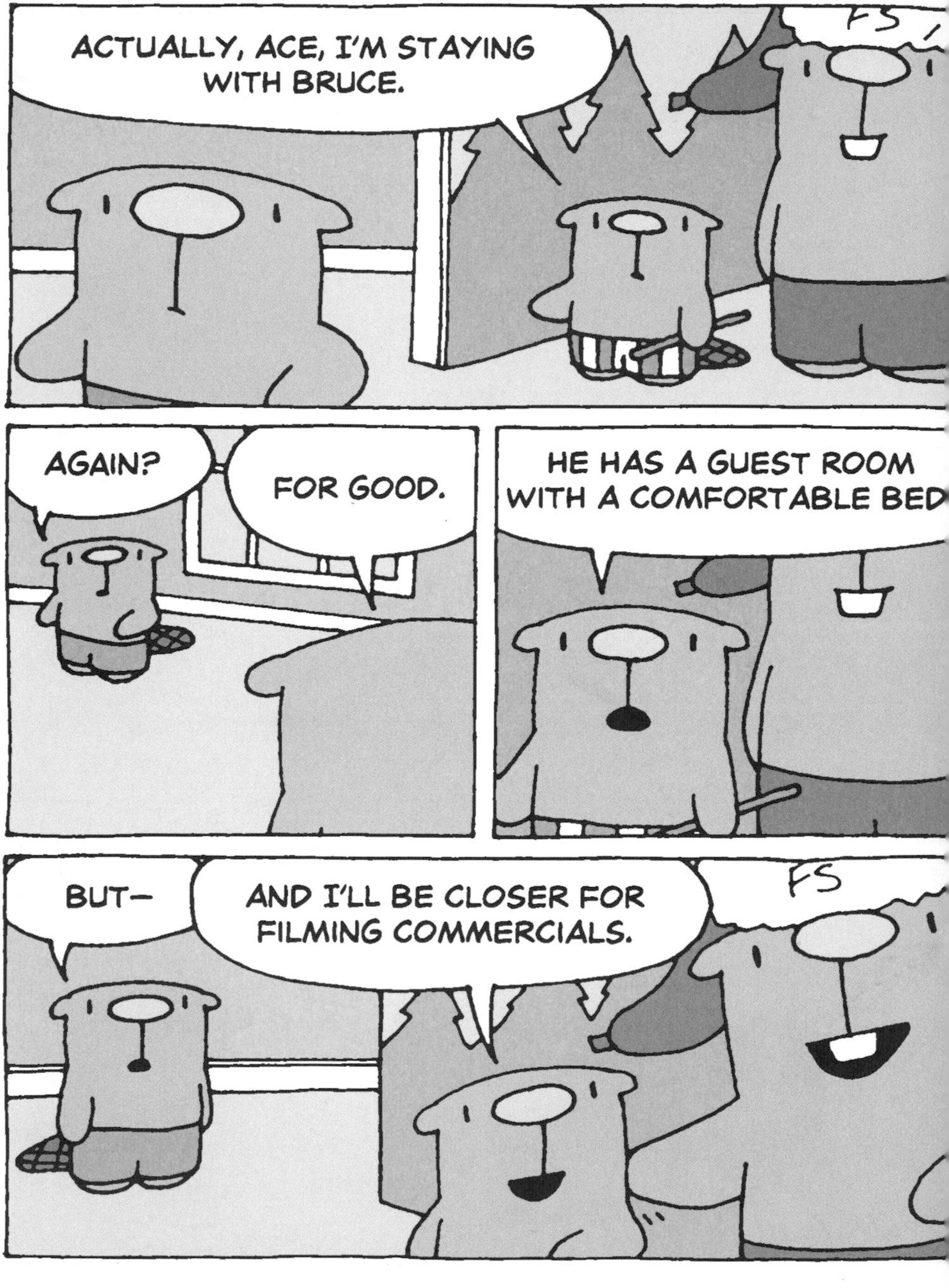
ACTUALLY, ACE, I'M STAYING WITH BRUCE.
FS
AGAIN?
FOR GOOD.
HE HAS A GUEST ROOM WITH A COMFORTABLE BED
BUT—
AND I'LL BE CLOSER FOR FILMING COMMERCIALS.
FS

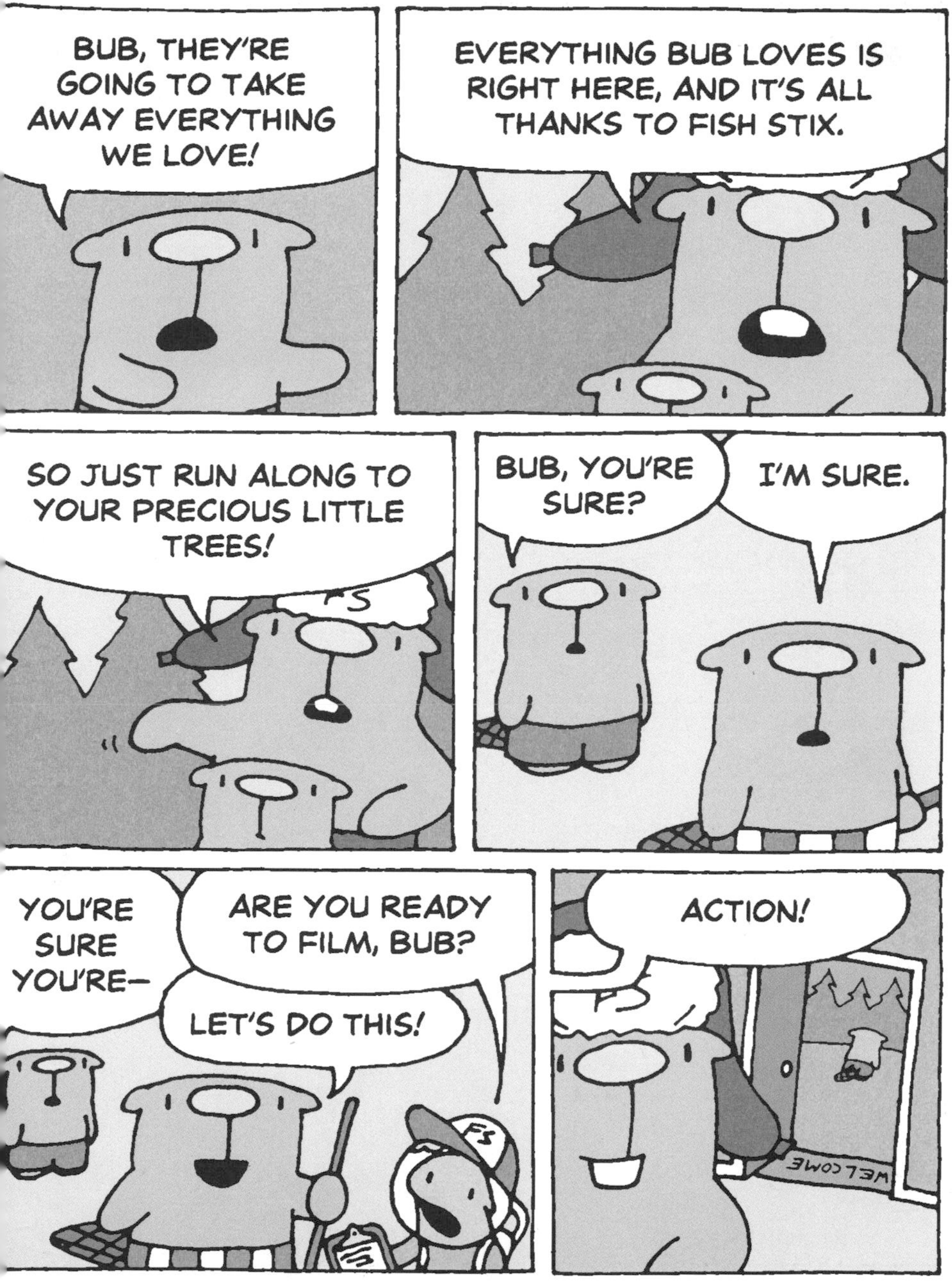
BUB, THEY'RE GOING TO TAKE AWAY EVERYTHING WE LOVE!
EVERYTHING BUB LOVES IS RIGHT HERE, AND IT'S ALL THANKS TO FISH STIX.
SO JUST RUN ALONG TO YOUR PRECIOUS LITTLE TREES!
BUB, YOU'RE SURE?
I'M SURE.
YOU'RE SURE YOU'RE—
ARE YOU READY TO FILM, BUB?
LET'S DO THIS!
ACTION!

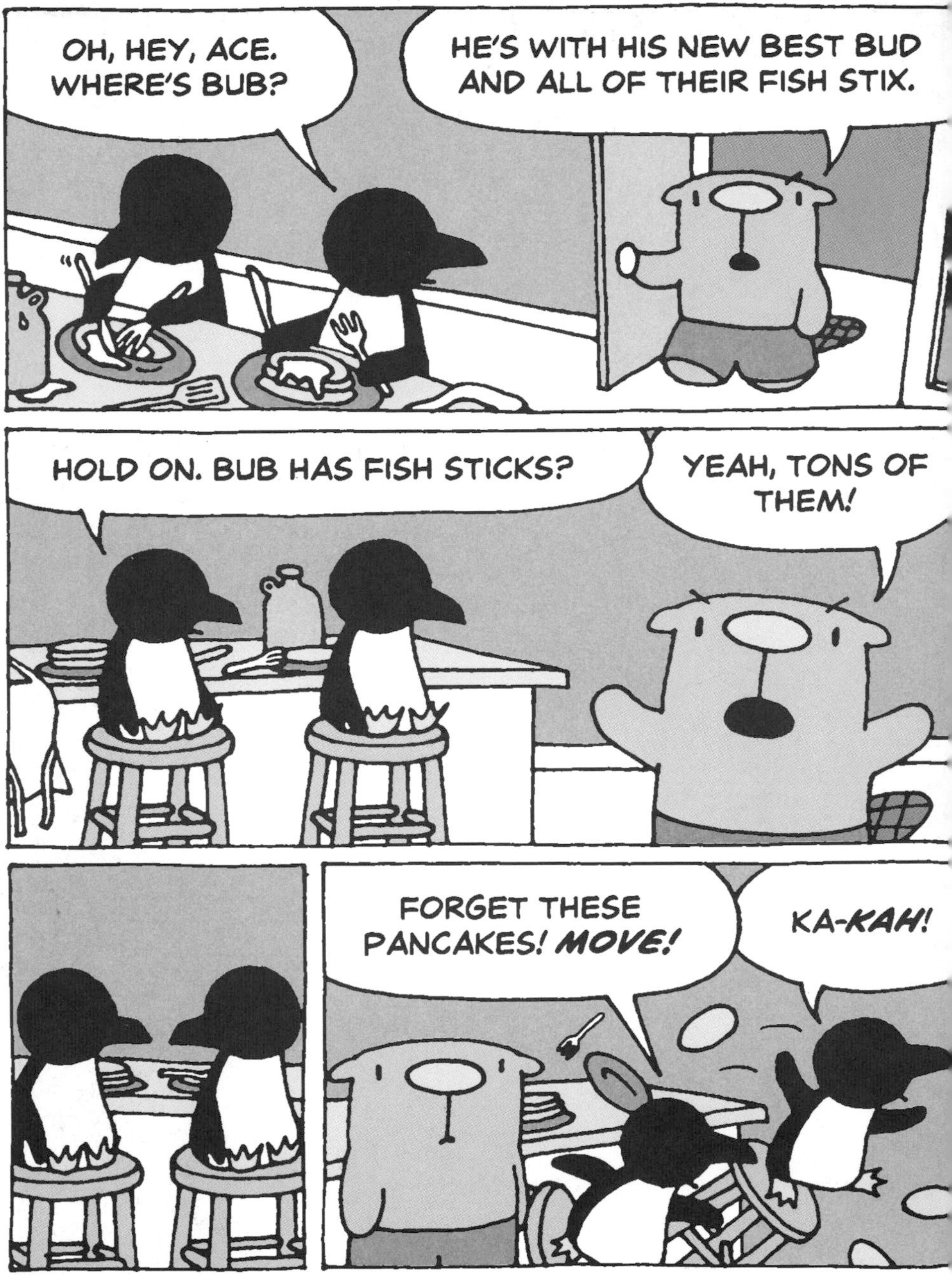
OH, HEY, ACE. WHERE'S BUB?
HE'S WITH HIS NEW BEST BUD AND ALL OF THEIR FISH STIX.
HOLD ON. BUB HAS FISH STICKS?
YEAH, TONS OF THEM!
FORGET THESE PANCAKES! *MOVE!*
KA-*KAH!*

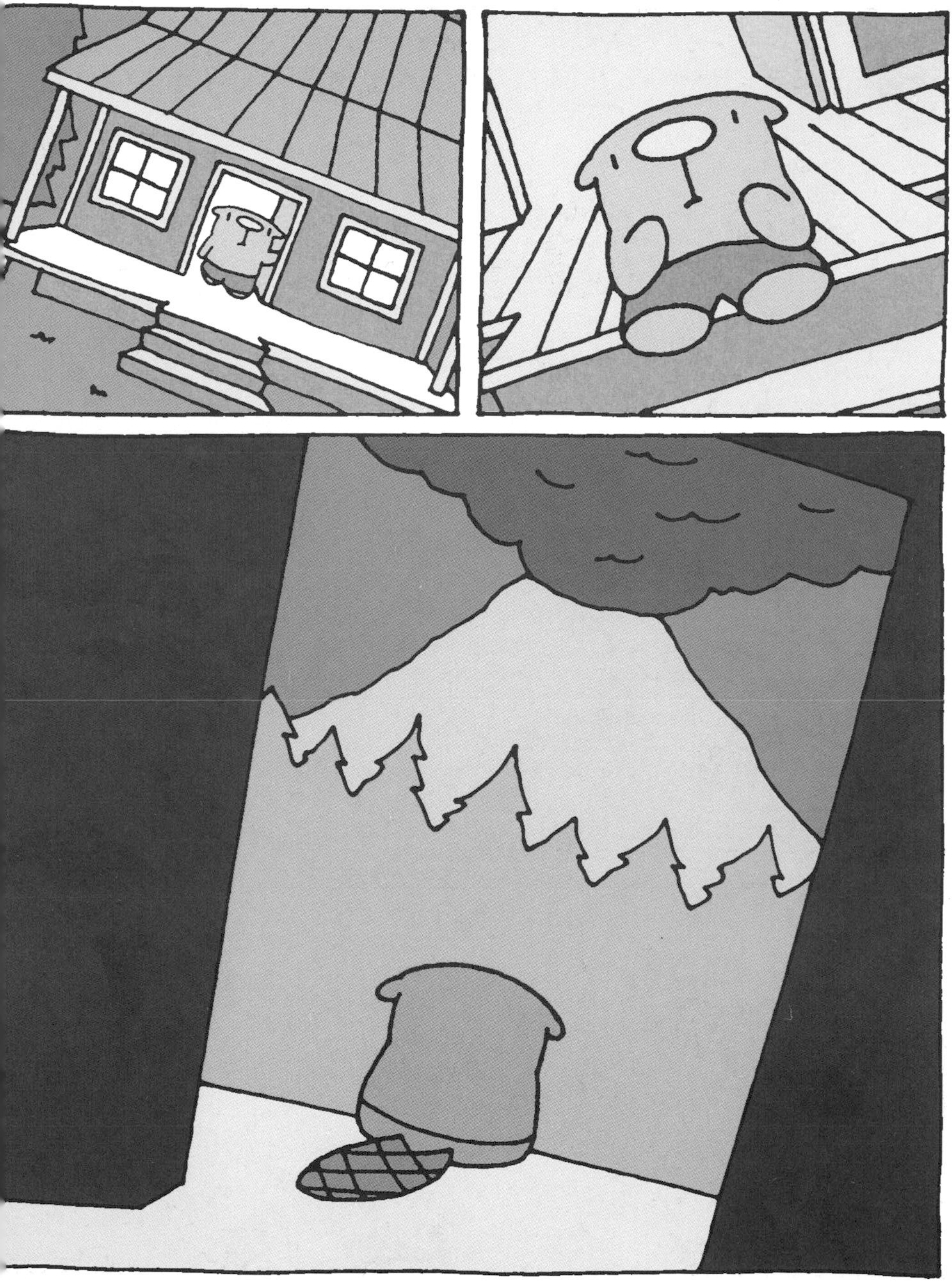

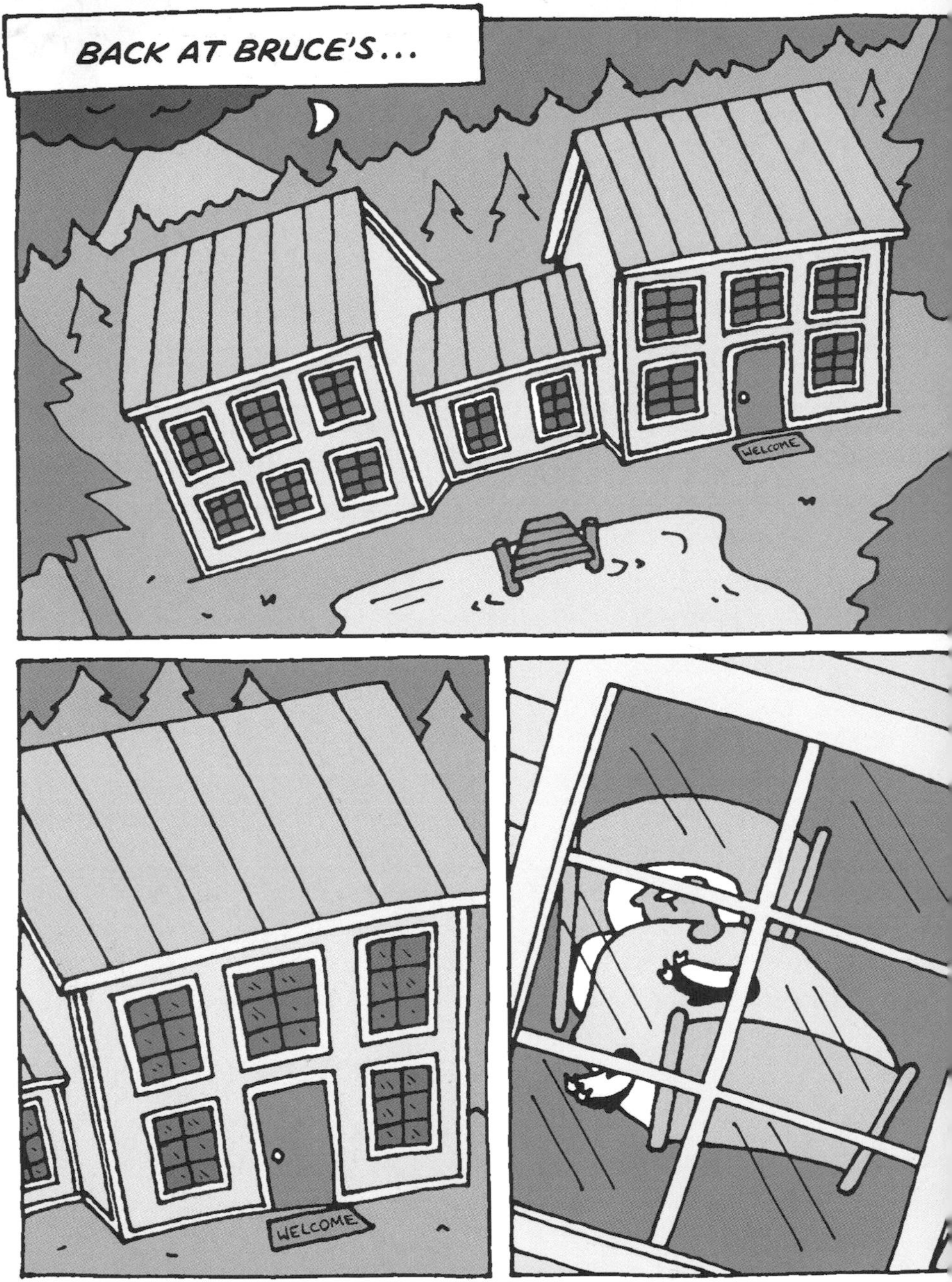
BACK AT BRUCE'S...
WELCOME
WELCOME

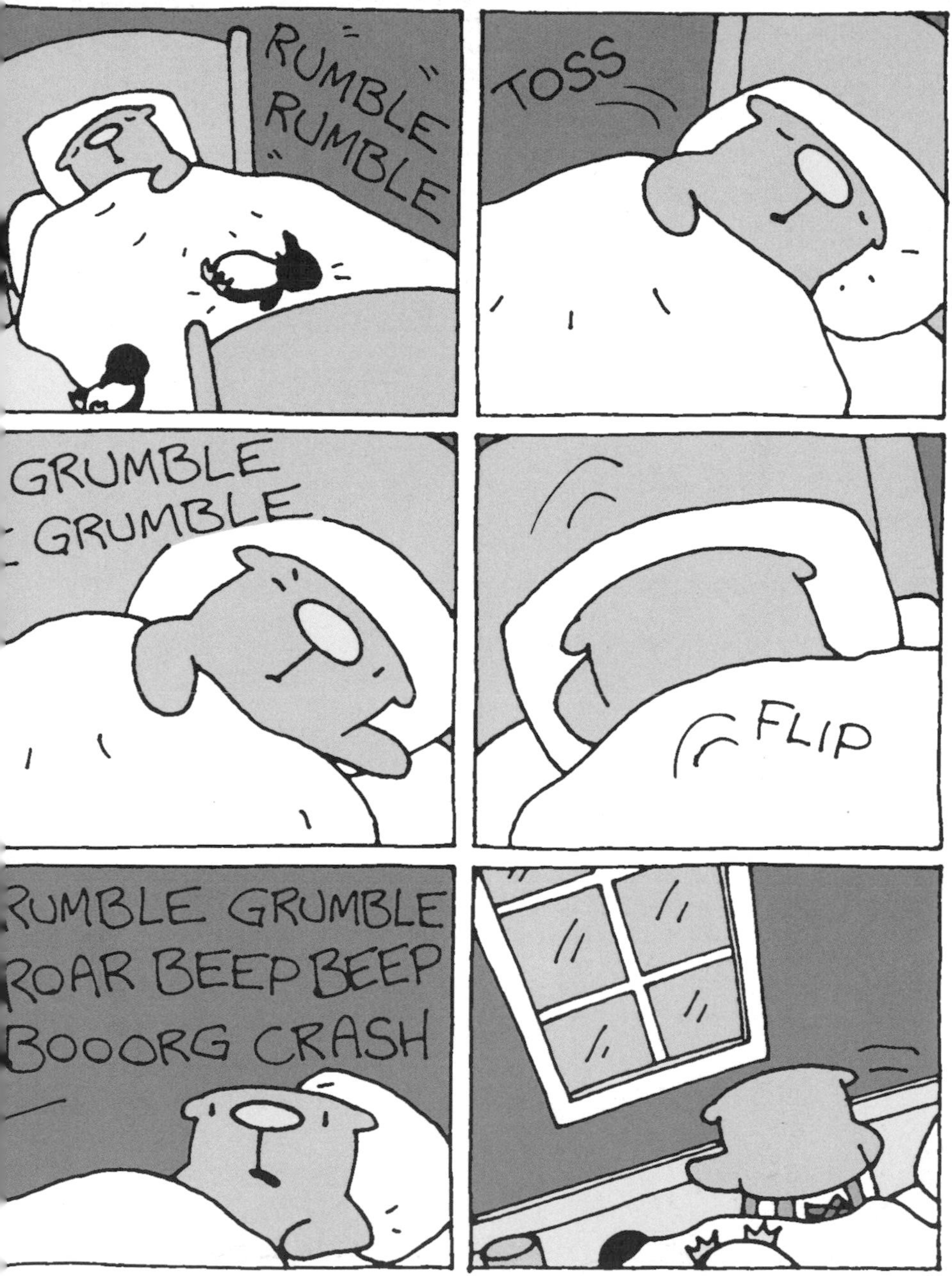
RUMBLE
RUMBLE
TOSS
GRUMBLE
GRUMBLE
FLIP
RUMBLE GRUMBLE
ROAR BEEP BEEP
BOOORG CRASH

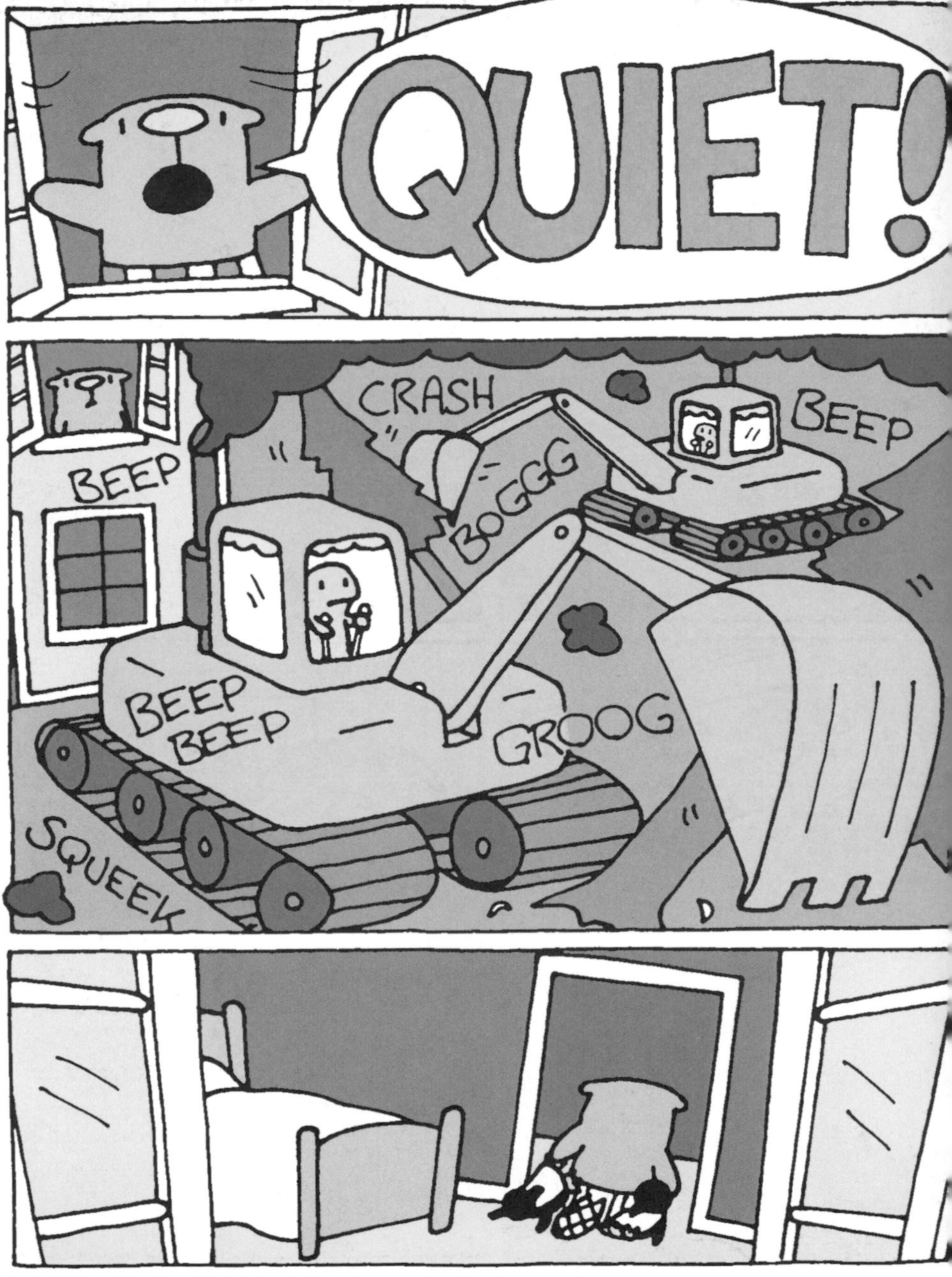
QUIET!
CRASH
BEEP
BEEP
BOGGG
BEEP BEEP
GROOG
SQUEEK

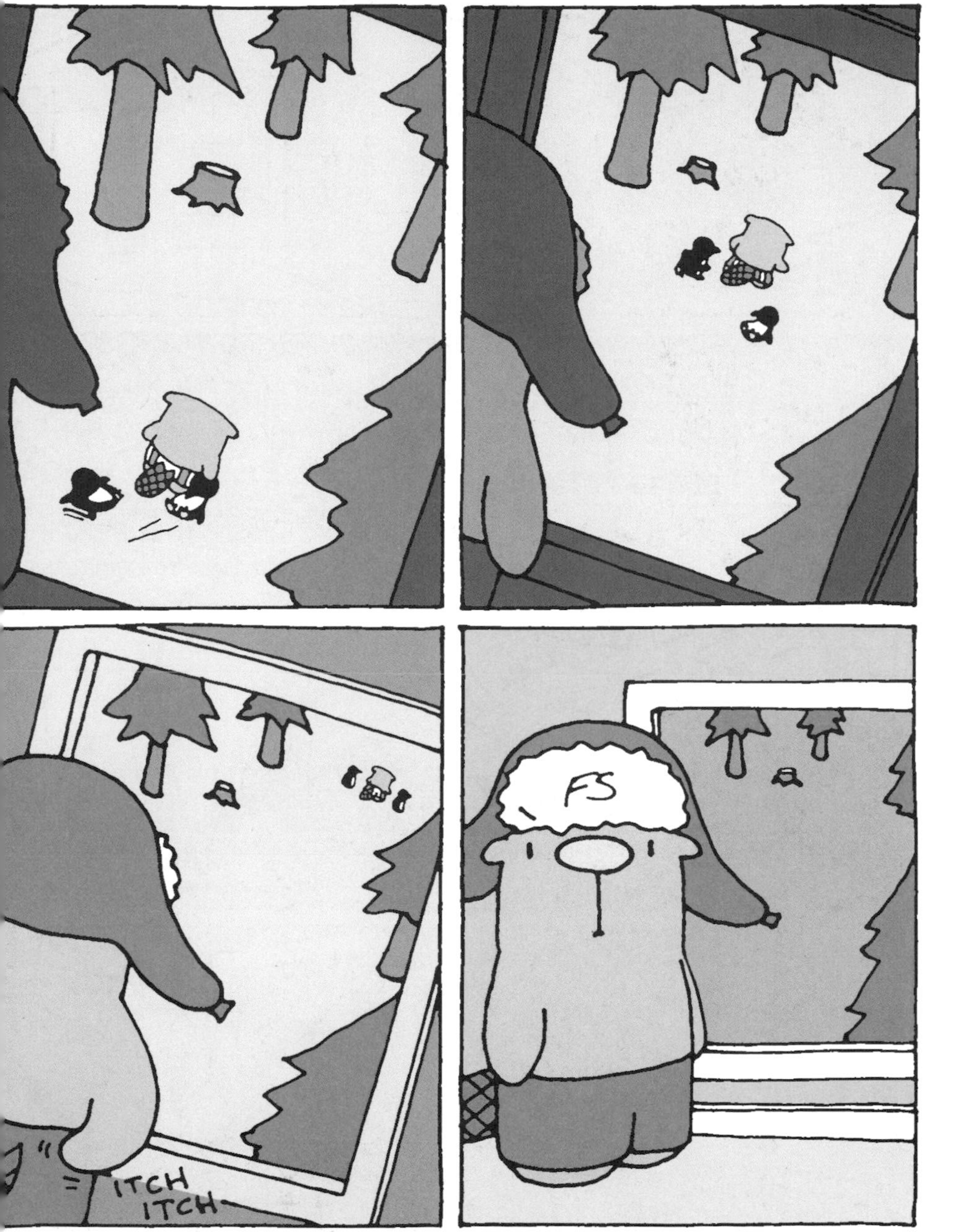
ITCH
ITCH

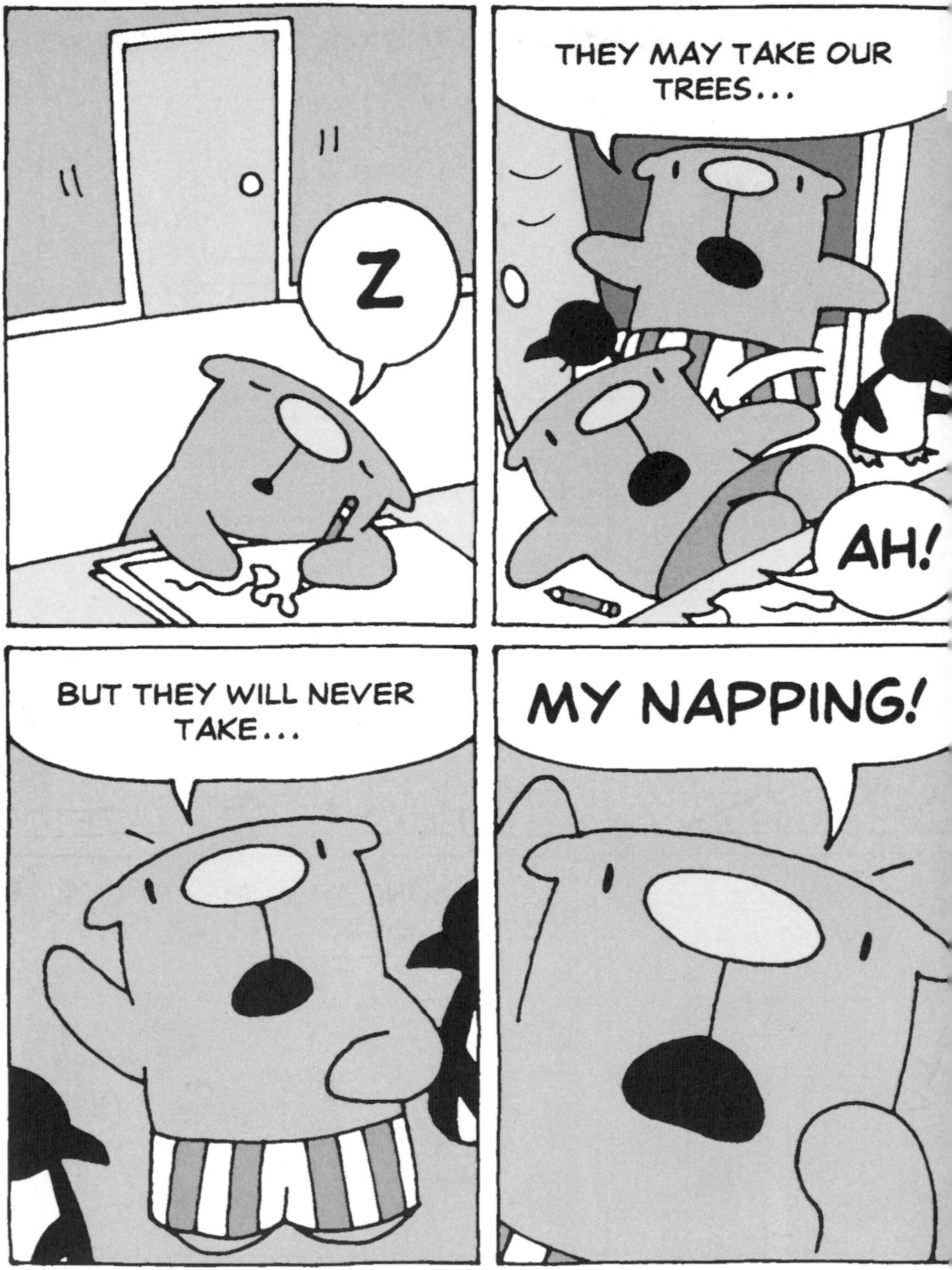
Z
THEY MAY TAKE OUR TREES...
AH!
BUT THEY WILL NEVER TAKE...
MY NAPPING!

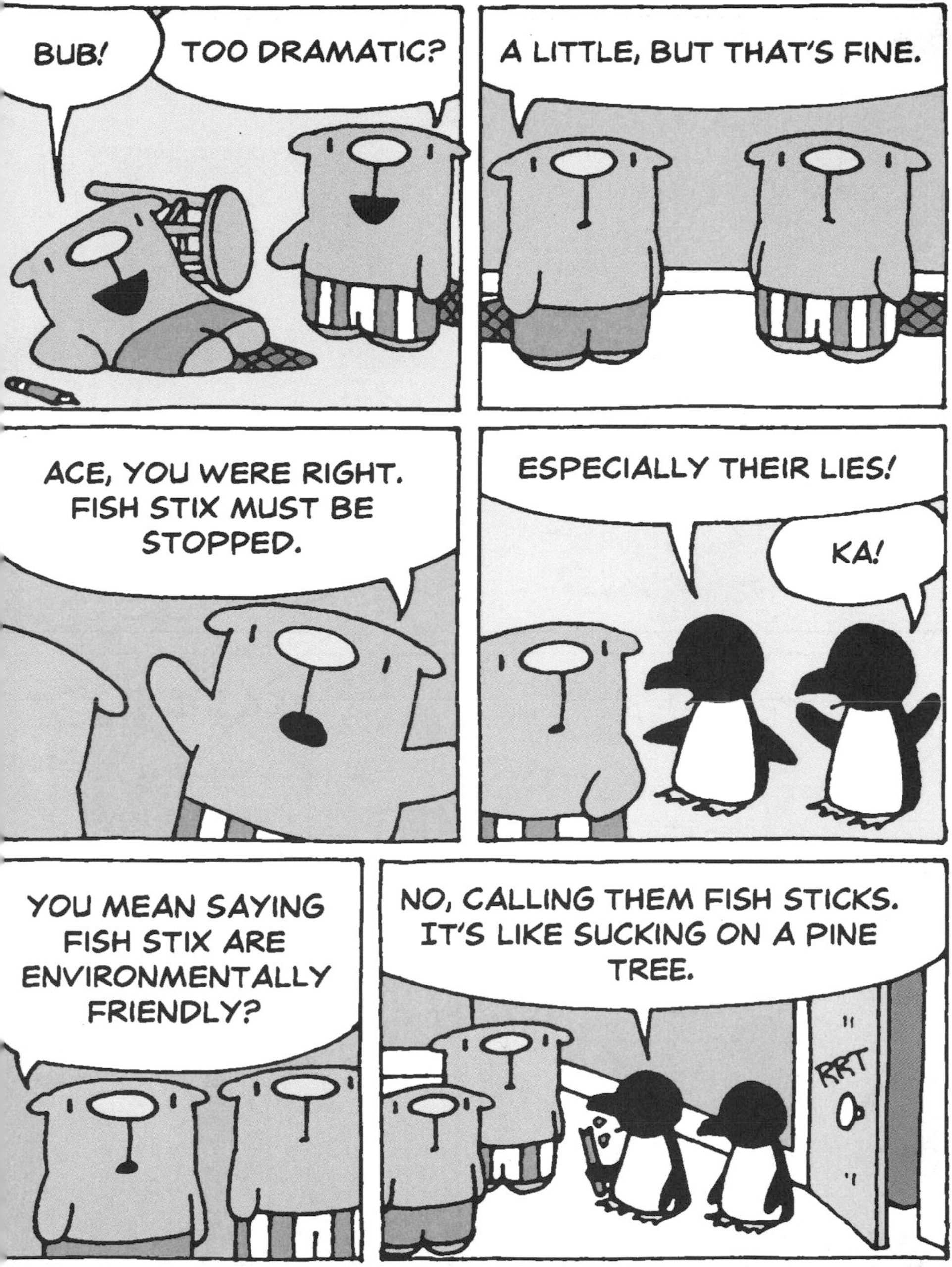
BUB!
TOO DRAMATIC?
A LITTLE, BUT THAT'S FINE.
ACE, YOU WERE RIGHT. FISH STIX MUST BE STOPPED.
ESPECIALLY THEIR LIES!
KA!
YOU MEAN SAYING FISH STIX ARE ENVIRONMENTALLY FRIENDLY?
NO, CALLING THEM FISH STICKS. IT'S LIKE SUCKING ON A PINE TREE.
RRT

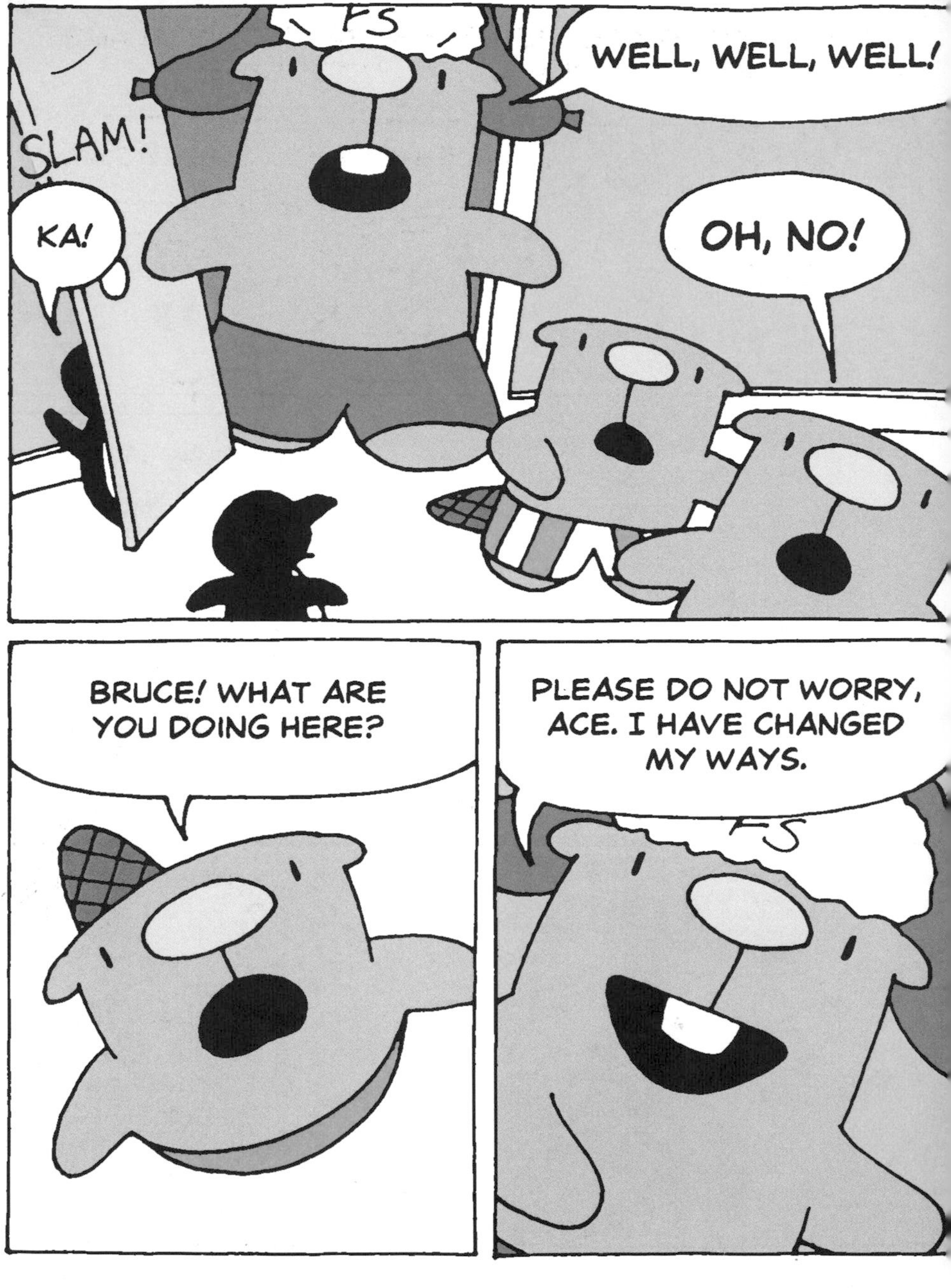

FS
WELL, WELL, WELL!
SLAM!
KA!
OH, NO!
BRUCE! WHAT ARE YOU DOING HERE?
PLEASE DO NOT WORRY, ACE. I HAVE CHANGED MY WAYS.
FS

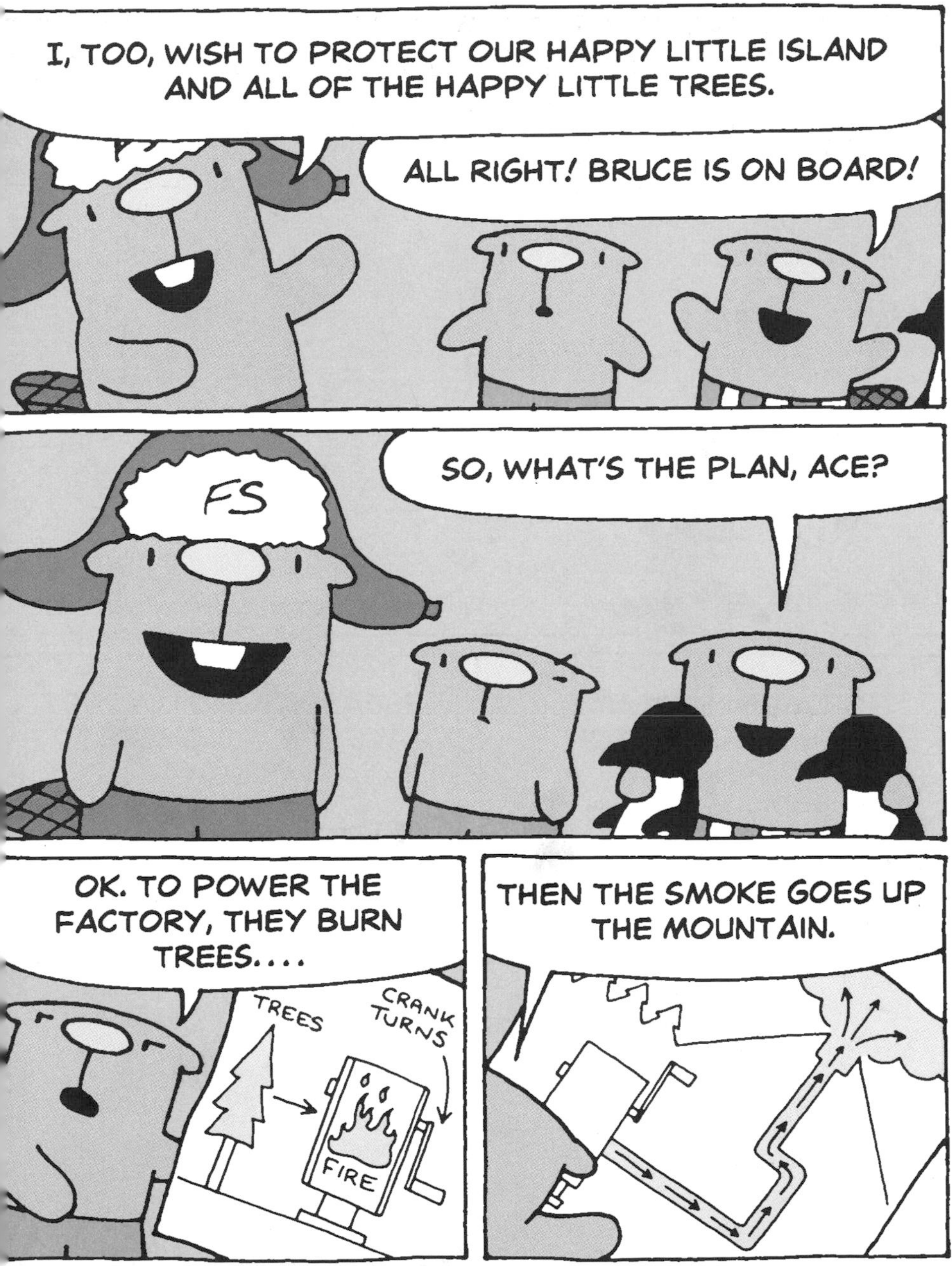
I, TOO, WISH TO PROTECT OUR HAPPY LITTLE ISLAND AND ALL OF THE HAPPY LITTLE TREES.
ALL RIGHT! BRUCE IS ON BOARD!
FS
SO, WHAT'S THE PLAN, ACE?
OK. TO POWER THE FACTORY, THEY BURN TREES....
TREES
CRANK TURNS
FIRE
THEN THE SMOKE GOES UP THE MOUNTAIN.

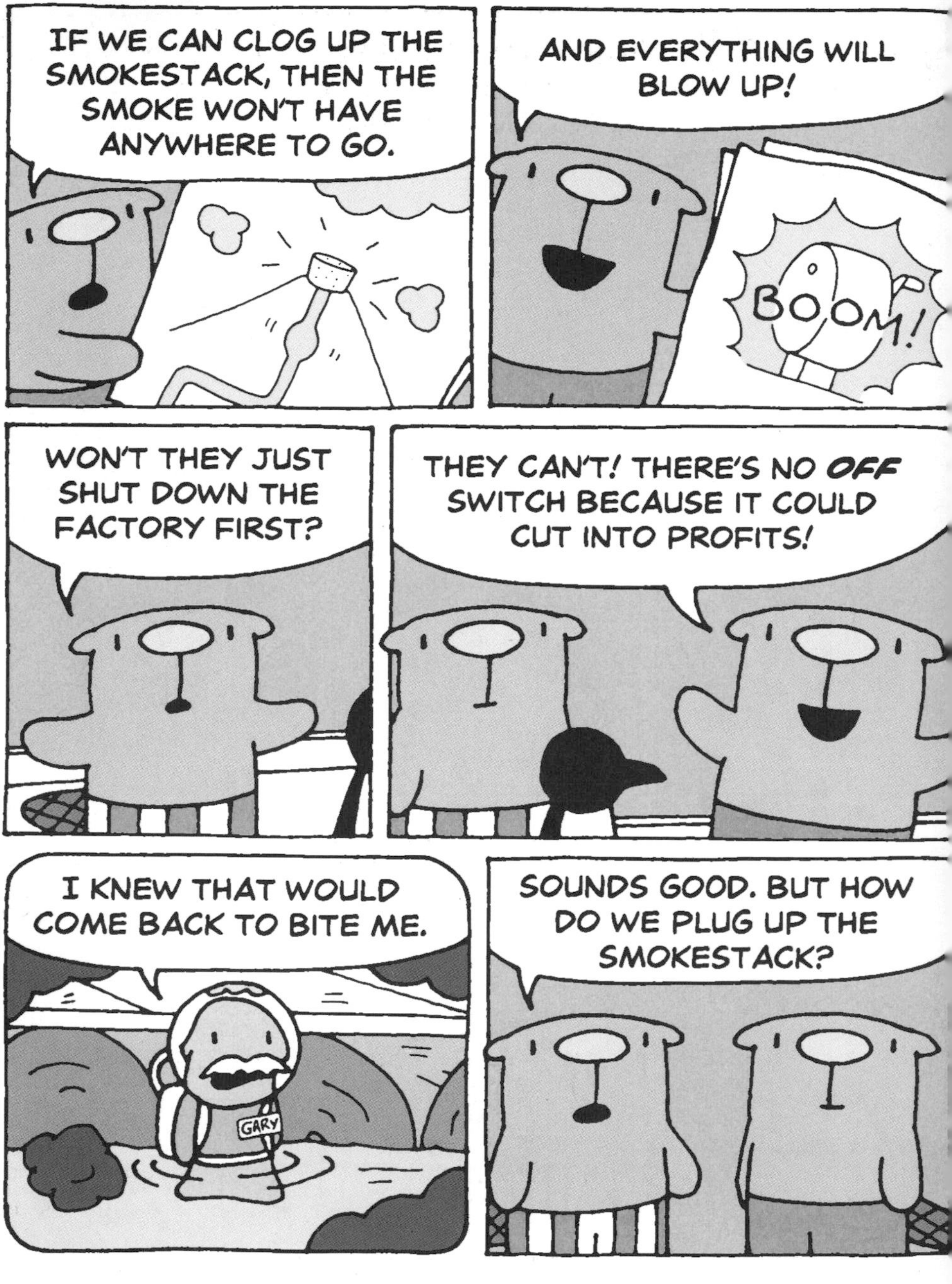
IF WE CAN CLOG UP THE SMOKESTACK, THEN THE SMOKE WON'T HAVE ANYWHERE TO GO.
AND EVERYTHING WILL BLOW UP!
BOOM!
WON'T THEY JUST SHUT DOWN THE FACTORY FIRST?
THEY CAN'T! THERE'S NO *OFF* SWITCH BECAUSE IT COULD CUT INTO PROFITS!
I KNEW THAT WOULD COME BACK TO BITE ME.
GARY
SOUNDS GOOD. BUT HOW DO WE PLUG UP THE SMOKESTACK?

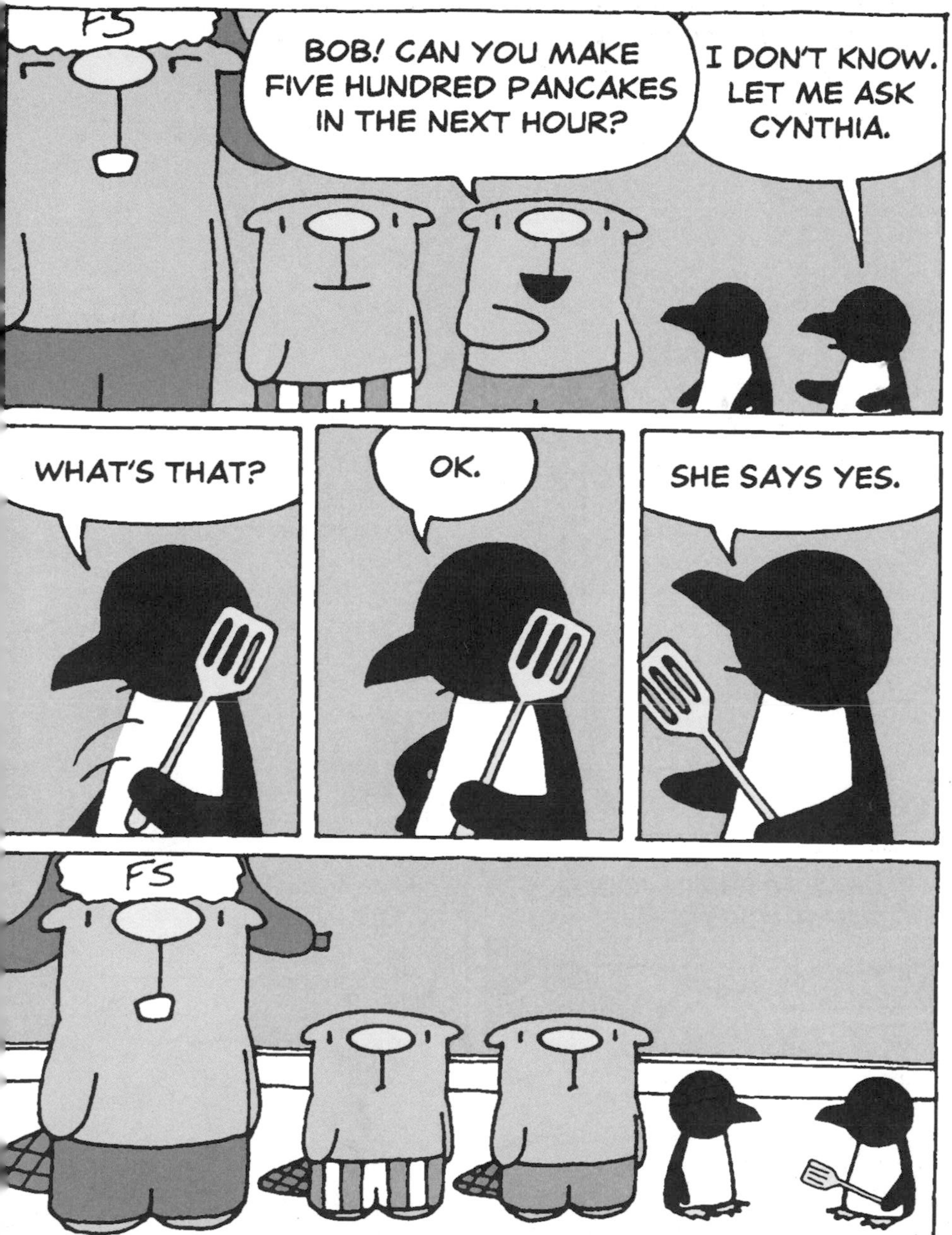
FS
BOB! CAN YOU MAKE FIVE HUNDRED PANCAKES IN THE NEXT HOUR?
I DON'T KNOW. LET ME ASK CYNTHIA.
WHAT'S THAT?
OK.
SHE SAYS YES.
FS

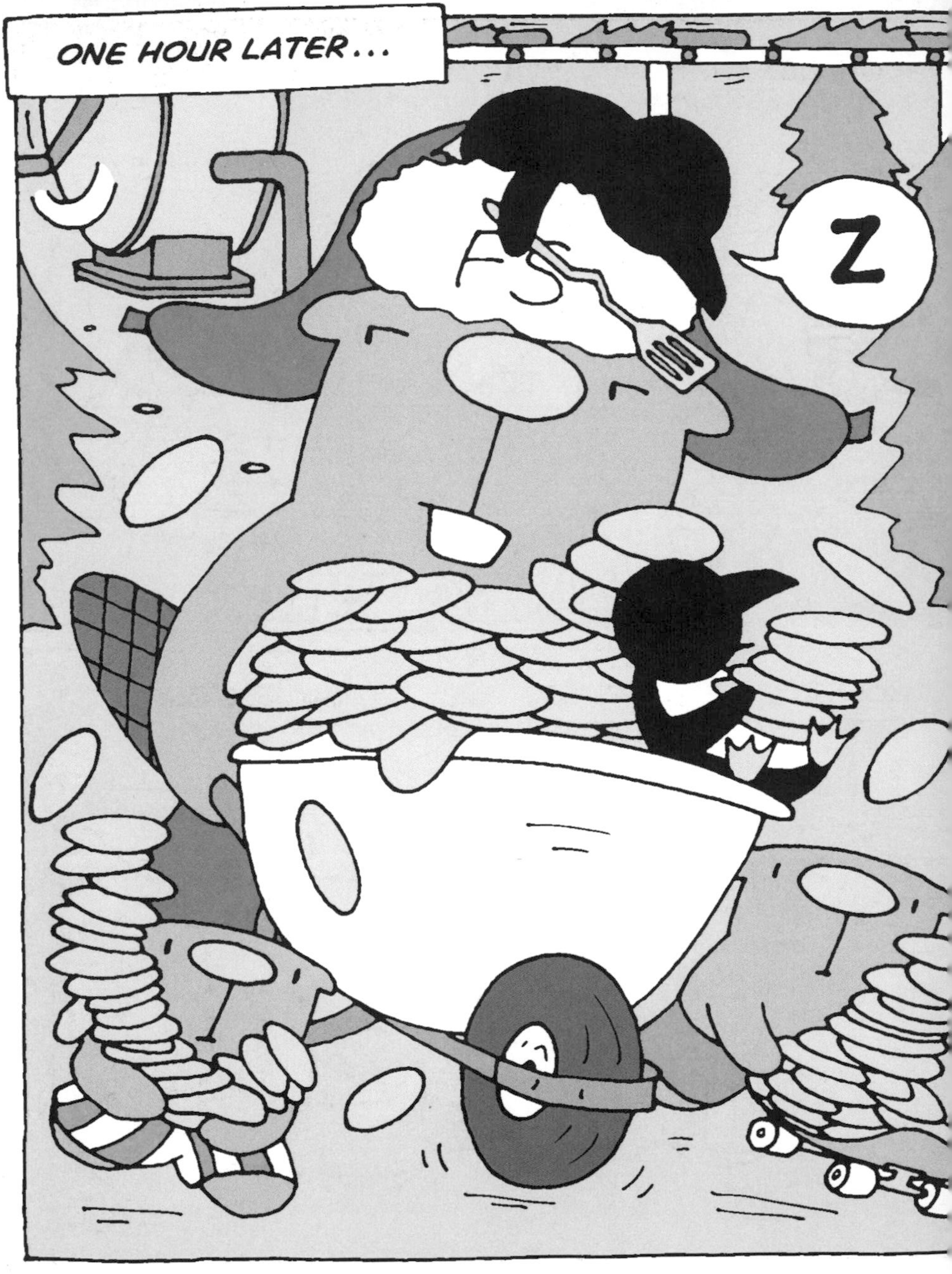
ONE HOUR LATER...
Z

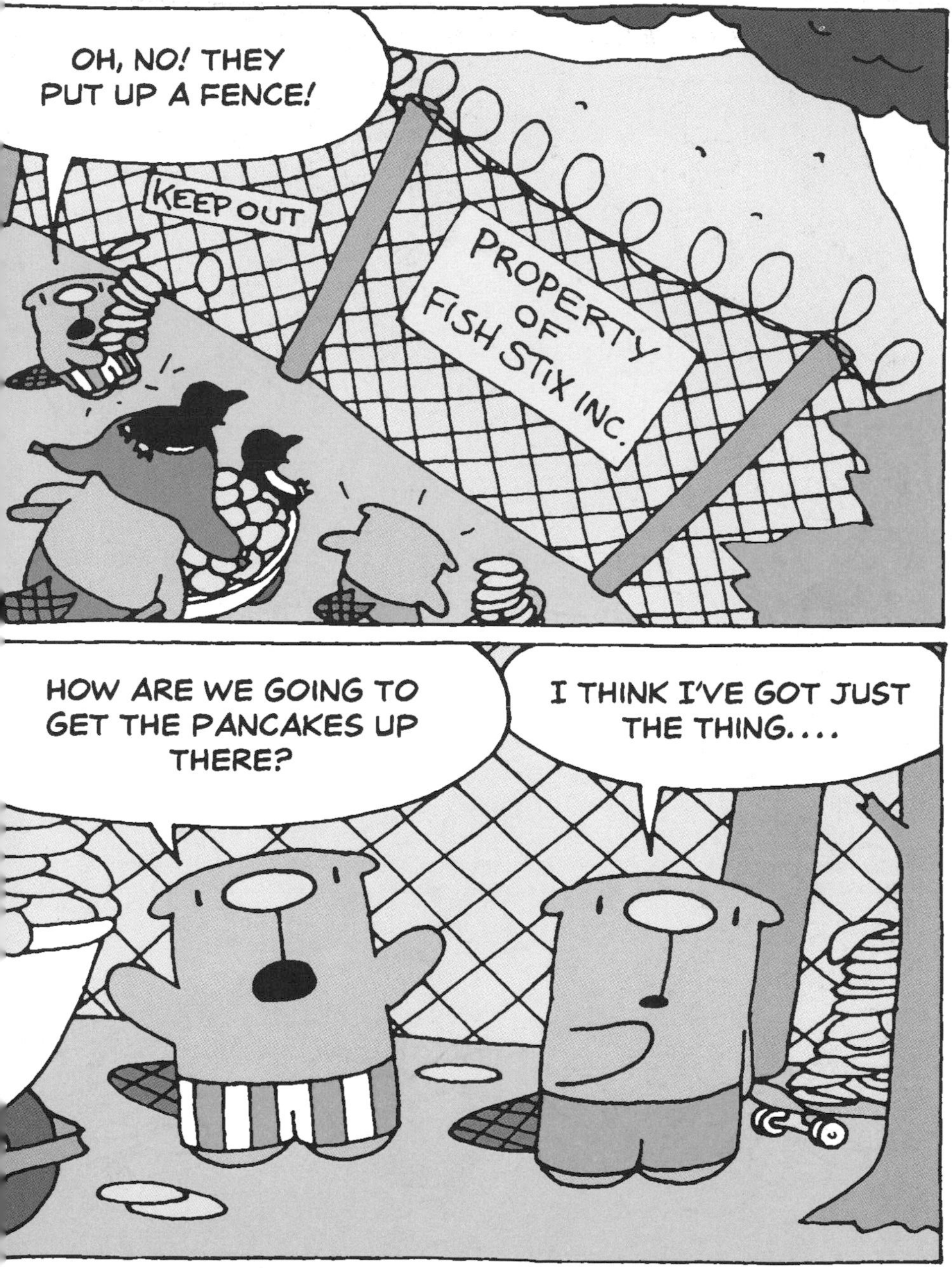
OH, NO! THEY PUT UP A FENCE!
KEEP OUT
PROPERTY OF FISH STIX INC.
HOW ARE WE GOING TO GET THE PANCAKES UP THERE?
I THINK I'VE GOT JUST THE THING. . . .

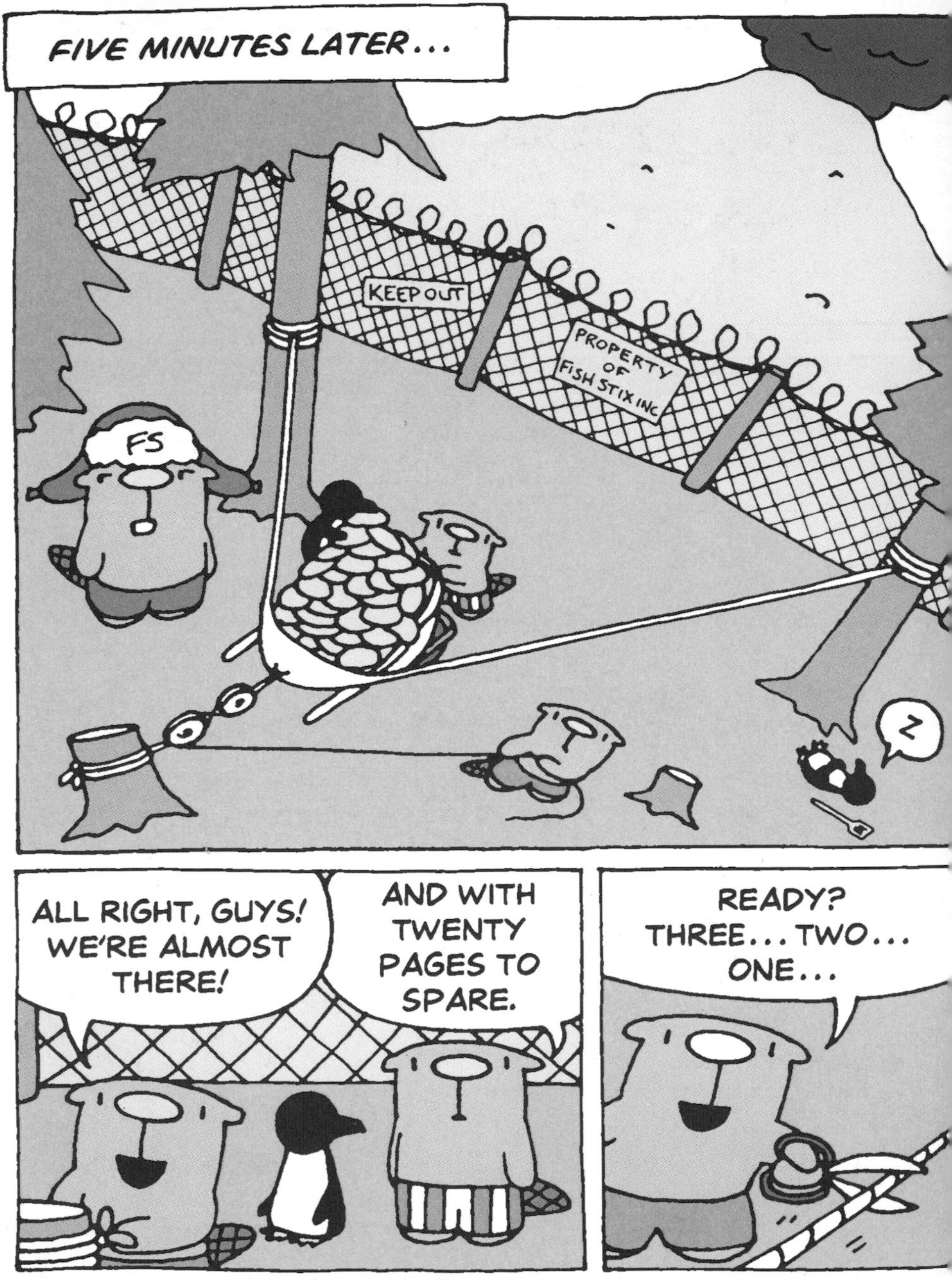
FIVE MINUTES LATER...
KEEP OUT
PROPERTY OF FISH STIX INC
FS
Z
ALL RIGHT, GUYS! WE'RE ALMOST THERE!
AND WITH TWENTY PAGES TO SPARE.
READY? THREE... TWO... ONE...

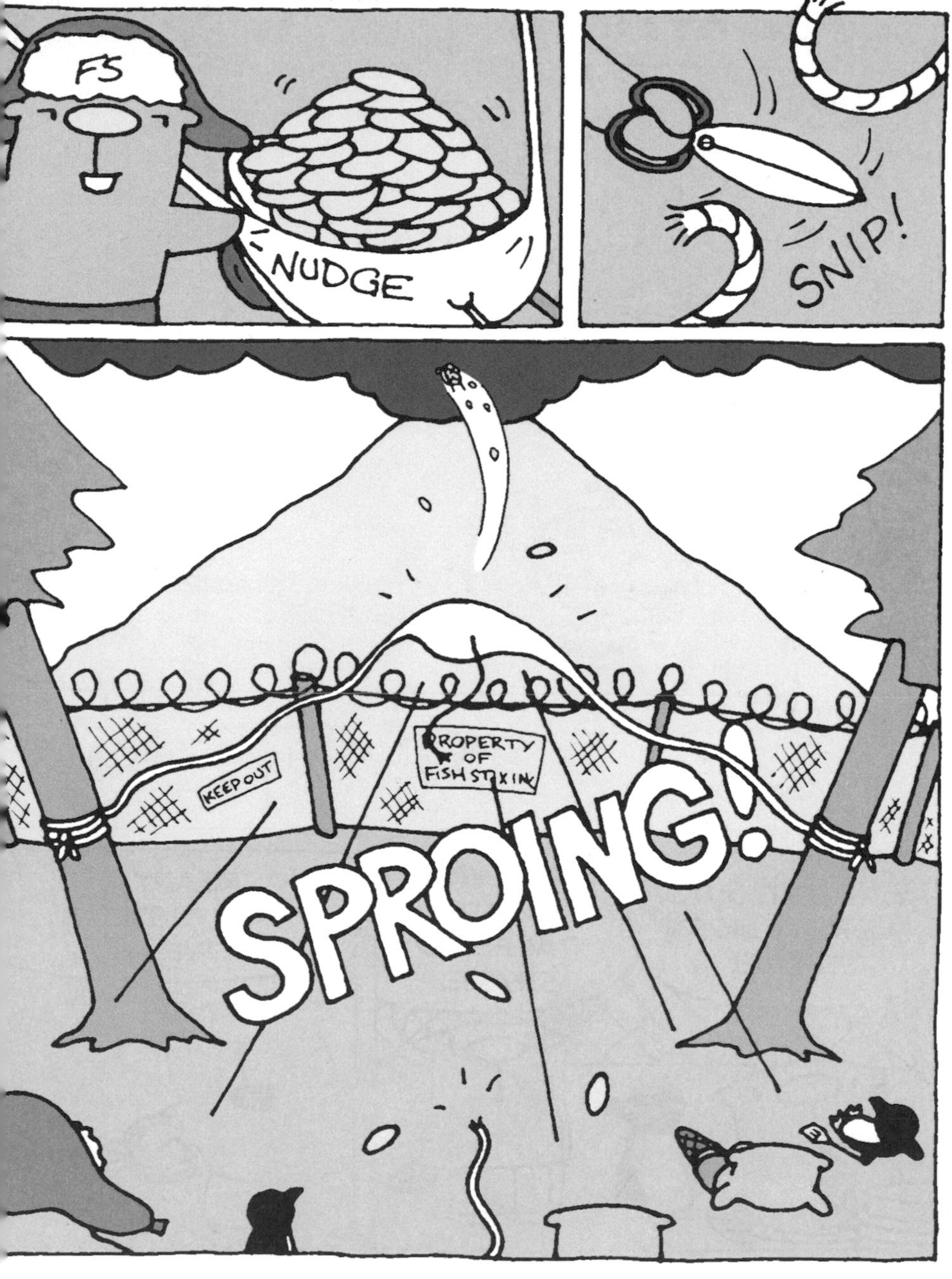
FS
NUDGE
SNIP!
KEEP OUT
PROPERTY OF FISH STIXINC
SPROING!

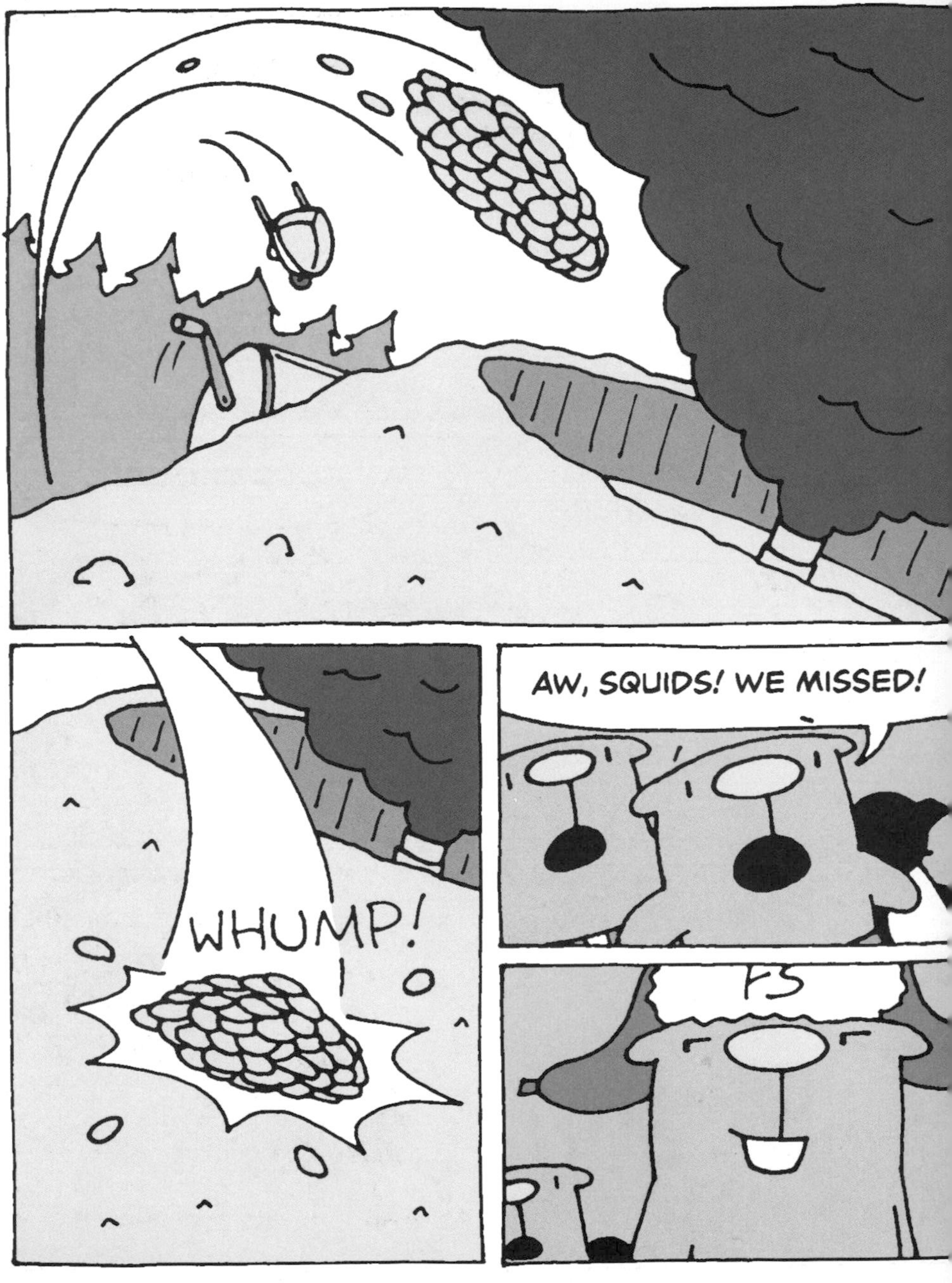
WHUMP!
AW, SQUIDS! WE MISSED!

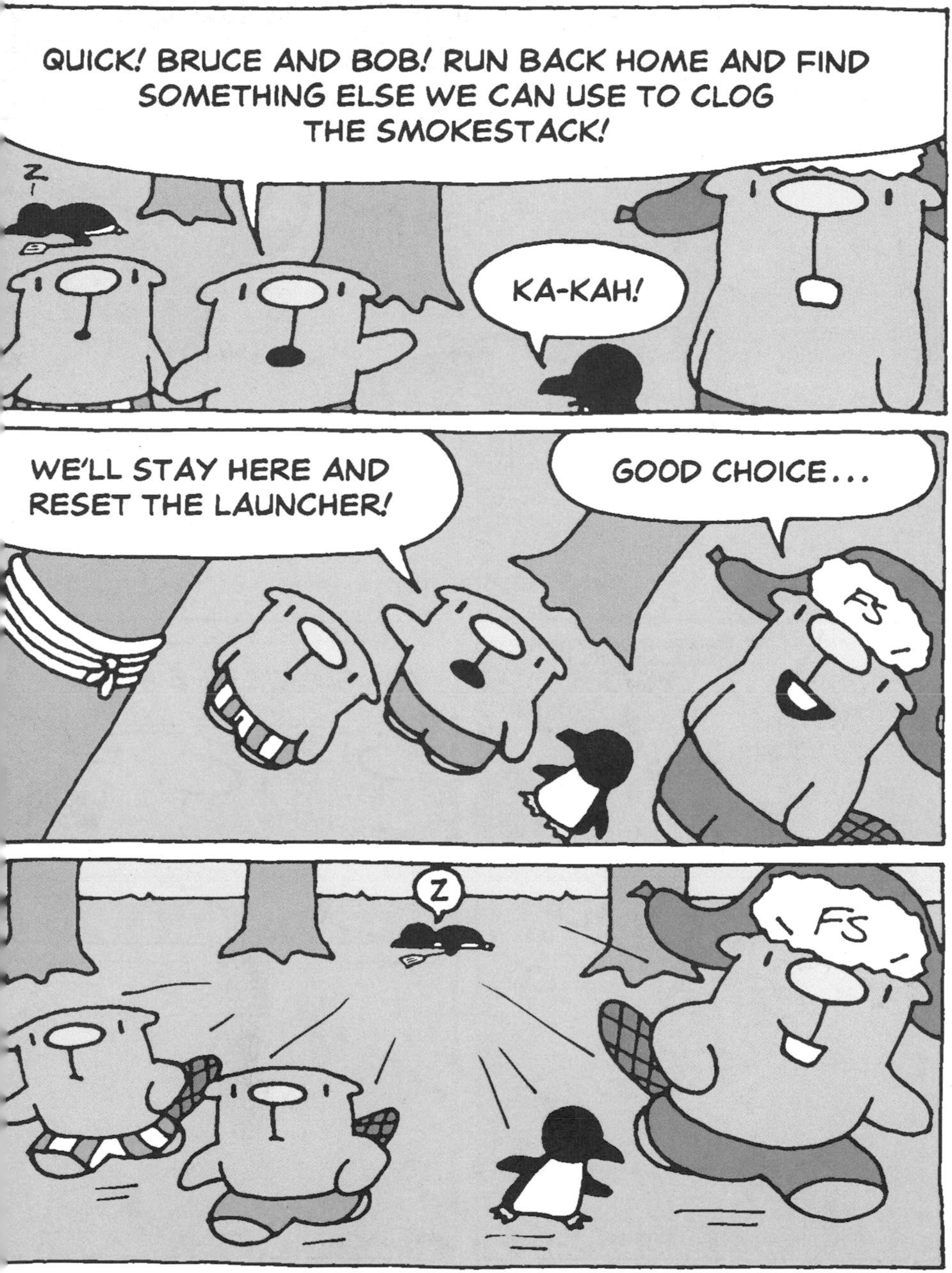
QUICK! BRUCE AND BOB! RUN BACK HOME AND FIND SOMETHING ELSE WE CAN USE TO CLOG THE SMOKESTACK!
KA-KAH!
WE'LL STAY HERE AND RESET THE LAUNCHER!
GOOD CHOICE...
Z
FS

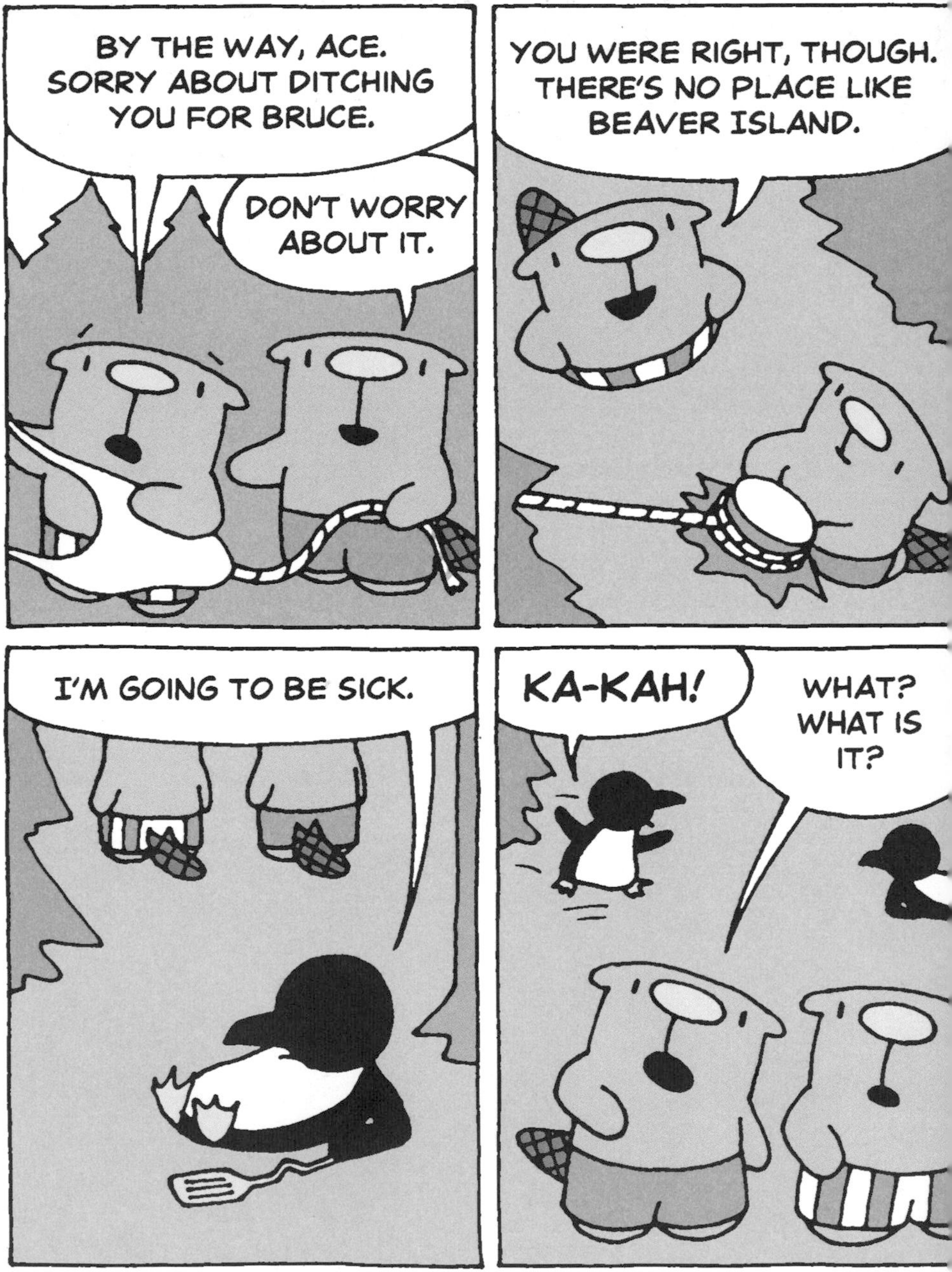
BY THE WAY, ACE. SORRY ABOUT DITCHING YOU FOR BRUCE.
DON'T WORRY ABOUT IT.
YOU WERE RIGHT, THOUGH. THERE'S NO PLACE LIKE BEAVER ISLAND.
I'M GOING TO BE SICK.
KA-KAH!
WHAT? WHAT IS IT?

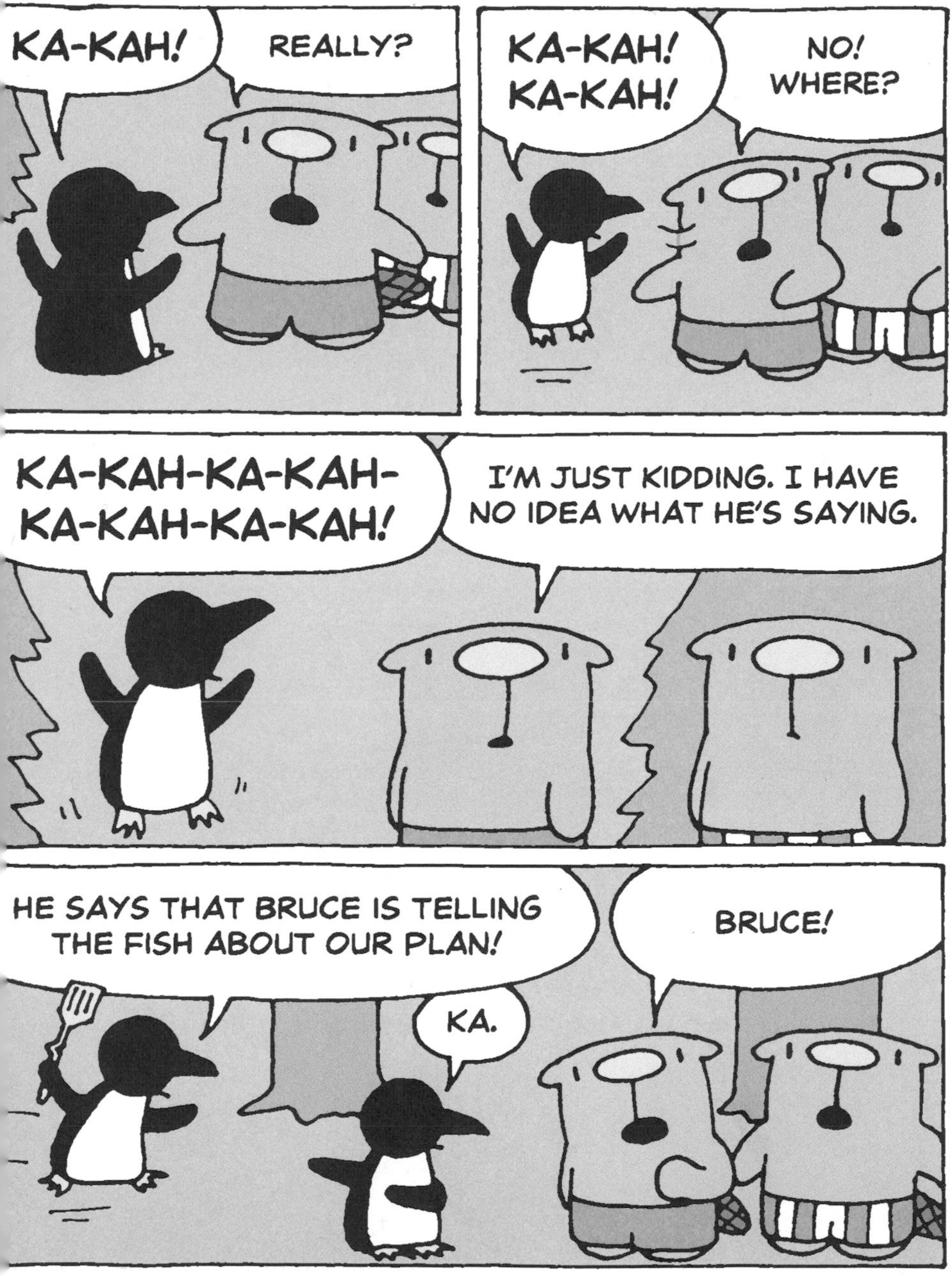
KA-KAH!
REALLY?
KA-KAH! KA-KAH!
NO! WHERE?
KA-KAH-KA-KAH-KA-KAH-KA-KAH!
I'M JUST KIDDING. I HAVE NO IDEA WHAT HE'S SAYING.
HE SAYS THAT BRUCE IS TELLING THE FISH ABOUT OUR PLAN!
KA.
BRUCE!

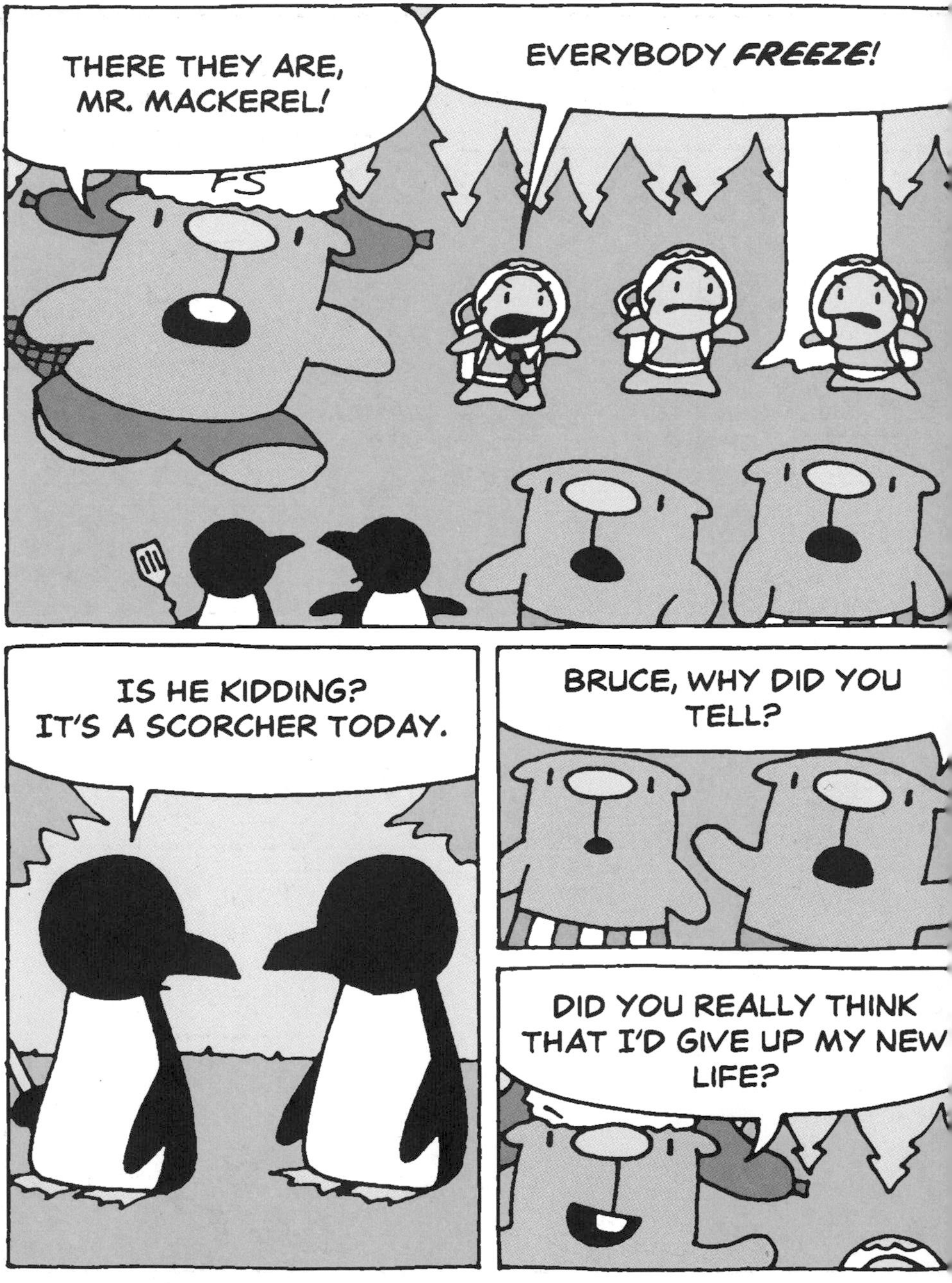
THERE THEY ARE, MR. MACKEREL!
EVERYBODY FREEZE!
FS
IS HE KIDDING? IT'S A SCORCHER TODAY.
BRUCE, WHY DID YOU TELL?
DID YOU REALLY THINK THAT I'D GIVE UP MY NEW LIFE?

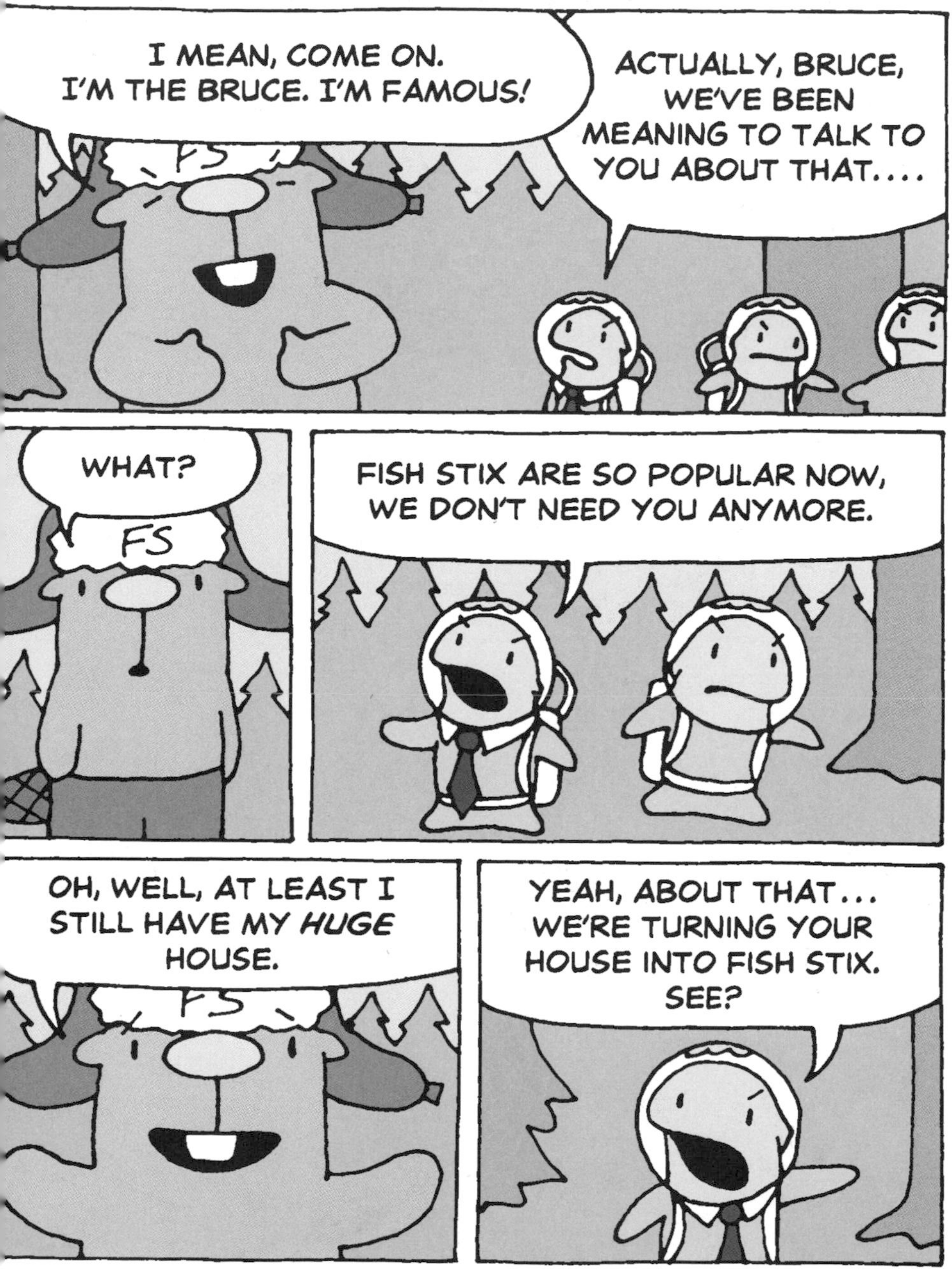
I MEAN, COME ON. I'M THE BRUCE. I'M FAMOUS!
ACTUALLY, BRUCE, WE'VE BEEN MEANING TO TALK TO YOU ABOUT THAT....
FS
WHAT?
FS
FISH STIX ARE SO POPULAR NOW, WE DON'T NEED YOU ANYMORE.
OH, WELL, AT LEAST I STILL HAVE MY *HUGE* HOUSE.
YEAH, ABOUT THAT... WE'RE TURNING YOUR HOUSE INTO FISH STIX. SEE?

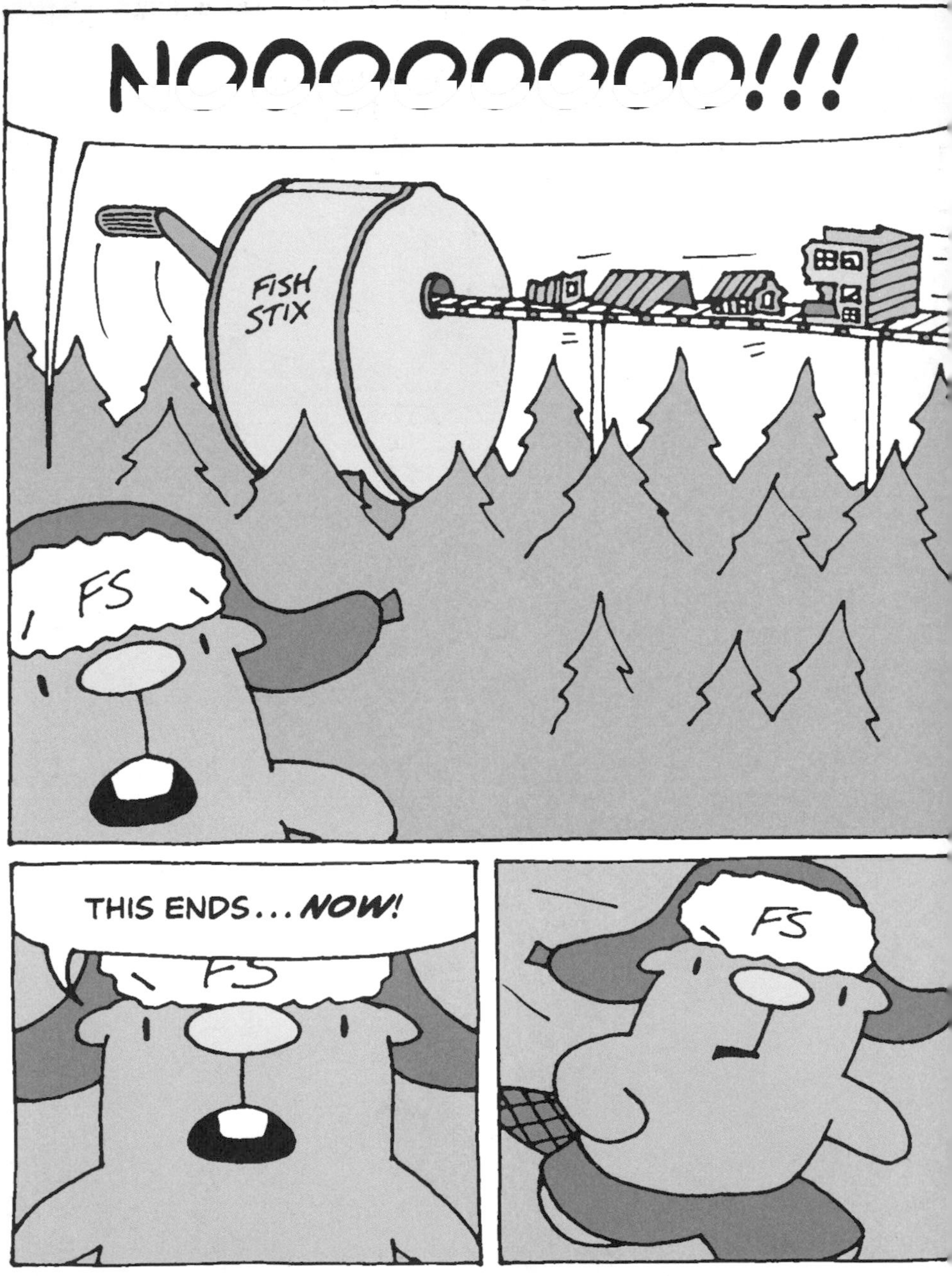
NOOOOOOOO!!!
FISH
STIX
FS
THIS ENDS... ***NOW!***
FS
FS

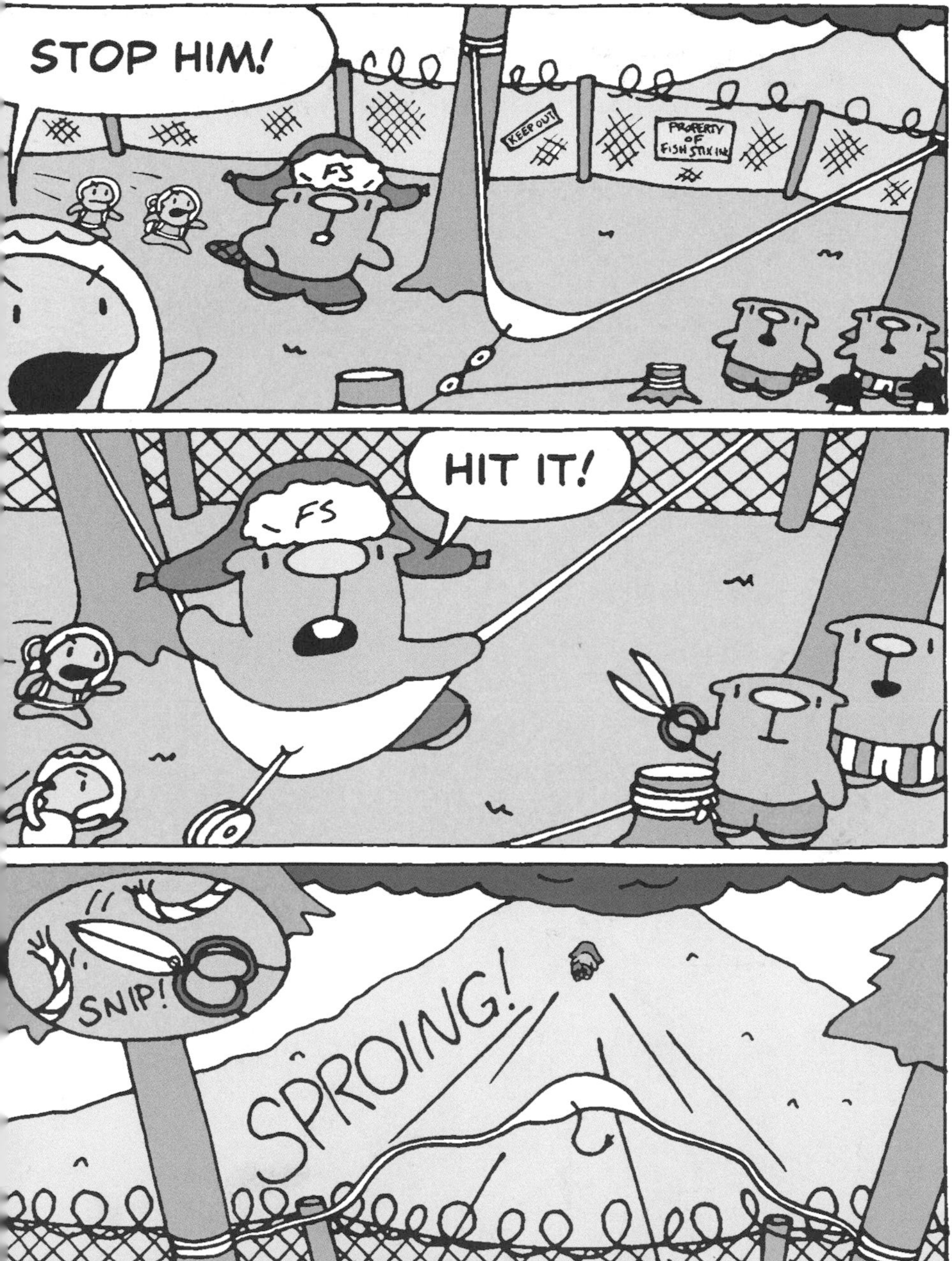
STOP HIM!
KEEP OUT
PROPERTY OF FISH STIX INC
FS
HIT IT!
FS
SNIP!
SPROING!

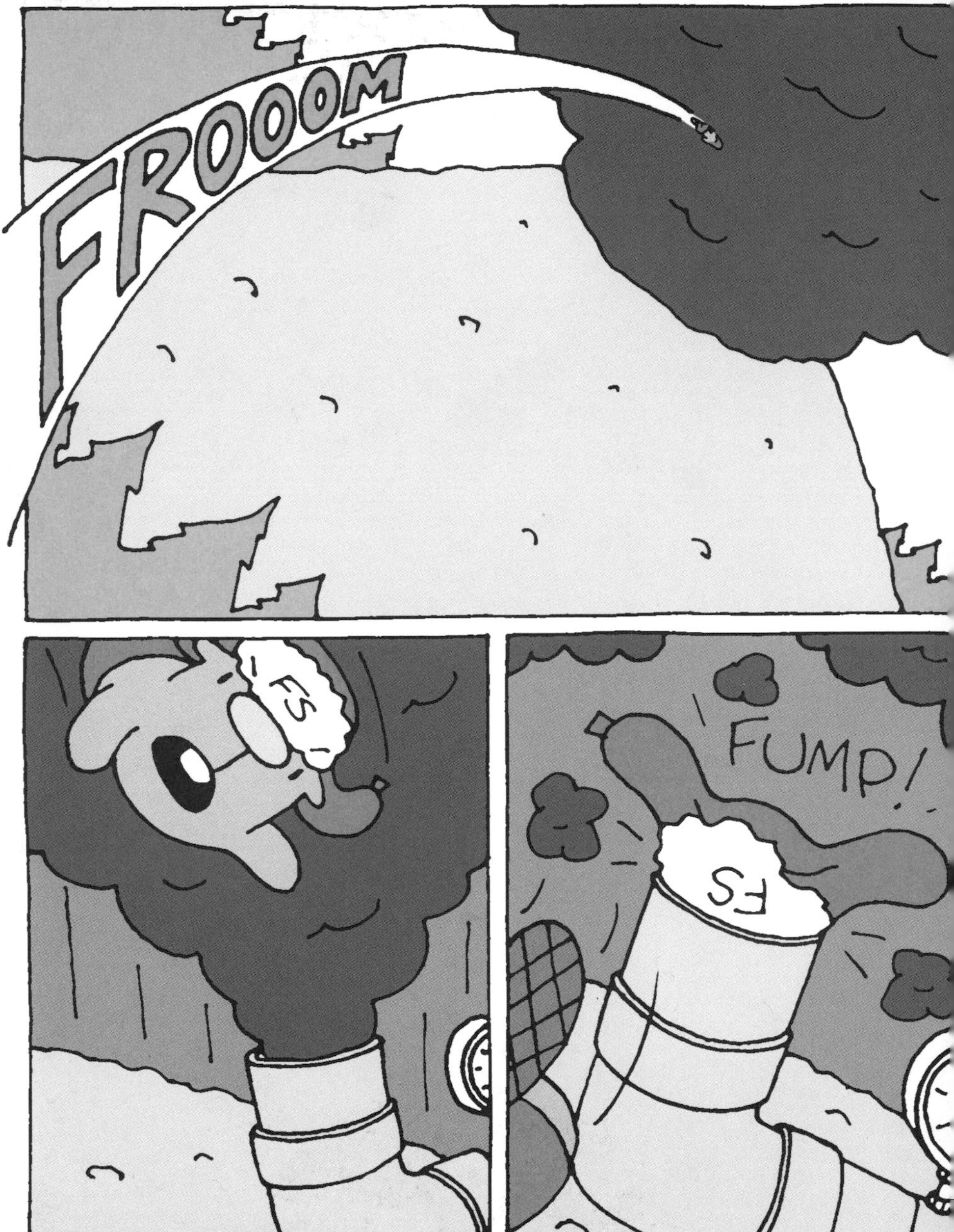
FROOOM
FS
FS
FUMP!

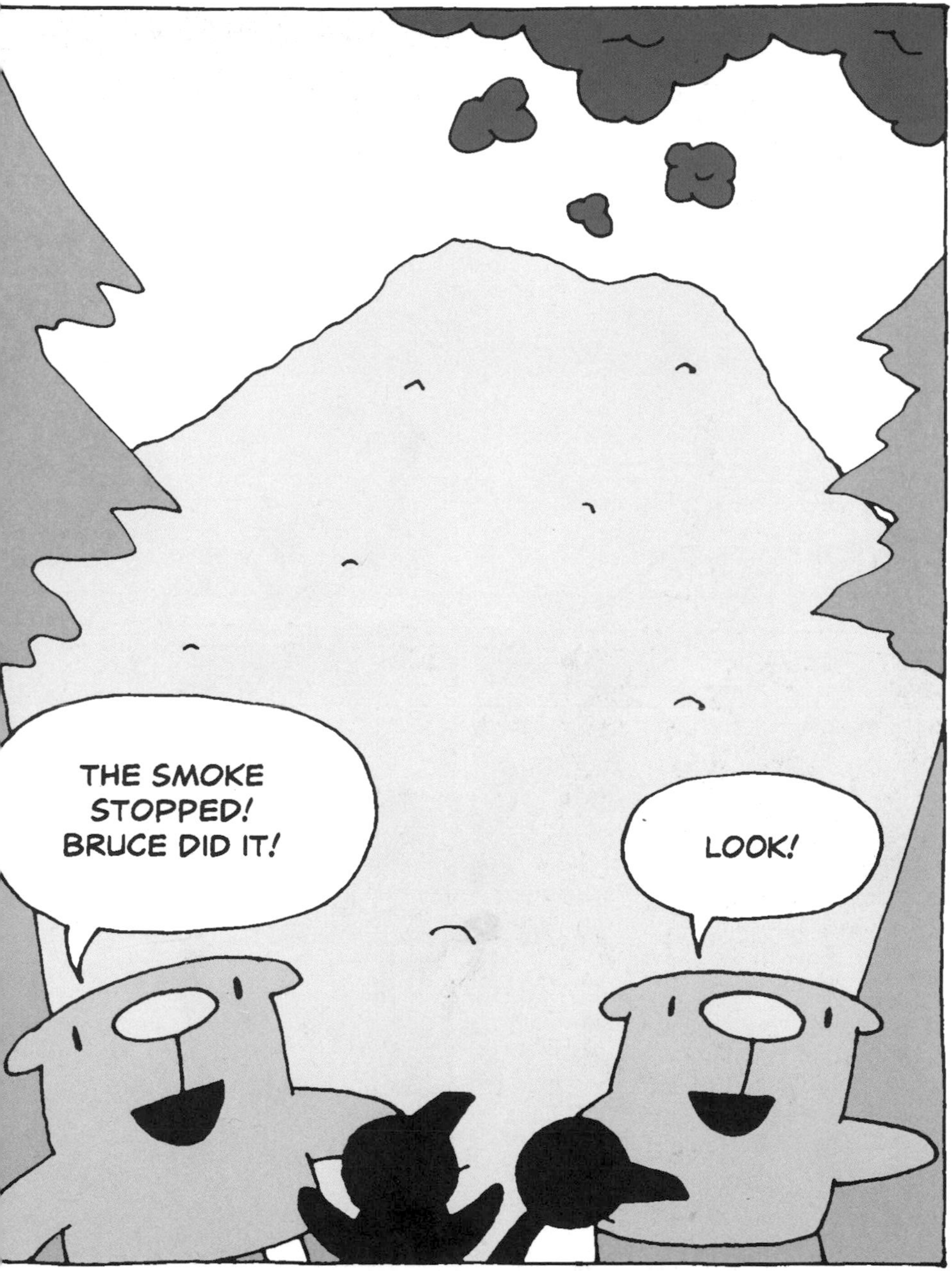
THE SMOKE STOPPED! BRUCE DID IT!
LOOK!

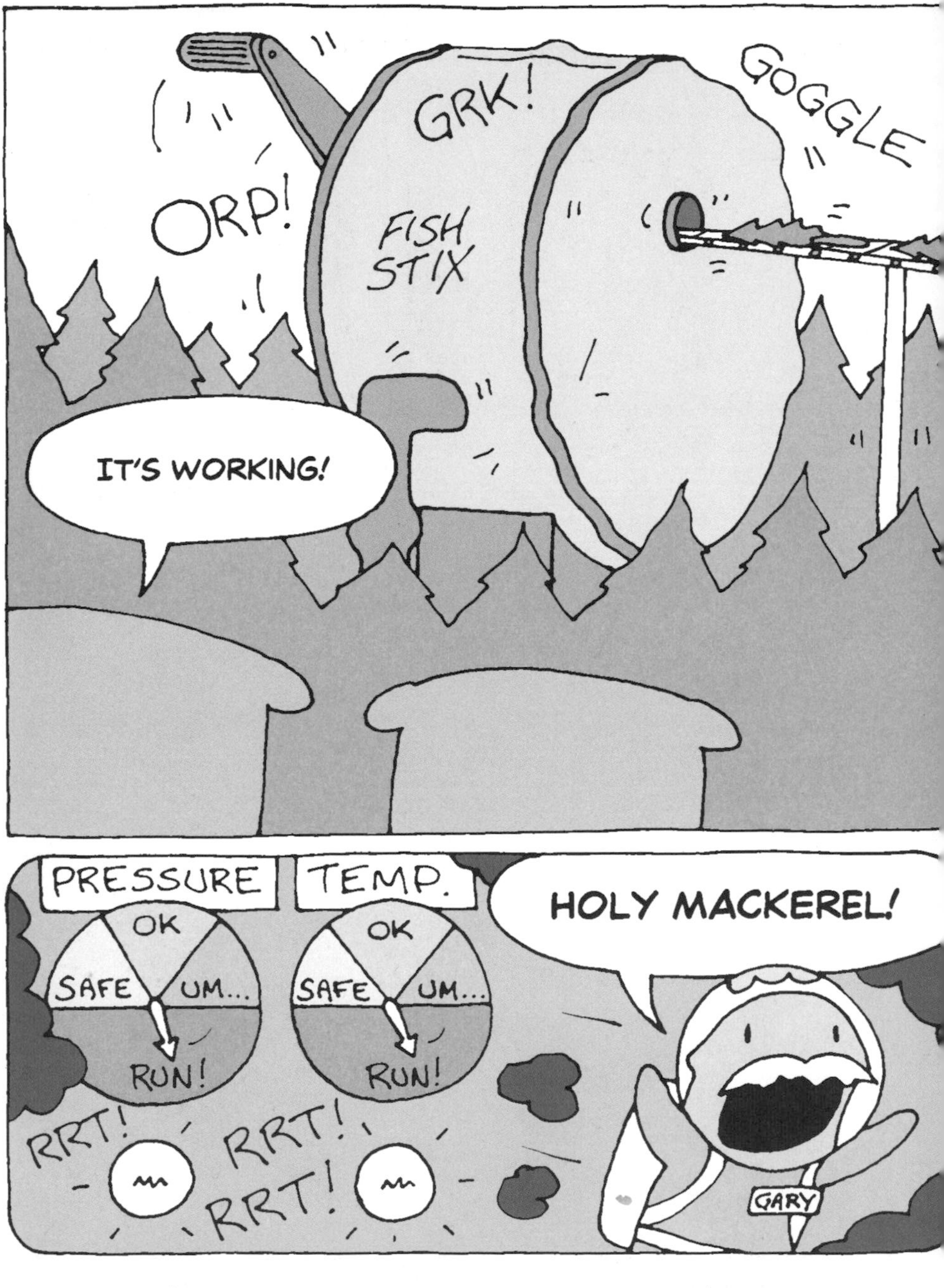
ORP!
GRK!
GOGGLE
FISH STIX
IT'S WORKING!
PRESSURE
OK
SAFE
UM...
RUN!
TEMP.
OK
SAFE
UM...
RUN!
HOLY MACKEREL!
RRT!
RRT!
RRT!
GARY

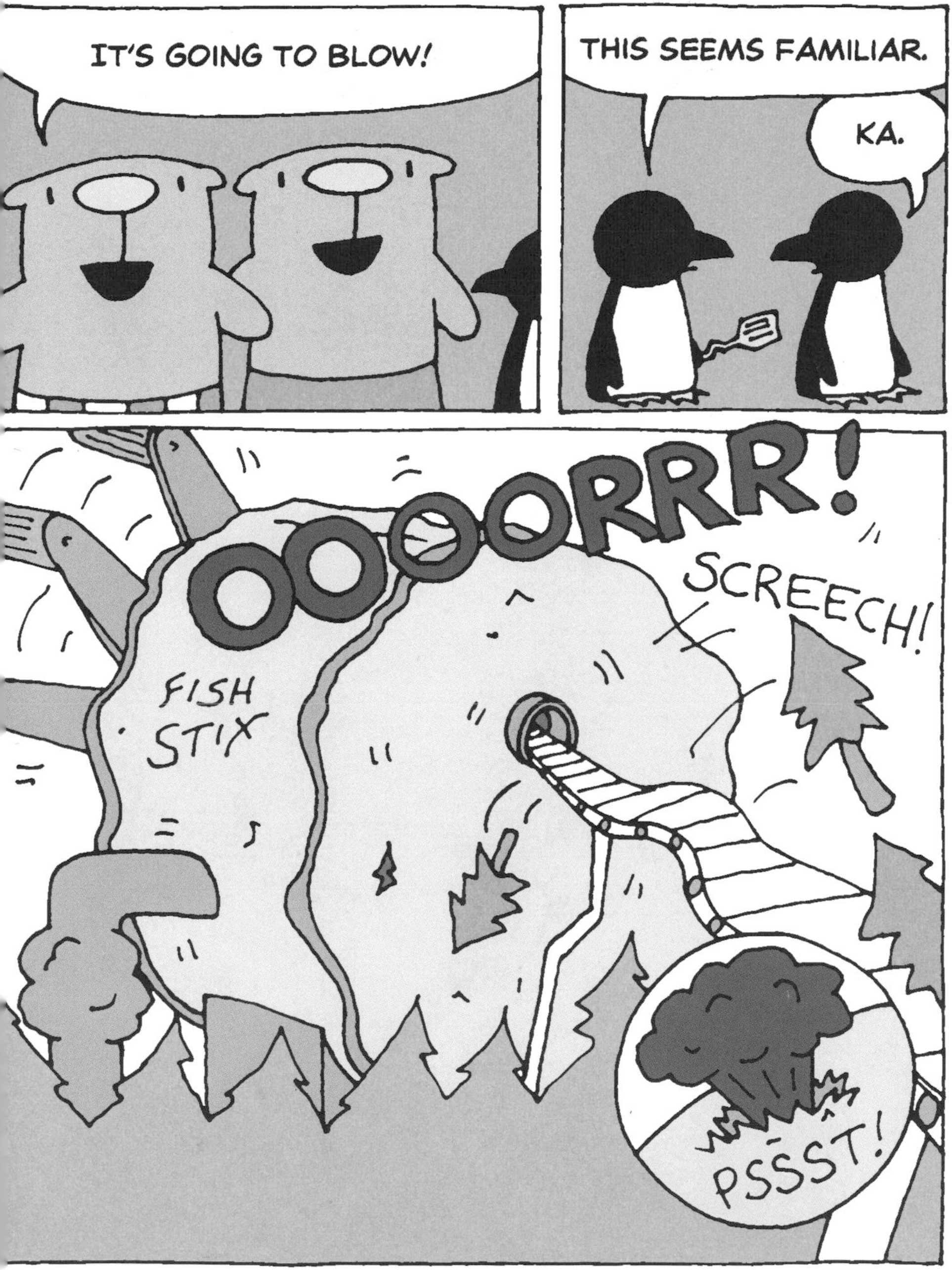
IT'S GOING TO BLOW!
THIS SEEMS FAMILIAR.
KA.
OOOOORRRR!
SCREEECH!
FISH STIX
PSSST!

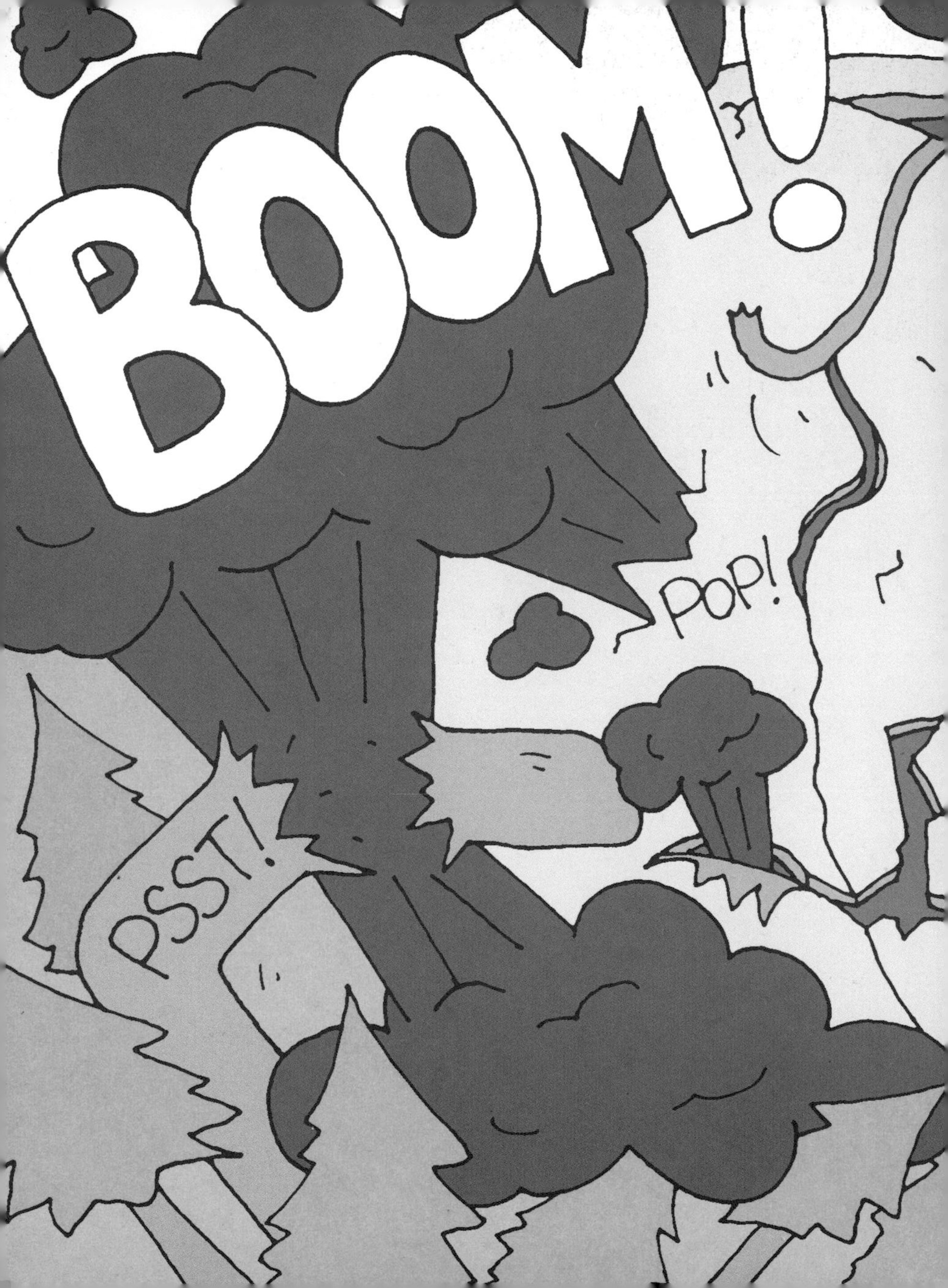
BOOM!
POP!
PSST!

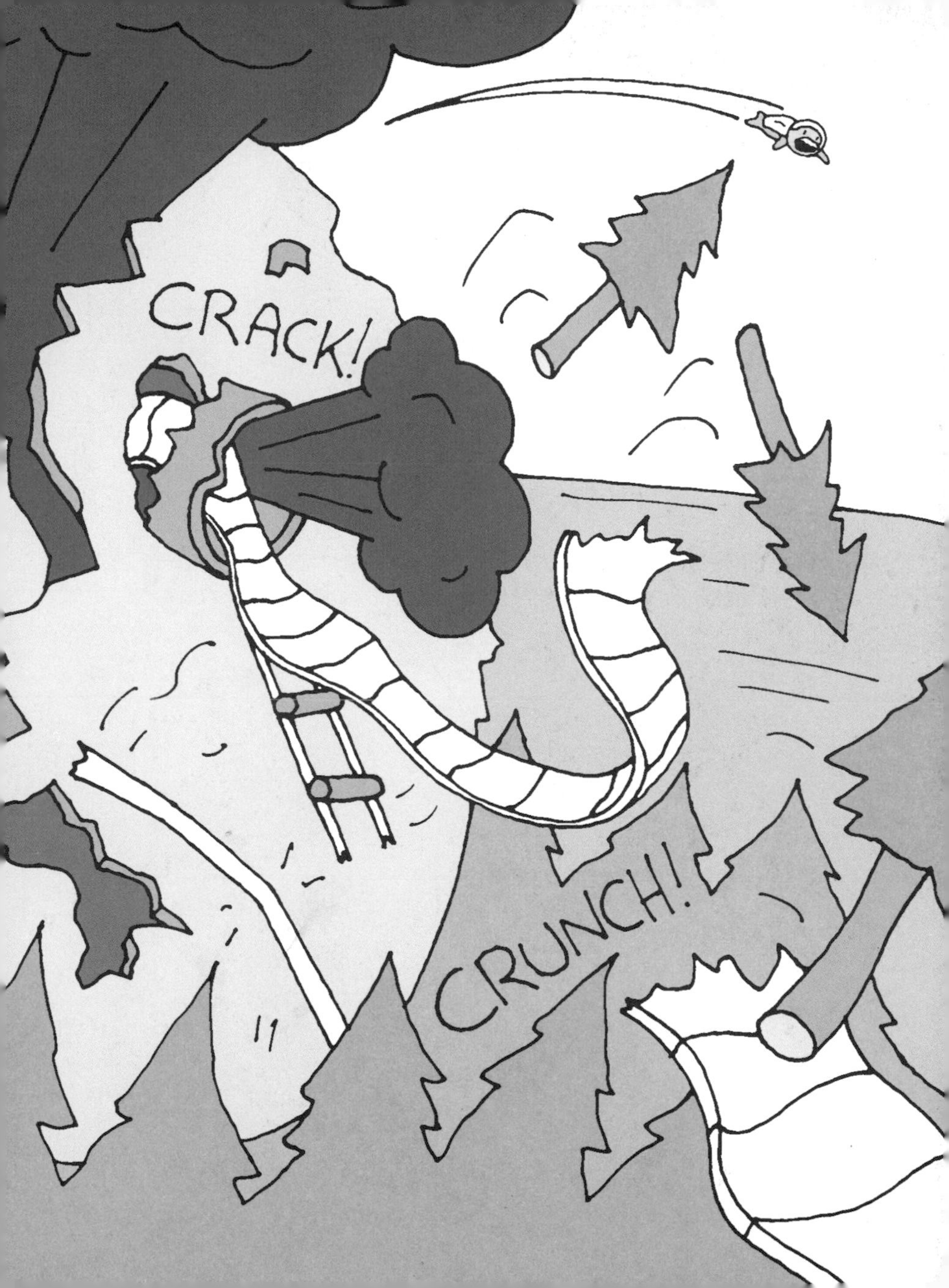
CRACK!
CRUNCH!

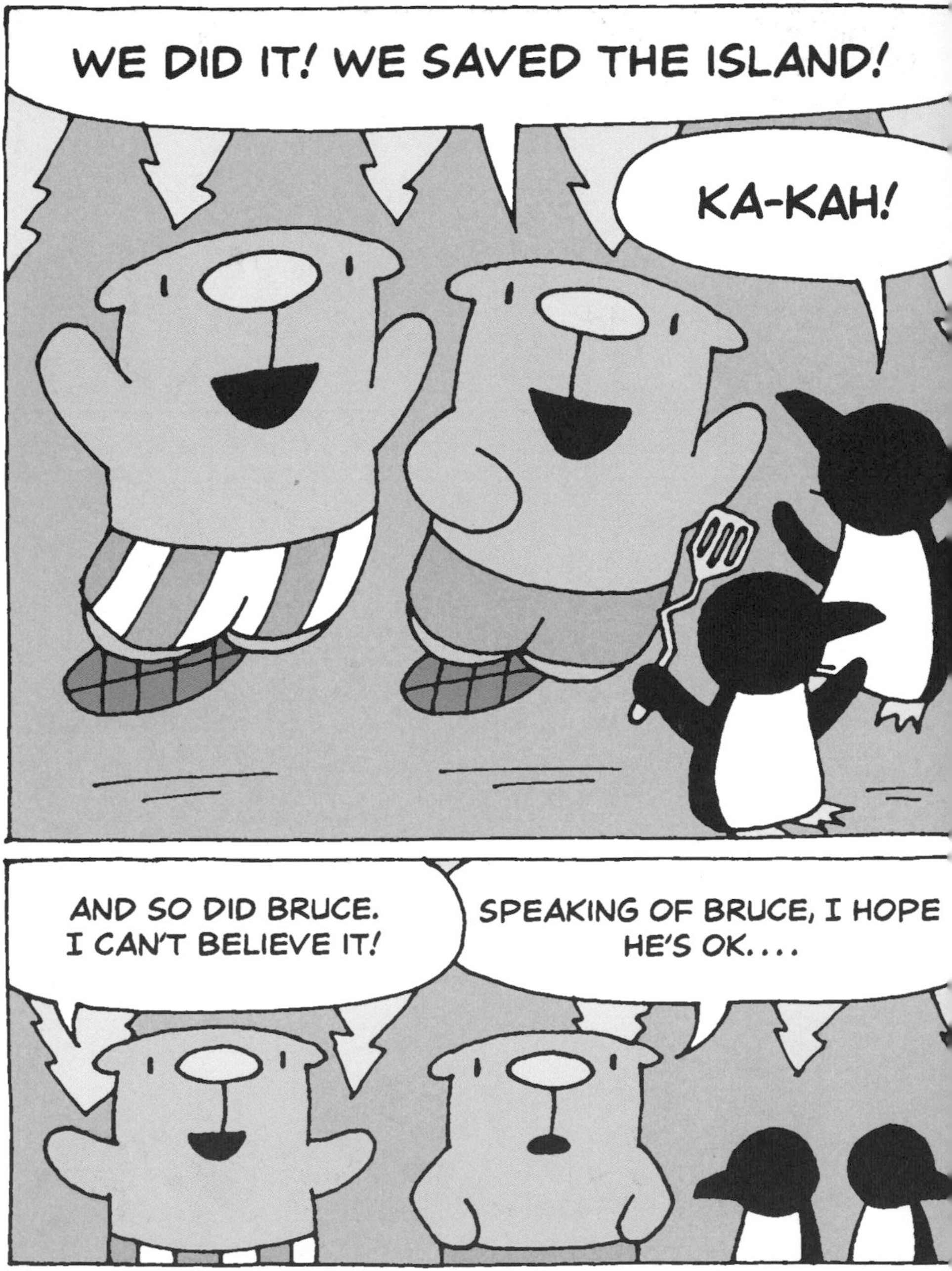
WE DID IT! WE SAVED THE ISLAND!
KA-KAH!
AND SO DID BRUCE. I CAN'T BELIEVE IT!
SPEAKING OF BRUCE, I HOPE HE'S OK. . . .

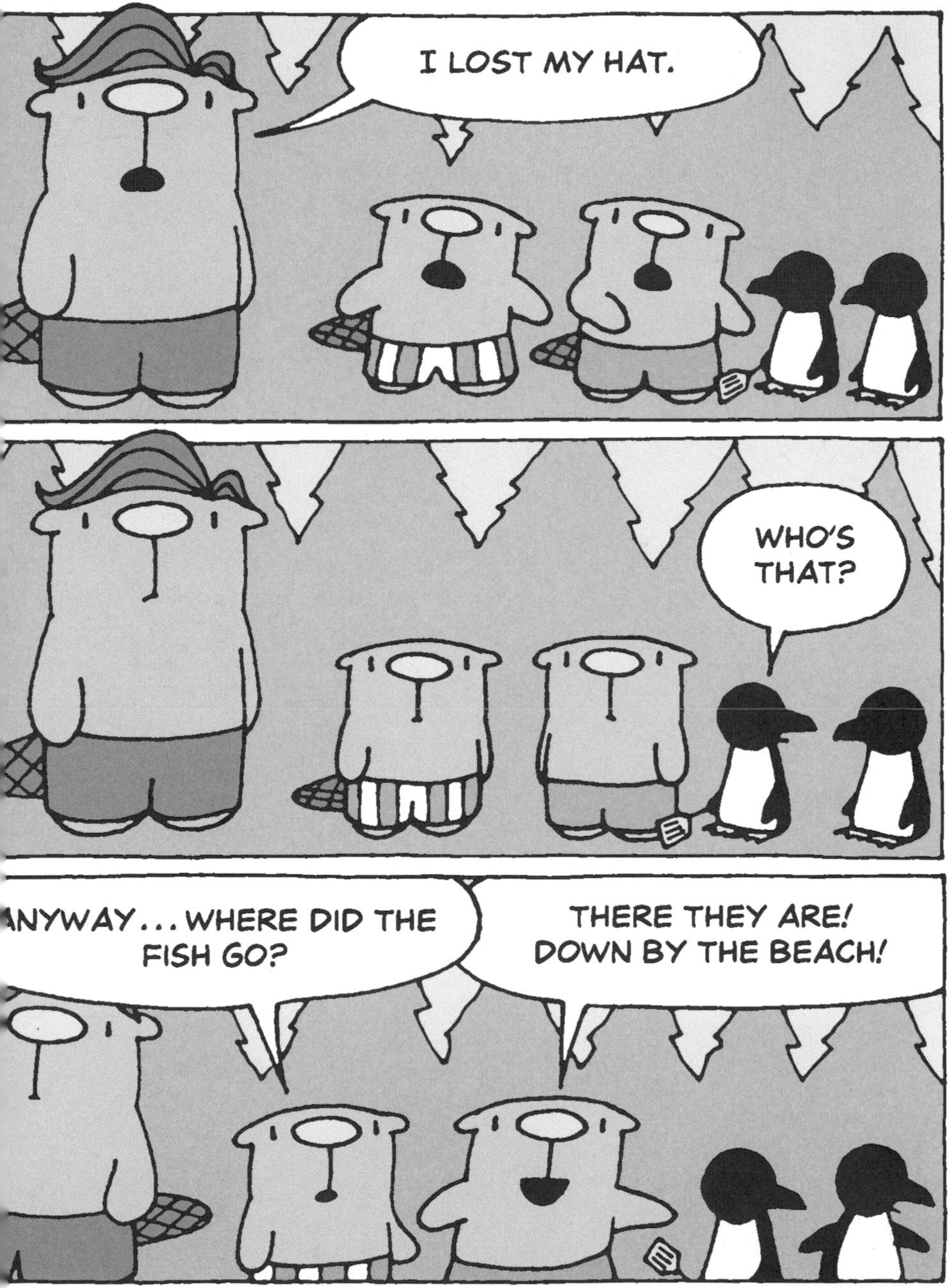
I LOST MY HAT.
WHO'S THAT?
ANYWAY... WHERE DID THE FISH GO?
THERE THEY ARE! DOWN BY THE BEACH!

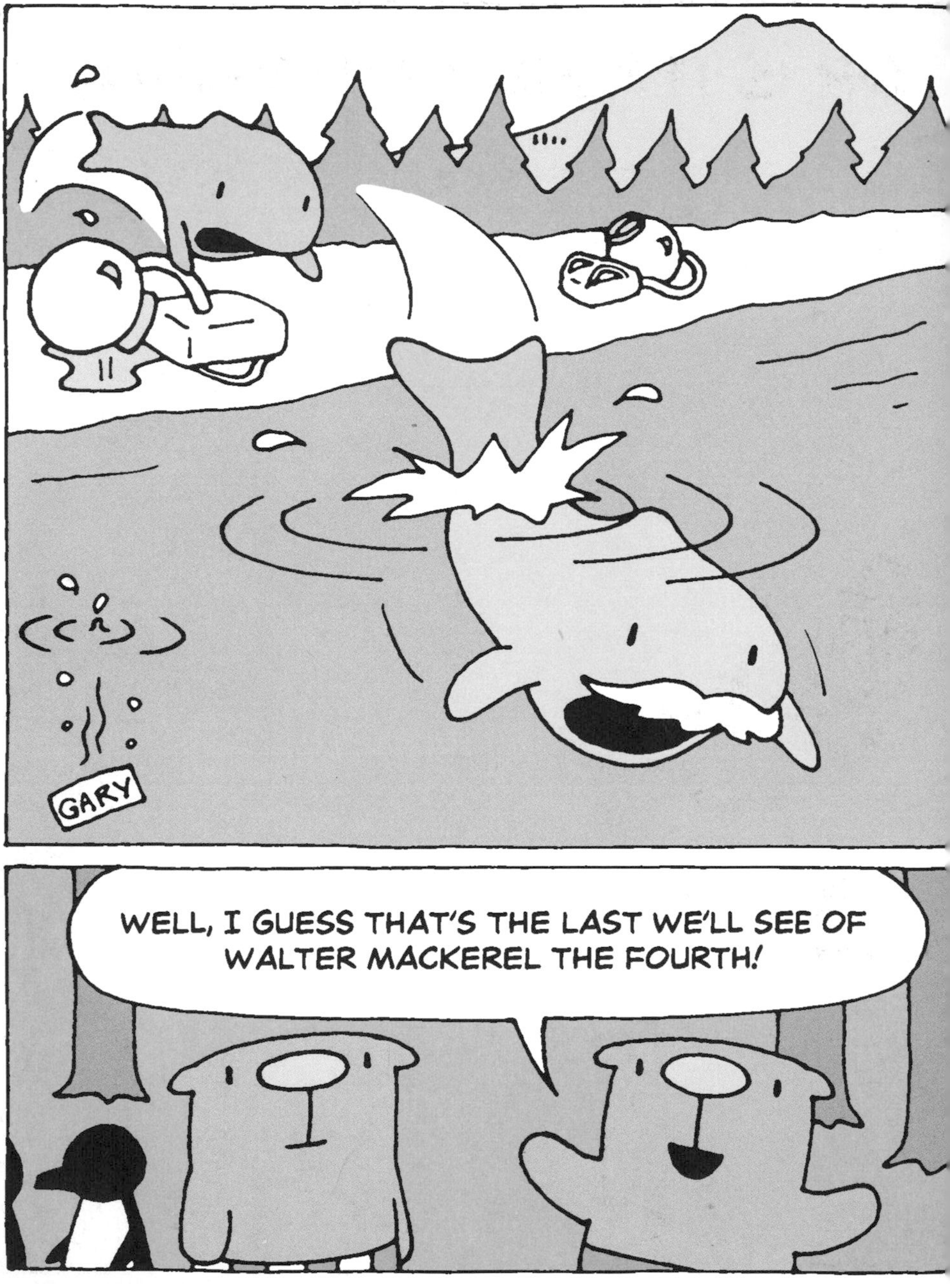
GARY
WELL, I GUESS THAT'S THE LAST WE'LL SEE OF WALTER MACKEREL THE FOURTH!

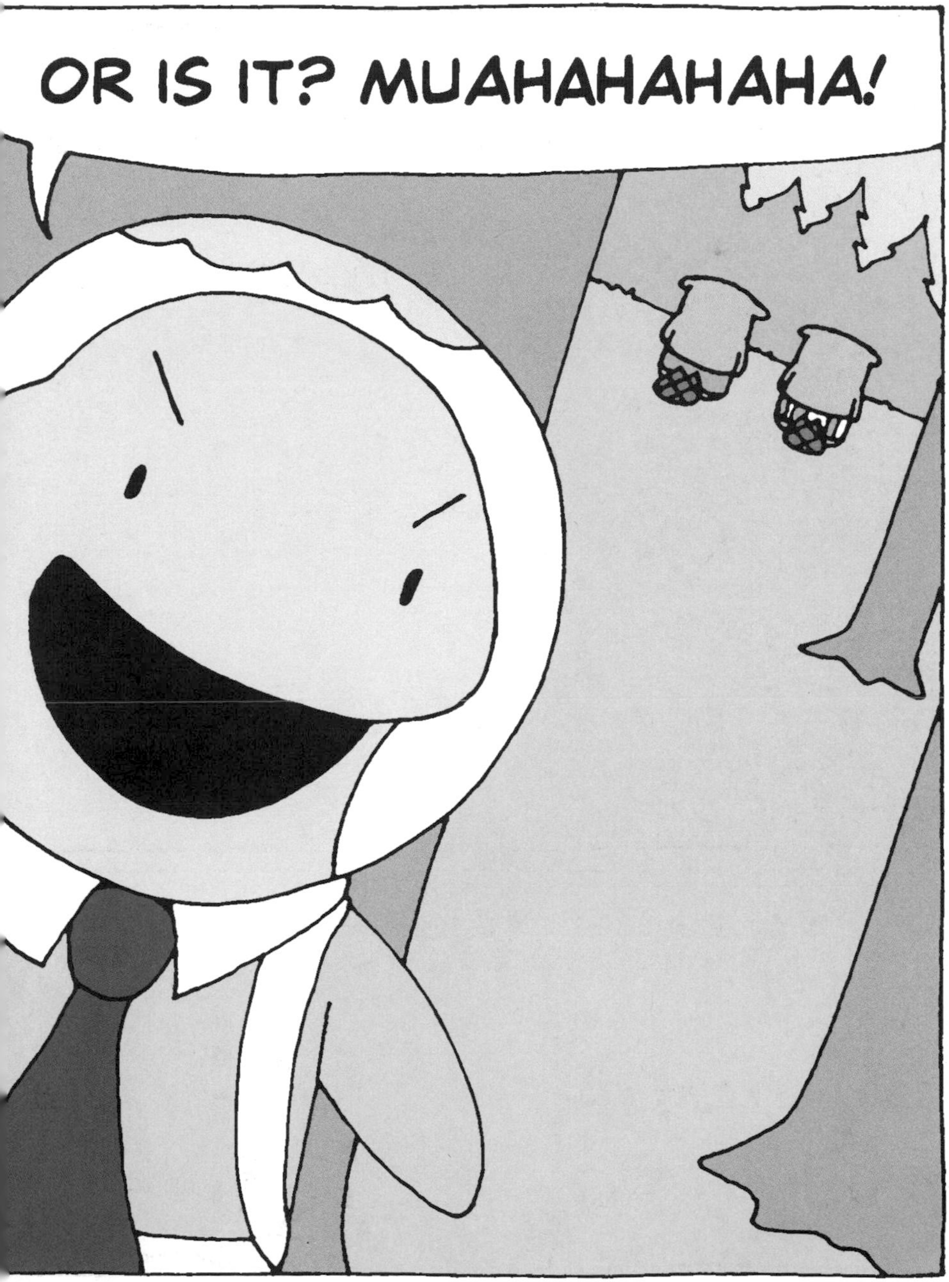
OR IS IT? MUAHAHAHAHAHA!

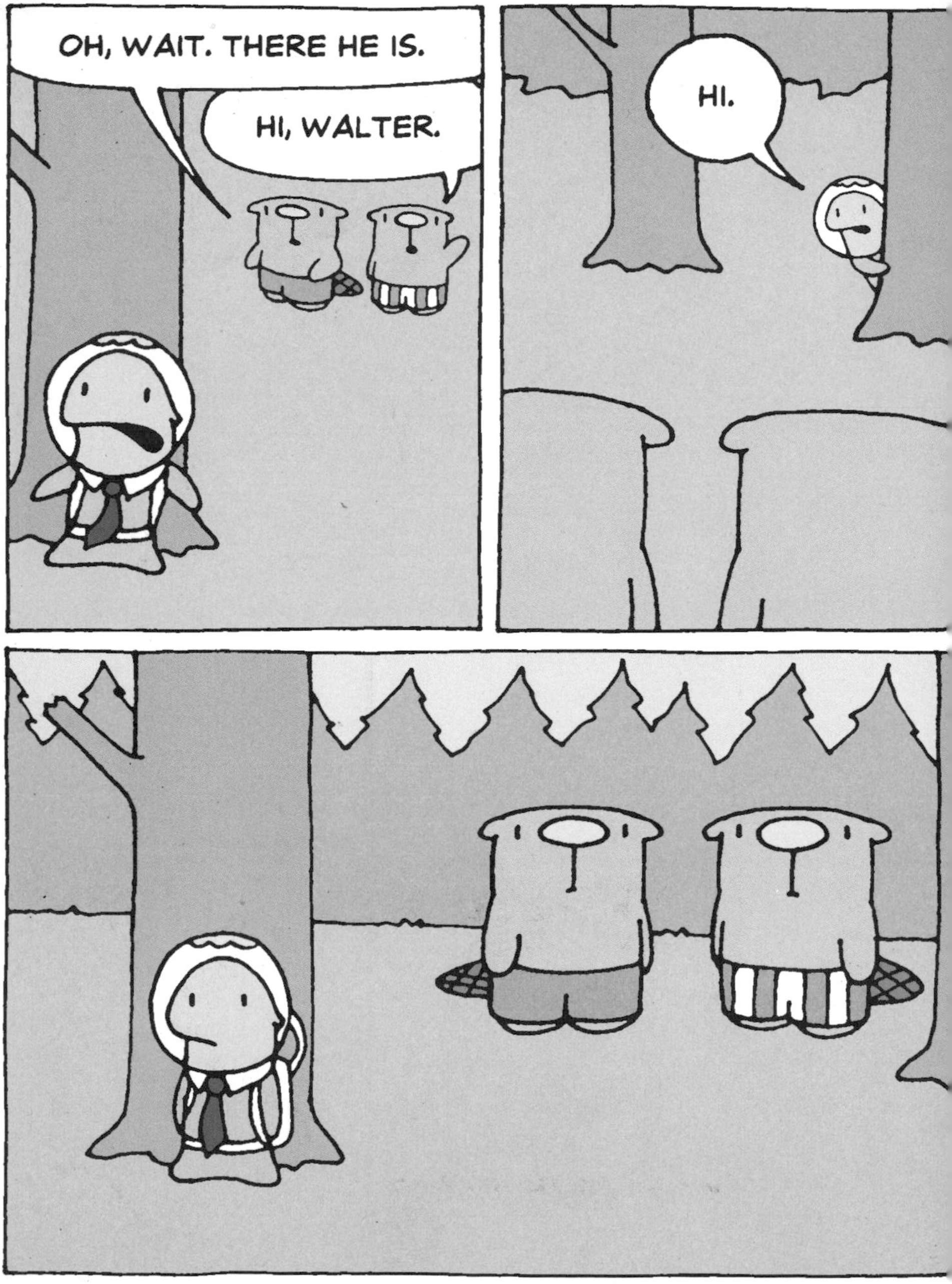
OH, WAIT. THERE HE IS.
HI, WALTER.
HI.